The Chase

D0878370

The Chase Runner Series

Book 1: The Chase

The Chase

The Chase Runner Series

By
Bradley Caffee

The Chase
Published by Mountain Brook Ink
White Salmon, WA U.S.A.

The website addresses shown in this book are not intended in any way to be or imply an endorsement on the part of Mountain Brook Ink, nor do we vouch for their content.

This story is a work of fiction. All characters and events are the product of the author's imagination. Any resemblance to any person, living or dead, is coincidental.

Scripture quotations are taken from the King James Version of the Bible. Public domain.
ISBN 978-1-953957-00-9
© 2021 Bradley Caffee

The Team: Miralee Ferrell, Alyssa Roat, Nikki Wright, Kristen Johnson, Cindy Jackson
Cover Design: Lynnette Bonner

Mountain Brook Ink is an inspirational publisher offering fiction you can believe in.
Printed in the United States of America

To Tirzah,
who helps me to be me

.

Acknowledgments

Thank you to my Lord and Savior, Jesus Christ, without whom I would not know the freedom to be the unique creation I was meant to be. Thank you for saving this "Willis" from a life of measuring up to the joy of knowing I am accepted. You have brought me to a place I never would have gone, much less considered attainable. Thank you for not removing my "thorns," so I could become the man I am today.

Thanks also to Tirzah, my wife and encourager, for allowing me to follow this crazy dream of writing. You have stood by me and not allowed me to give up, even when the manuscript sat around for months untouched. You've put up with countless days of me disappearing into my laptop and celebrated each milestone. Thank you for being the keeper of my dreams.

My kids, who have patiently waited while dad finished "one more paragraph." You both amaze me every day as you become the unique people God created you to be. I hope my pursuit of this dream has shown you they are possible.

My agent, Sarah Freese, who took on a writer who promised he was done "playing at his writing." You believed me and believed in my work when so many tried to tell me it would never happen.

My editor, Miralee Ferrell, thank you for giving this unknown author a chance. Willis, Perryn, Jaden, Kane, and the others' story is deeply personal to me, and I am humbled that you would help me bring them to life on the page.

To the incredible publishing team at Mountain Brook Ink, thank you for teaching this new author all the things about marketing a debut novel and supporting other authors. You and the fellow authors at MBI have been so welcoming from day one.

Lauren, my dedicated first-reader, for putting up with my endless emails and for championing the character of Sheila. You saw Willis and Perryn's story unfold from the beginning.

Becca, Greg, Kyla, Lauren, and Nikayla, my superhero team

of beta-readers, for taking time away from the craziness of life to help me develop this story. So much of where the book is today is because of you five.

Carrie Givens, the first editor to ever look at my work, for putting up with my overuse of adverbs and giving me amazing counsel to navigate the world of publishing. You were the first to tell me this story was meant for more.

Janeen Ippolito, who brought her A-game to make this story so much better, even though I won the edit in a raffle. My writing has never been the same.

Steven, my "cattle prod," who gave me the final nudge to finally sit and begin writing.

To all my friends and readers who kept me moving forward with their never-ending pleas to read the manuscript and nagging requests for official release dates. You put up with my promises that the book would one day make it to print for so long. I hope it was worth the wait.

Chapter One

Sweat dripped from Willis's forehead to the metal floor. His breaths seemed to echo off the walls of the empty training room on the Western Alliance space station, returning each pant of recycled air to him as if taunting his efforts. Normally a place of action, the silence of the cavernous sphere unnerved him. He'd skipped out on his team at the morning meal to spend time on the track alone. None of the other racers practiced solo, but that is what it meant to lead the best team in the Western Alliance. This last part of the track could decide which team won the next run, and he was not about to lose. The moving walls had caught him off-guard again and knocked him off his feet. He silently cursed the track before him as he rubbed his sore shoulder. He still bore bruises from the previous track they'd been forced to run, and he had no desire to add to them.

The Western Alliance was one of three alliances that could afford to place their training centers in space where the administrators had complete control over their training environment. The rest of the alliances been forced to choose terrestrial training grounds. Some were even petitioning the World Coalition to outlaw the orbiting stations saying they gave their alliances unfair advantages, which they did. As the recipient of those advantages, he wasn't going to argue. If it got him home—if it helped him live up to the legacy of the Thomson family—he would take any advantage he could get.

The track was inside the training sphere that crawled with a beehive of hexagonal panels. Each metallic panel that made the interior of the ten-story room was interchangeable, allowing the track to be altered each month to present new challenges. As no one could predict the exact nature of the next year's Chase, the track was designed to simulate any variable, including environmental controls so the administrators could change the conditions to match different Chase environments. The track was unpredictable, and that made them—made him—some of the best trained racers in the entire Coalition.

Staring in front of him, he watched the moving parts protrude in and out. "Right, right, down, left, over." He whispered the sequence to himself, committing it to memory. In all likelihood, he would be the member of his team to reach this point of the race first, and he had to be prepared.

Thunk. A wall dropped suddenly from above, and he added an extra 'down' to his sequence. A blow to the head there would mean the difference between winning and losing.

Standing, he returned to the start of the long room. He closed his eyes.

Willis, you've got this.

Opening his eyes, he sprang forward. Ducking to the right, he extended an arm to push off the far wall. He drooped underneath another wall and kicked to the left to avoid a third. The overhead wall he'd noticed shot downward, and he dropped into a roll.

The sequence flowed through his mind, and he grinned as he passed the wall that had struck him earlier. Springing from the exit, he slowed to a stop on the open track beyond. Hands on his knees, he panted heavily and turned to look at the way he'd come.

"Gotcha," he whispered to the empty room.

Satisfied he was ready for their training run later, he exited to join his teammates in the common room. The annual Chase had ended, and everyone would be gathering to watch the victory ceremony.

"Quick! Grab the camera!"

Sheila hated covering the annual Chase. The endless crowds

who'd traveled from around the world to see something that was no longer original. It made her sick. Those who couldn't afford a privileged seat in the surrounding stands gathered according to their alliances in front of the stage. The black velvet curtains behind the podium and the matching skirt around the foot of the stage made the unbearable sun seem more oppressive. She kicked herself for uncovering her supervisor's budget mistake five years ago. Now she was in exile covering news that wasn't truly news.

The Chase happened every year, at least every year since she could remember. The alliances around the world each put up their best team to compete to win the right to change the Law. One law. That was it. Other than that, the Law never changed. The Law mandated everything. The Law mandated her clothing to identify her as a woman from the Western Alliance, a pants and jacket combination with the yellow and black Alliance insignia on the sleeve. The Law mandated that her father's business was taxed to the point of extinction. The Law mandated that she eat, sleep, and drink the amounts dictated. She resented the Law, but it ruled her anyway.

She frowned as she examined the one spot left where they could get a clear shot of the girl. Standing at the edge of the mob near the stage steps, she sighed in frustration. The angle would have been better on the right side of the stage. *The shadows are all wrong here.*

The bright sunlight burned her squinting eyes as she looked along the front of the stage. Pritchard, whom she'd shared press rooms with at several inter-alliance events, stood there gazing in a mirror. She rolled her eyes as he practiced several versions of his smile.

"Hey, Pritchard!" she called. "I don't suppose you want to trade spots, do you?" Glancing at Sheila over the mirror, he lowered his arm and adopted one of his rehearsed grins. She groaned. "I would have gone with smile number two." The last comment was too quiet for him to hear over the growing noise, but she privately enjoyed the moment at his expense.

"Sheila." Prichard finally responded. He handed the mirror

to an assistant and skirted through the growing crowds.

She sighed. She hadn't meant for him to come over.

"Sheila, my impetuous competitor." He held his arms wide as if he was going to embrace her.

She raised her eyebrows at the comment. "Me?" She gestured to herself. "Last I checked, you were the one whose news stories were as fake as the material in your suits."

He appeared offended but quickly smiled again. "Fake? Oh no, my darling. I may have—" He paused. "I may have *embellished* a few details, but that's because I know that it is drama the viewers want."

"Drama? Spend any more time in front of that mirror, and your viewers will have more drama than they can handle."

He harrumphed. Shaking his head, his lips curled as he spoke. "At least I haven't been demoted to a junior journalist for my alliance, Ms. Kemp."

The comment stung. "And yet here we both are, reporting the same exact event and sweating under the same sun."

"I am here because I chose to be. I chose the great privilege of reporting on this world-changing event. I don't imagine you are here by choice." She frowned, making him beam again. He had beaten her.

Her scowl deepened. She regretted ever talking to him. She turned away.

"Ms. Kemp?"

"Yes, Prichard?" She sighed.

"I suggest if you want a proper spot in front of the stage next year that you get here early. As for my spot, you can't have it." He glanced around, smirking. "The shadows are going to cause fits for the camera aperture. Your viewers, if you have any left, will think you are sick with how washed out you're going to appear."

"I know. Thank you, Prichard." She was tiring of him and couldn't hide the disdain in her voice. He grinned and slipped back toward his cameraman.

Fun's over, Sheila. Get this over with, and you're done for another year.

4

"Focus on me, but get ready to transition to the stage once she's up there." She stared at her cameraman to make sure he'd heard her. "Do you want me to get the chairman in the frame?" Tony smirked.

She gritted her teeth. He knew how much the chairman bothered her. After losing her banter with Prichard, she chose not to answer him. "Make sure you get the girl. Chuck will kill me if I miss this one." Everyone was buzzing about the girl who had won the Chase this year. The phenom from the Joint Mediterranean States was supposed to blow everyone away, but another racer had tripped in front of him causing his fall, resulting in a twisted ankle. There would be outcry from his government and certainly an investigation, but no one would care. All they cared about is that this nobody had somehow crossed the finish line first.

"What's this girl's name again?" Tony scrunched his face in confusion.

"Shreya," she responded.

"Shreya? Shhhhreeya. Shhriieeeyyyaa," Tony went on making odd shapes with his mouth as he overemphasized the syllables of her name. "What ever happened to normal names like Susan or Jenny?"

"She's not from the Western Alliance, doofus. Different alliance, different culture and language." She rolled her eyes. That is why he was behind the camera.

Music suddenly filled the air with triumphant anthems silencing conversations across the lawn. Reporters instantly straightened their stances and fixed their hair. This was the moment. Sheila pulled at the collar of her grey jacket, picking off a couple of fallen blonde hairs. She should have worn the blue one. The right corner of the collar on this one never lay flat.

Holding her microphone to her chin, she stared into the lens of the camera and imagined the blank stares of millions of people at home. Person after person would be seated with their glazed eyes staring at the screens in their homes to see the surprise of the year take the stage.

The music shifted to the over-the-top patriotic sound of the World Coalition anthem followed by violent applause causing her to wince. Out of the corner of her eye, she saw the chairman taking the stage.

A man of average height, Chairman DeGraaf had to pull the front of his robes up to avoid tripping on the stairs. He breathed heavily in the heat of the afternoon, the consequence of an ill-timed heat wave that had hit this year's race. His wire-rimmed glasses had slid partially down his stubby nose and sweat glistened on his face. His gray, thinning hair was carefully placed along his scalp, but the sweat had plastered it to the skin. He appeared miserable in his black, red-trimmed robe meant to remind the world of the mournful years after the Great Collapse before the Law brought order.

He was followed by a delegation of twelve deputy chairmen and chairwomen. Each one of them was garbed in traditional clothing designating the allied region they represented. Representation was a loose term in the Coalition. The allied regions did not get a vote, and their deputy chair was nominated from within the Coalition.

Sheila peered past the entourage to see the winning girl. There she was.

Sheila exhaled slowly as she followed the movement of the seventeen-year-old. The girl was beautiful. Her black hair was pulled backward and allowed to hang naturally behind her. She had been dressed in a purple and gold silk sari which flowed perfectly around her form without causing her to appear beyond her age.

"A symbol of hope and equality, this year's champion truly embodies all that is good about the Chase," Sheila reported to the camera. Tony's smirk and raised eyebrow reminded her to remove the snarkiness from words like 'hope' and 'good.' She couldn't help it. Her father had been loyal to the Western Alliance, supplying the Alliance centers with training helmets. To repay his loyalty, the government had stopped paying for them and levied huge import taxes on his materials. As she described the alliances that the various officials represented, she recalled the day government officials showed up to arrest her father for failure to pay the import prices. She never saw him again as he disappeared among the masses the Alliance referred to as 'rehabilitation candidates.' The arrest had been nothing more than a covert way for the Alliance to assume ownership of his helmet designs. The Chase gave everyone the hope of change, but nothing ever changed.

"Despite the protests from Mediterranean officials," she continued, "the crowd seems eager to welcome this young beauty into the long line of enshrined champion Law-changers." Sheila could feel the words passing her lips as she described the scene for the camera, but she couldn't hear them. It was the girl's eyes. Her shape and forearms showed the years of training, but it was her eyes that betrayed a lost childhood. The tears rimming her lower eyelids gave away her terror. She smiled to pass them off as a sign of her assumed joy.

She's not ready. The realization suddenly filled Sheila's mind.

"Greetings and welcome to the loyal citizens of the World Coalition." DeGraaf, blotted his forehead with a handkerchief and tried to quiet the crowd with his other hand. "The humility of my office grants me the great honor of displaying this year's shining example of the purity and greatness of the Law. The Law that protects us all."

"The Law is good!" came the robotic response of the crowd.

"The Law that preserves us all," DeGraaf held his arms wide.

"The Law remains!"

"The Law that saves us all," finished the chairman, clasping his hands together.

"The Law is good!"

"Our beautiful world was thrown into turmoil," the chairman continued, "when the Great Collapse threatened to undo our way of life. Corrupt nations scrapped and warred over the simplest of goods. Conflict became lawlessness. Lawlessness became anarchy. "Then came the Law. Drafted by our long-departed generations to govern and preserve the beauty of humanity, the Law stands perfect and unalterable, save for once a year when a young man or young woman has proven themselves in the field of contest." He shook his head slightly and looked down as if mourning. "Not a battle where lives are lost or destroyed. Much of history has been plagued by conflict. Rather they chose a contest where the brightest and fittest alone could achieve victory. Our young people are our future." The chairman paused to let the words echo through the crowd. His eyes slowly moved over the faces in front of him. "The wisdom of the Lawmakers was to help the next generation own the Law by drafting a new law each year following the annual Chase. Only the most dedicated young people could compete in so difficult a challenge as the Chase, and it is their dedication that will shape their generation. Youth are unfettered by the burdens of adult life, having not yet succumbed to the bias and politics of the world that once brought about the Great Collapse. Only one so untouched can change the Law with pure intentions. Such was the foresight of the Lawmakers that a tested and loyal youth would be worthy of drafting the newest law.

"Representing the Union of Free Southeastern Territories, this year's winner will demonstrate the blessing of the Law by imposing new grace upon us."

With that, DeGraaf stepped aside from the podium and motioned to Shreya. Sheila's lips curled. He hadn't used the girl's name. He probably didn't even know it.

Trembling, Shreya stepped onto the platform and stared at the masses hushed to hear her words. Her eyes nervously scanned the people as if watching for a way to escape.

I can't believe they didn't prepare her. Sheila shook her head. While the favorites were often drilled in their alliance's greatest needs, the younger racers often had little knowledge outside their training. Regions were strictly prohibited from telling their racers what law to pass, and racers were often drugged and questioned pre-race to see if they'd been coached. Now, an unprepared teenager was to shape the future of her people. Shreya's lips, glossed perfectly and shining in the sunlight, parted into a tremble. "On behalf of the glorious culture of the Union of Free Southeastern Territories," she spoke trying to keep her voice from shaking, "I declare that the people of that alliance receive a tribute of one-tenth of all the annual food rations from the other eleven alliances."

Dear God. She has no idea. The law would create bitterness between alliances and effect little real change. A moment when the world could be bettered was lost to short-sightedness. Sheila guessed the girl had grown up in poverty and feeding her people at the expense of other alliances had been motivated by ignorance and not malevolence. Amid the thunderous applause, Sheila turned to the camera.

"There you have it, folks. Time will tell how *profound* an impact this new law will have on the World Coalition." She rambled on with her impressions of the law hoping Chuck wouldn't notice her sarcasm in the comment. She'd hear about it if he did.

But nothing has changed. She hated covering the Chase.

Chapter Two

Willis leaned against a post and picked at a loose thread on his jacket as the other trainees pressed into get a better view of the Western Alliance broadcast of the victory ceremony. A few shots of the crowd drew his attention in the hopes of catching a glimpse of his parents who attended every year, but all attention was on the unlikely winner. *That's how the Chase goes. One wrong move by an unprepared racer could ruin the chances of those destined to win.*

"Hey, Willis, that gonna be you next year?" a voice came from the corner, possibly from a member of Green Team. He chose not to answer.

"When are we up today?" Jez, his teammate on the Red Team, wormed her way through the racers to stand beside him in the common room of the Western Alliance Training Center.

A hush spread over the room. Even Willis looked up. All eyes fixed on the monitors as the nervous girl passed the new law. A collective sigh filled the room as she finished speaking. The moment was over. That year's Chase was over. Conversation in the common resumed, ignoring the reporter named Sheila Kemp who was commenting on the girl's decision. Willis joined others in shaking his head at the new law. Jez impatiently grabbed his wrist to pull the schedule card in his hand closer, reminding him he hadn't answered.

"We have the track right after the goldies." He checked once more to be sure he was right.

Jez clicked her tongue in disgust. "That's all we need, a track smelling of hair spray and nail polish."

"Careful, Jez. Joanne has them working hard. They may seem all glitter and selfie shots, but we can't let up. They're right up there with Black Team." The goldies, as many called them, were the all-female Gold Team. Their obsession with themselves was ceaseless, but that didn't mean they weren't true racers. Willis had done the math and knew that one good run would be all they needed to take over second in the standings.

The common room made up most of this half of the space station and resembled a university recreation hall with the section to his right hosting various amusements meant to occupy the trainees in their downtime. These were rarely used since most trainees spent all their spare time preparing for the next run. Monitors lining the walls meant to resemble windows displayed live images of the stars around the orbiting station, but one could switch the screen to display various scenes from around the Western Alliance. Tables, normally occupied by strategizing teams, filled the bulk of the space. The wall to his left contained a window opening into the gym, complete with its color-coded sections to designate the equipment as belonging to a specific team of trainees. Behind him was the archway that led to the rest of the facility.

The station was designed around the training sphere, the largest structure which contained their practice track. Jutting from the side of the sphere was the main corridor, off which the team barracks stuck out like ribs, ending in a rectangular area that contained the common room and gym. An outer ring contained the mess hall, administrator's offices, medical wing, and various other areas that didn't concern the racers.

Despite the size of the space, the normally separated teams stood tightly and mixed together competing for the best view of the broadcast monitor. Willis wore his standard uniform, made up of pants, a black shirt, and a red waist-length jacket trimmed in black. Others wore similar outfits, except with their own colors, which kaleidoscoped as each glued their eyes to the screen to see the results of the Chase. The broadcast shifted to review a highlight reel of the winner's run and career leading up to the Chase.

"Who is she?" someone asked.

"No idea. Never heard of her," came another voice.

"Everyone will tomorrow. Man, seventeen, and she won it all."

Seventeen. Willis stared from the back of the room, leaning on a table. *How could she win at seventeen?* Antonio DeLuca was supposed to have won this year. In a short-lived cooperation effort between alliances, he'd trained at the same junior training center with Willis as a child, where their competition was often heated. A close finish in a training run led DeLuca to lose his temper and attack another racer. When the Western Alliance sought to discipline him, the DeLuca family smuggled him back to the Joint Mediterranean States and out of the jurisdiction of the Western Alliance. Willis had been relieved to see him entered in the Chase this year, as they were both eighteen. He was the racer who stood to challenge Willis next year, but he'd been entered early when the pool of racers appeared thin. He was a supposed lock for the win, and his use was expended. Racers got one shot at the Chase. That was it.

"Seventeen?" Willis searched the faces around him to see if he'd heard correctly.

"Yep. And going home a hero."

Going home. It was an idea as foreign to Willis as breathing outside the protective walls of the space station. He had never gone home. Placed into training before he could remember, he never truly knew his parents, yet the Chase reminded him of them every year. His parents, racers themselves, were often held up as demonstrations of the beauty of the Law, the greatness of the Alliance, and importance of his genetic heritage. Yes, he would serve the Western Alliance, but more to make his parents proud. Becoming a Law-changer was the lone way he grasped how to do that.

"The girl's a half-wit," Jez snarled into his ear, glaring at the images of Shreya. Her nails dug into the muscle of his arm, which she'd taken after examining the track schedule, right through the red sleeve of his team jacket. She curled her lips in disgust at the screen. "How dare she assume the place of superior racers. Her alliance should have pulled her before she embarrassed them with a stupid law."

Willis shook off her clawing grip but allowed Jez to go on without interruption as she spouted more venom at the girl on the screen. Food rations would have little effect on the Western Alliance—the WA—or any of the other larger alliances. The people were well cared for as long as they obeyed the Law.

He had rubbed the back of his left ear with his thumb when Jez had mentioned 'superior racers,' a habit he had since childhood. The tattooed code, a number one, on his ear which sat above a bar code that identified his famous parentage indicated he'd been genetically recoded once in his life. Recoding was a process by which a racer's memory and consciousness was transferred to a genetically modified copy of their physical body. A low gen-code was a badge of honor and prestige among racers, and it meant he wasn't in the habit of losing. The tattoo had one small flaw as if the needle had slipped. The skin was raised at that spot ever so slightly, perceptible to the touch. It brought comfort to Willis to know he still had his low gen-code. It told everyone else that, in the Western Alliance, *he* was a superior racer.

Unless they competed in the Chase, racers weren't allowed to retire until age twenty-one, and recoding was practiced even at the earliest stages of childhood training. Scanning the room, Willis noted that none of the racers present were even close to retirement. Over the span of his training, Willis had watched others face frequent recoding during their developmental years if they didn't perform, and he knew a couple of the racers on the station to already have high gen-codes.

It was a reality none of them discussed, though it was always on their minds. Most preferred to leave their gen-code as private a matter as they could.

More than his height, strength, or well-toned body, Willis's famously low gen-code told everyone a story. He was a natural, his talent not genetically manufactured. Among the racers on the station, everyone expected he would compete in the Chase or retire long before his recodings were used up. It gave him respect as a leader. He rubbed the bump behind his ear once more for good measure.

"D-d-d-d-dex, gonna t-t-t-t-trip again this week?" Willis's thoughts were interrupted by the high-pitched mocking voice of Toad, another of his Red Team members. At least that's what they called him. His real name was Lester or something like it, but Toad was more fitting his character. "You sure it wasn't a relative of yours who tripped that guy in the Chase?" Toad added.

"St-st-st-stop, T-t-toad," Dex stammered, retreating from the area. His glassy eyes betrayed the hurt caused by Toad's ridicule of his stutter.

"Toad, lay off." Willis rolled his eyes and sighed as he approached Toad from behind.

Toad smirked and continued his rounds to the lesser racers in the room. The kid was relentless in his teasing of the other trainees, but he wasn't being untruthful. Dex had speed, for sure, but couldn't keep from tripping over himself, leading to several Blue Team failures. More than once, Willis had leapt over the kid as he lay sprawled on the track.

"Back off, maggot," came a stern voice.

Willis chuckled to himself. Toad had turned around right into the enormous body of Creed, the leader of Black Team. Willis couldn't help but laugh at the thought that Toad had overreached this time.

"Touch me again, and I'll squash you." Creed wasn't kidding. Mario Creed stood solidly flanked by the rest of the Black Team. Jen Walker and Casey Stone, the female members of the team, stood on either side of Creed with their arms crossed. Casey's twin brother, Zeke, stood next to his sister, running his hand through his unkempt hair and staring to the side absentmindedly. Since the Black Team solely used each other's last names, Creed called him Stone-zee to distinguish him from his sister. Much larger and impressive in their black uniforms, they towered over Toad as his face flushed to match the color of his red uniform. The ceremony done, most trainees were gawking at Toad's idiocy.

"Try it, and we'll see who ends up recoded after the next run." Toad was talking too big a game. Willis glanced over at Kane, the fourth on his Red Team, who stepped forward behind Toad. Creed wouldn't hesitate to find an excuse to hammer Toad if he believed he could get away with it. Kane silently laid a giant, dark hand on Toad's shoulder. Creed was an imposing presence, built with a huge frame that could crush someone of Toad's underwhelming size, but he was nothing next to Kane who stood like a giant among the group. Kane's behemoth size made Toad appear even more pathetic. For a second, Creed's advance was halted as he contemplated Kane's addition to the situation.

Seeing the various teams intent on watching the standoff between the two largest racers in the room, Willis turned to Jez. "Better get Toad out of here before Creed decides taking on Kane is a good idea."

With a nod from Willis, Kane began pulling Toad toward the door despite his protests. A fight no longer a possibility, the rest of the trainees began to disperse.

"Why do you even put up with that red-haired runt?" Jez's eyes narrowed at the scene.

"He's a good racer. That's why," Willis retorted. He believed it, though he too, sometimes questioned whether the annoyance of Toad's manner was worth it.

Jez turned to him, an expression of cynicism on her face. "A racer who made his former team look foolish to impress you. He told those guys they were running the course at half-speed that day. He knew you were recruiting."

Willis tilted his head, keeping one eye on the door to make sure Toad didn't escape Kane's grip, and spoke softly. "I'm not stupid. He may have hamstrung a few teams in his wake, but he's raced with the best. Remember, I made him run the course against another team before I picked him up."

"I-I don't think you're stupid." Jez retreated. Her dark eyes brightened as she looked up at Willis, her hand raising to move her straight, jet-black hair behind her ear. For an instant, her hardened appearance softened, and Willis noticed how attractive she could be when she wasn't angry. She had delicate features when they weren't hidden behind fierce eyes. He pretended not to see her studying the side of his face for a moment and then turned to glance at her.

She quickly glanced away and restored her usual cold appearance. She trusted him. That was important. She was an elite racer, trim, but all lean muscle. Her gen-code was a nine, low, although not as low as his. She could probably lead a team of her own. She'd chosen to stick with the Red Team, which made them that much better. He needed her trust for his team to remain elite, even if he never could truly return that trust. He couldn't have her leaving the team—or worse—trying to take his place. He had no doubt she wouldn't hesitate to backstab almost any other trainee in the room. She despised other racers, especially those of the Green or Blue Team.

Green Team was above average, but no real threat to the leading teams. Nico, their undersized team leader, overstepped when he took on a team of his own. Willis had considered recruiting him for Red Team around the time he'd added Jez, but Nico accepted leadership before he could act. It was a good thing too. Nico had peaked as a racer and would have become a liability.

Black Team was merely a few points behind first place. Creed had introduced a military form of discipline to their training, and it'd launched the team into second place. Willis had to push Red Team daily to keep them out front. Willis reminded himself that Creed's team practiced immediately after his own and showing up late wouldn't give his team any extra time on the track today.

Then there was Blue Team. Dead last.

Chapter Three

Perryn gasped as she bolted up in her bed. Glancing quickly around the room, her thoughts raced, trying to collect themselves. "My name is Perryn," she whispered. "I am a racer for the Western Alliance. I run for Blue Team. I will survive to retire from training." Her heart slowed as she repeated her rehearsed reminders. She examined her hands to make sure they were hers. She never felt like herself for days after waking from a recoding, and she hated the feeling.

Pulling her feet over the side of the bed, she breathed deliberately to test if her new lungs worked. For all the improvements the recoding was supposed to make, she never felt stronger. As a child, she could always sense that she was a little bit faster or stronger, but those sensations stopped years ago. She did remember twisting her ankle slightly during the race, and this new ankle showed no signs of the injury.

"At least that's something." She rubbed her legs and arms, assuring herself they were truly hers. She tried to remember her recoding, but all she recalled were emotions. Horror and dread filled her with no memory as to why. The Alliance had done its job preventing her from remembering what happened in the medical wing of the station.

The mirror showed the face of a teenage girl that she recognized as herself. Brown hair, brown eyes, and a heart-shaped face like that of her mother. The hatch next to her revealed a fresh blue uniform fitted for her average frame, this time with a yellow team leader armband folded neatly atop the pile. All team leaders wore one. Seeing the band passed to her meant only one thing—their team leader Diego was dead. She choked as she picked it up.

"Breathe, Perryn. Move forward, exactly like every other

time." Her hands shook as she dressed.

Still fixing her dark brown hair behind her head, she found the hallways were vacant when she exited her room. The corridor to the mess hall was usually a flurry of activity in the mornings as teams shifted between the common room, mess hall, and training sphere. It wasn't until she found no one eating at breakfast that she realized what day it was. The Chase had taken place during her recoding. Everyone would be gawking at the screens to see what was happening.

She grabbed her food tray from her panel on the wall and headed for the common room.

The common room was a jumble of colored uniforms jockeying for position to see the end of the Chase. From the chatter, she gathered that someone had fallen during the race and an unexpected winner was about to pass a new law. She could hear the crowd on the monitors chanting about the Law in response to the chairman.

She didn't care about any of it. She would never run in the Chase. All she desired was to stop being recoded and make it to twenty-one so she could retire and leave this place.

Not every nation practiced genetic recoding. Some alliances saw recoding as disgusting, an impure practice. Others couldn't afford it. Everyone knew the truth, though. Alliances like hers who practiced recoding won almost every year. Finding naturally talented racers was difficult, and recoding allowed alliances to focus on the few exceptional ones they had. In addition to allowing racers to almost instantly overcome serious injuries like her ankle from the previous race, each recoding was meant to systematically minimize the genetic flaws in a given racer's makeup, but Perryn understood too well that the process wasn't without cost.

The recoding process gradually altered the runner's personality, and she struggled to remember who she was before she began training. The young girl who started with dreams of a becoming a famous Chase runner were gone, replaced by a loser with a high gen-code. All that was left was the shadow of herself in the mirror, but that is what it meant to be a part of the Western Alliance. Loyalty to the Alliance meant doing whatever it took to win. Loyalty meant days like this one where she woke an invader in someone else's body.

Though not as frequent as in her childhood training, recoding was still a monthly possibility. It meant little, though, as the improvements it gave her this late in her training were small and gave her no advantage over the other more talented trainees. There were limits. The WA had seemingly perfected the process, but even they were scarcely able to get to the hundredth recoding before the genetic material was beyond use. You either raced well enough, or you were recoded. You raced, or you were recoded into extinction.

Extinction. She fingered the new yellow armband. *Is that my fate?*

"St-st-st-stop, T-t-toad," came Dex's voice across the room. She turned in her chair to see Toad mocking her teammate. She gritted her teeth as she considered trying out her newly recoded fists on Toad's freckled face. Dex couldn't help who he was. He was tall and gangly with sandy-colored hair and could run like the wind, but his habit for tripping at the worst moments of the race crippled his confidence. He was a bluey like her. They were all rejects of the system. Some kind of commotion was taking place between the Red Team and Black Team, but she wanted nothing to do with it as soon as she saw that Dex was left alone.

Her anger quickly melted away as she returned to the arm band in her fingers.

"What am I going to do with this?" she whispered to herself. She stared at the stars on the screen wishing she could escape to one of them.

"Hey, P-p-perryn. You wake up okay?" Dex waved at her as he approached.

"Yeah," she responded, not wanting to get into a conversation.

She curled the armband in her fist so he wouldn't bring it up. "You?"

"Woke up early this time. Got to see the whole Chase run this morning!" He was trying to be cheerful, but Perryn could still see the hurt in his blue eyes from Toad's comment.

"Hey, don't worry about what Toad said," she comforted.

"Oh—that." He was suddenly downcast. "It's fine."

"No, it's not. Just because he's one of those arrogant Red Teamers doesn't mean he can abuse anyone he wants."

"Don't tell him that. If he keeps trying to pick on Creed, we won't have to worry about him much longer."

Perryn chuckled at the idea. "Is that what is going on over there?" She gave a slight grin.

"Yeah," Dex's smile returned. "He's so short, I'm not sure Creed could swing low enough to hit him." Dex's face flushed in embarrassment when she didn't laugh at his joke right away. "So, you think it might be us next year? The Chase, I mean."

Perryn's frowned. She opened her mouth and closed it without speaking. She looked again at her hands. "Let's get ready for today."

Dex bounced off to the barracks. He was young and one of the newest to the station.

She threw the arm band onto the table in front of her. She didn't want it. As far as she was concerned, it still belonged to Diego.

Blue Team had long been the band of misfits put together to ensure the better racers were never recoded at the elite levels. Recoding came with risks and ultimately the death of the racer. The formation of Blue Team became the Alliance solution to maintain the threat of recoding without putting the elite racers in any real danger. Young, eager runners who had little hope of being elite were often advanced early and 'blue-teamed.' She had been one of them, coming to the station full of hope to find that she was constantly recoded and would ultimately be replaced when she either died or retired.

Diego had changed that. He was the first to pull the Blue

Team together as a group. He'd noticed the strengths of the group and played into them. After a few runs, he had the team threatening to overrun Green Team in the training runs. Last week was the closest they'd come until Dex fell, taking out Diego and Amber. Perryn had tried to rescue her team by getting to the front but couldn't make up the ground. She didn't have the wheels. The team had been recoded a couple days later to try to enhance their DNA, but Diego's hundredth coding ended in his death. The doctors always attempted the hundredth coding, trying experimental techniques to break the 'coding barrier' as they called it. It never worked.

He doesn't understand. Not yet anyway. She went back to staring at the screens.

"Look at her! As if I'd post our picture with her in the background!" Cleo laughed. Starr and Lacey cackled in unison to the mocking comment.

Perryn had been trying to ignore the three goldies since they'd approached her previously quiet side of the common room.

"All right, ladies, this one's for the fans." Cleo waved the others in closer. The three in their gold uniforms leaned as Cleo reached out to snap their latest selfie shot. Their uniforms had been altered to their liking, as much as was allowed within regulations, and each had done their hair in a different, yet perfectly manicured style. All three wore matching gold lip gloss.

"Finished yet?" Joanne sighed. The Gold Team leader stared at her teammates as they posed and smiled for the camera.

"Never!" Starr rebutted. "We're never done giving our fans some love."

"Seriously, Jo, you need to chill," Lacey agreed.

"Come on. We have the track for the next hour. If we're going to overtake Red Team this year, we've got to figure out that second level," Joanne called as she started for the archway.

"What—" Cleo started.

"—ever!" Lacey finished. "Can we leave Jo out of the calendar this year? She's no fun to be around when she gets all serious like this."

"One more, Jo." Cleo held the camera out to the other two. Without hesitation, both assumed a 'candid' pose that emphasized their best side. "Sweet, ladies. Let's catch up to Jo before she cracks."

The three girls started their model runway exit from the common room. As they passed the last row of tables, Cleo turned and placed her manicured nails on the corner table. "Oh, and Perryn, don't waste our time trying to sneak into one of our shots again. Like any of *our* fans wants to see *your* face." The three girls didn't disguise their laughter as they walked through the archway.

Perryn sat at the table without acknowledging the comment. She had been there long before those three had shown up, but she hadn't the energy to argue with them. Not that they'd get it, anyway. Logic wasn't exactly their friend. Silently, she cursed the goldies. For all their glamor, they were good racers—good enough not to be stuck on the Blue Team.

She sat in silence as racers slowly drifted out of the room to prepare for the day of training.

Chapter Four

Willis's eyebrows creased as he watched the Gold Team's mockery of Perryn in the corner. He nodded his head toward the exit, and Kane had to keep one huge hand on Toad to drag him from the common room. Toad, feeling over-confident with Kane around, had continued his blustering. Willis smiled. Toad appeared like a tomato as his flushed face was indistinguishable from his blazing red hair.

Jez crossed her thin, muscular arms in disgust and stormed out behind them.

Willis's stomach clenched as he checked the time. *They're distracted. I hope they don't bring all the fuss over the Chase ceremony and law-passing to the track.*

He eyed Perryn as he approached the archway. She sat facing away from the silver table with an untouched meal sitting behind her. His eyes lingered on her brown hair, noting a few strays that hadn't quite been pulled back with the rest of her hair and hung down the sides of her head, an imperfection that he'd always liked from afar. He imagined it meant she was easier to talk to than some on the station, though they rarely spoke. He bit his lip, wondering if he should speak to her.

Perryn's gaze was fixed to the monitor as if she were watching for something. Her arms hung limp as both hands rested on her lap. As he got closer, the arm band on the table explained her indifference to her surroundings. It was the same band he wore, the one that all team leaders wore.

"You guys almost had Nico's crew last week." He cringed as the words came out of his mouth, and she frowned. She obviously wanted to be left alone. "Look, I'm sorry about Diego. He was a good kid."

Perryn's eyes left the screen as she turned to stare at Willis. The dampness of tears still clung to her lower eyelids. He hadn't noticed that. He saw dashed hope in her brown eyes.

"He was our first real chance," she whispered. She reached for the arm band.

Startled at her vulnerability, Willis stood motionless. He should say something comforting. The silence finally awkward, he didn't have a choice. "At least you get to be team leader."

Oh, the stupidity. That was insensitive. She was right. Diego had been their real hope.

Perryn's hands balled into fists, crushing the arm band in her grip. She stood, her chair scraping the floor as she kicked it out of the way. She gazed up at him, not angry, but determined. For an instant, she stood taller, and Willis saw that she had strength left in her. Then, it was gone. Her momentary fiery eyes dimmed to their usual exhausted appearance. Without a word she turned and walked to the archway.

His parents were famous for saying that everyone had a role in the Alliance. Blue Team had theirs. Recovering from recoding meant lost track time, which then meant less training. They could never keep up with the other teams. Willis sighed heavily. It was a lousy card for anyone to draw, but the Alliance understood what it was doing. The system of protecting the elite racers while recoding others kept the Western Alliance competitive in the Chase, winning every few years. Winning is what mattered. It was in moments like these that he wished he could ask his parents to explain it all to him.

Reaching the archway, he watched Perryn from a distance as her brown ponytail swayed with her tired steps. He shook his head and hoped that he'd never experience what she was going through. He rubbed at his ear, reminding himself who he was, as he headed to change for their training run.

Chapter Five

"I can't do it," the woman whimpered, her voice cracking with sorrow.

"It's the only way we can save him. They'll take him away as soon as he's walking," a male voice nearby pleaded. Sadness dripped with every word.

The soft sound of unstifled sobs filled the air with a tangible anxiety. "What if he hates us for it?" she continued. Her voice muffled as she buried her face in the man's arms. A long moment passed as they wept together.

"He won't. Not when he's old enough to understand," he said, caressing her face with his hand. "Here, you hold him. I'll take care of it. You don't have to watch."

Pain. Excruciating pain.

Willis had been experiencing the dream for as long as he could remember, but he still had no idea what it meant. The images were too fuzzy. The faces too blurred.

And the pain.

Not that the pain was real. He knew it was the idea of pain, but it felt real until he woke up. A few seconds of inspection were all that was required to realize his body was covered in sweat but still intact. He swore his right leg ached for an hour after each dream, but it must be imagined. His hands shook as he wiped the perspiration from his forehead.

Who were the people in the dream? Why did he keep dreaming about them? The answer wouldn't come to him. It never did. Once, he'd entertained the notion that they were his parents, but he'd dismissed it. That made no sense to him. Every instinct he had about his parents said they were kind, alliance-loyal parents who had gladly handed him over for training, and he had years of letters from them to prove it. The images he saw in the dream didn't fit with what he knew to be true. Even when he focused, the indistinct faces felt barely out of reach. His breath shuddered as he tried to calm himself. *It's a dream—nothing more.*

He stared in the mirror over his sink, studying the lines on his face. His short, medium-brown hair sat matted and sweaty on his head. Dampening his fingers, he tried to straighten it. He studied his own blue eyes and debated if he understood what was asked of him this year. Thoughts of the previous day's practice run at the track invaded his attention. The team had worked the top level for most of their hour. If they could shave time off their start, there was no way the other teams could catch them.

He tapped a button and a panel next to his bed opened, revealing a single, fresh red uniform. He pulled them on—the son of two racers, he was a superb physical specimen, designed to be an elite runner. A separate racing uniform, a single, conforming piece would appear in the same place in time for their training run later today.

The red lights of his barracks greeted him with their indirect glow when he entered the hallway.

Willis stopped at the edge as he turned into the main corridor. The door to the track was open, and the smell of metal and recycled air came from the door. This current track had five levels and formed a tight cubicle structure that appeared to float in the middle of the empty sphere except for the few beams that hooked the entire track to the outer panels. As usual, he used their first run of the week to do a complete run-through of the track. The team would then shower, and over their next meal, try to determine which parts of the track were problematic. The rest of the week would then be focused on these areas alone rather than constantly running the entirety of the track.

Even after spending the entire run on the top level yesterday, Toad still hadn't mastered the first obstacle. *Toad better have some answers.* Willis had tried to offer suggestions, but to his frustration, Toad wouldn't listen. Willis silently rehearsed the various points he'd cover with Toad at breakfast. He insisted on a detailed strategy. It was the kind of leader he liked to be, but the thoughts kept him up late. Perhaps his weariness explained the occurrence of the dream.

Toad's height was his liability, and the team knew they'd have to assist to get him over. He continually stumbled as he climbed the wall, driving Jez insane with irritation. *Jez was probably up all night fuming.* He chuckled to himself. At least breakfast wouldn't be boring.

"You're going to keep your mouth shut, that's what!" Jez spat into Amber's face. She pinned the Blue Team runner to the wall, her right forearm pressing the girl's left jawline. "You think I'm going to take pity on a bluey like you?"

"I'm not sure I'm the one to be pitied," came Amber's muffled voice.

Willis took in the scene as he approached them outside the Blue Team dorms. What Amber had done to elicit the violent reaction, he couldn't imagine. Jez would snap her neck if she believed she could get away with it. He should probably tell Perryn to talk to her team about watching what they said.

"You little good-for-nothing. How dare you!" Jez's eyes went wild. "How many times did they recode you over there, huh? Came here with no number, simply to get tagged by this Alliance. Serves you right for running from your alliance, you little traitor."

"You think your captain would like to know?" Amber smirked.

Jez whipped her head around to see that Willis was a few steps away. Her teeth were bared in a furious grit.

"You going to introduce me to your new friend, Jez?" Willis joked.

"We were about done here," Jez responded. Without warning, she reared back and slammed Amber's head into the wall. She crumpled to the floor holding her right temple, blood appearing between her fingers. "You shut your face, dirtbag, or there will be far worse coming."

"One day, Jez. One day your little secret is going to catch you. I've seen it. They kept files on all the elite racers where I came from. We studied them. You act tough, but I know who you are." Amber began to slink away, still holding her head.

Jez's nostrils flared as she stepped toward her, but Willis caught her arm. Jez lived as though she loathed everyone, but it bothered him to see her react so violently. He couldn't imagine what Amber knew that would make her respond like this. He could feel every muscle in Jez's body ready to unleash her hatred. She yanked at her arm trying to free it.

"Jez, look at me," Willis spoke softly. Daggers shone from her eyes, a sharpness that lessened when she peered into his. "Let her go. That'll land you a week in an isolation chamber, and that's not what we need." Her body relaxed, and her breathing slowed as she listened.

"The bluey better keep her lies behind her teeth," Jez hissed.

"What was she talking about?"

"Nothing. Lies."

"You sure? I heard what she said. What does she know about you?"

"It's nothing. Leave it. I'll deal with her later."

"I think she got the message already." Willis took a deep breath and glanced in the direction Amber had walked. He dismissed the idea of going after her. It would make Jez angrier if he continued to intrude, and he needed to direct her energy. Today's run was the most important thing. "We need to focus if we're going to get through practice today."

Jez sighed and shot a glance to either side as if not wanting to meet his eyes. "Okay. Seriously, what a—"

"Seriously, I'm hungry," Willis interrupted, hoping she'd let it go. "Let's eat. Save some of that fire for Toad. He'd better get today's run right."

"Or I'll beat the snot out of him," Jez whispered as they walked.

The mess hall was plain, square with color-coded tables for each team. The smell of vitamin enriched eggs and fruit filled the air. Like nearly everything else on the station, it was designed with function in mind. Willis liked that. No distractions—all business. It kept Red Team fixed on their next run. The walls were the light source in the room, lighting every direction with a fluorescent glow. Next to each table were four panels, one for each team member. Willis walked up to the one labeled with his name, scanned his fingerprint, and removed the tray from the space that appeared in the wall.

Toad was already at the table, keeping his head down, when he and Jez arrived. Willis supposed he wasn't ready to make eye-contact after yesterday's practice.

Jez slammed her tray down on the table next to Toad making Willis jump.

"You'd better get it right today, or so help me, I'll hurt you into next year's Chase," she barked, shattering the near silence of the room.

"I don't want to talk about it." Toad said. Willis glared at him to make certain he understood that Jez wasn't kidding.

The few people in the mess hall looked up at Jez's outburst before returning to their meals.

Willis marveled that Toad was idiotic enough to mouth off to Creed but cowered at the prospect of facing Jez. A noise to his left revealed Creed's Black Team, arriving together as per their precise schedule. They ate in silence, preferring to discuss team business in private. To the right, Nico was busy instructing the greenies in quiet whispers. Behind him the gold table sat empty except for Joanne. The other goldies were probably still prepping their hair.

In the corner, he saw Perryn once again ignoring her meal. One hand held up her droopy head like she hadn't slept much. Dex sat nearby stuttering his way through forced conversation, but she didn't appear to be responding. She still wasn't wearing her arm band. If Chief Administrator Blacc caught her, he would cite her for uniform code. As he considered walking over to her to warn her, Jez continued her tirade.

"You little runt, yesterday was supposed to be a simple run through level one. We're supposed to be working on the second level today, but no, we have to return to let you mess it up one more time."

"Okay, Jez. He gets it." Willis tried to calm her as he sat down opposite Toad. Kane was to his left eating almost silently. He never talked in meetings. In fact, Willis had never heard him talk more than a grunt here or there. He was big enough to break almost anyone in two. Willis didn't know how he could spend life on the station in silence. *What did they do to him in that prison?* Rumor was that Kane had been imprisoned for murdering someone, a person in a subway tube or something, but no one knew what was rumor and what was fact. Whatever it was, the Alliance apparently believed his ability to race outweighed his crime and sent him here. Willis was just glad he was on his team.

"See, Jez? Willis is okay with it," Toad shot back.

"Toad, she's right." Willis corrected quickly, afraid Jez might turn on him. "You get one shot today on the track to figure out that jump, and we're moving on. If you get recoded this week, I'm not going to cry about it." Toad's head returned to its downward angle. "We run the track right after Blue Team today, and I want to make the most of this practice."

Willis was in his element. This was where he thrived. He was an elite racer, but his real gift was leading the team. Teamwork was critical. The Chase took place over two days. The first day was a team event, and it determined the start for the individual race the second day. While the Chase was ultimately won by a single racer, it could be lost by a team that couldn't work together.

He walked them through the obstacles they'd work on today. Kane nodded in silent agreement as Willis assigned him the task of hoisting Toad over the level one hurdle. Level two would require Jez, their best climber, to run ahead and shimmy up a pole to release the rope needed to cross a gap. Willis would handle crossing the wire web himself. Each obstacle had to be crossed by at least one team member who would hit a button right beyond. That button would briefly make the obstacle easier, giving an advantage to the teams that leveraged the abilities of their members the best. One blown assignment could mean costly seconds. The team hung on every word. Even Toad, who rarely stopped running his mouth, paid attention.

Willis was born for this. His parents had both run in the Chase before he was born. The Western Alliance had barely missed a win that year, his parents getting edged out by another runner. There was celebration anyway, though, because the conclusion to their training for the Chase brought the announcement of his parents' relationship.A few months after the Chase, the Alliance watched as his parents had married, started a life together, and followed with the news they were pregnant. Willis was the hope of the Alliance. People had often told him this. The son of two elite racers would surely have the genetics to win the Chase. His parents' occasional note to him said as much. He knew they meant to be encouraging, but he daily felt the pressure.

He arrived at the training station at a record young age, and the years hadn't brought disappointment. Recoded once, too young to remember why, he led the best team with a year to prepare for the Chase, and it was his race to lose.

"Suit up. We train in one hour." Willis dismissed his team, the last to leave the mess hall.

Chapter Six

Sheila picked at her meal on the flight. She was rehearsing her speech to Chuck, her editor. *Chairman DeGraaf's failure to remember the name of the young winner highlights the flaw of a system where any nobody, given the right circumstances, could become a Law-changer.* The words from her report repeated in her head. She would have to answer for her critical comments about the chairman and the Coalition. Chuck didn't like any unwanted attention from the Alliance censors. All was supposed to be well and good in the Alliance—all the time. She knew differently. Anybody who had eyes to see the world around them knew differently.

Even the plate in front of her spoke to the unevenness of this 'utopia' that had been created. Her supersonic airliner was state-of-the-art. A single column of plush seats ran the length of the roomy cabin. Flight attendants kept constant watch on the passengers, seeing to their every need. The Alliance had spared no expense for the planes it sent, carrying dignitaries and authorized press to the Chase. They wanted them to arrive in style to show the world what happens when you were a dominant presence in the Chase.

That is, to the extent they could.

The flight had been restocked in the United African Cooperative where the race had been held this year. They had been hit hard under sanctions levied upon them for attempting to cheat at the Chase three years ago. A runner had attempted to break onto that year's course before the day of the Chase. It was a foolish move, and he barely made it a quarter mile before he was discovered and arrested. The Coalition had made an example of him to the world, returning him to his alliance after weeks of interrogation and punishment. He hadn't been seen since, likely dealt with by the justice that can come from a mob of people.

Food rations and supplies had been limited to near crippling levels, yet the UAC was expected to host the Chase this year. The development of the course had nearly bankrupted the Cooperative. The Coalition had done its job well.

She'd been there. She picked the camera angles to fill the lens with the stage and ceremony, but all the while one eye had remained fixed on the poverty behind the camera. Children in rags. Mothers half-starved giving what little they had to children with even less. You would never know these conditions existed in the world if you were from places like the Western Alliance.

"Would you like something else?" The flight attendant interrupted her thoughts.

She stared down at the ugly piece of processed meat covered in who-knows-what. This was probably more than most of the people in the Cooperative ate in a day, and yet they'd stocked their plane with what they had. A lump of guilt rose in her throat as she entertained the idea of not eating it. A pile of greasy, nutritionless mush sitting on the tray of a luxury airliner, it was a silent testimony of the world that few grasped.

"No. Thank you," she replied.

She was sure her stomach would make her pay for this. She picked up her fork.

Chapter Seven

"Don't forget the new plan for level two. Toad, you'll hold until Jez gets past her first obstacle. Got it?" Willis's gaze froze on Toad for a second as he gave last minute instructions outside his barracks.

"Yeah, I got it." Toad smirked.

"Do you?" Jez's lip curled. "Ruin this run, and I'll—"

"He's got it, Jez," Willis interrupted. "You good, Kane?"

Kane nodded.

Jez's lips pressed as she motioned for Toad to focus, but Willis wasn't worried. After the early mishaps of the week, the team had put together three perfect practices. Each had worked hard, preparing themselves. Even Toad had set aside his usual constant mouth to get this track down. They were ready for today's run—and good thing. With all the excitement over the annual Chase, the Chief Administrators had moved the monthly elimination run up to this week to get the teams into focus. The last team to have a runner cross the finish line would be recoded.

"Let me check you guys out." Willis stepped toward his teammates. A year ago, his yellow leader's arm band had been too loose and caught on a wire. The mistake nearly cost them the race. Since then, he made a habit of checking their uniforms before each elimination run. Their racing uniforms were made of a single, heavy duty material designed to allow for a freedom of movement. Theirs were entirely red save for the black stripes that ran from forearm to wrist and knee to ankle. The other equipment they used was a set of training helmets, required by the Alliance for safety during training.

"Toad, your sleeve is bunched up on your left arm. Jez, your helmet strap is twisted on that same side. Kane, check that left shoe." He double-checked his arm band one more time. "Bring it in."

The three stepped toward him. He laid his hands on the shoulders of Kane to his right and Jez to the left. The others did the same to each other in a sort of loose huddle, except that Jez reached up her right hand and covered Willis's hand. He ignored the gesture.

"Team, the Alliance is counting on us this year." Willis nodded to each of them.

"You mean they're counting on you, Will," Jez corrected. "*You* are the hope of the Alliance."

"It may only take one racer to win, but it takes a team to get him there. We're a team. We train as a team. We run as a team. We win as a team."

Nods came from everyone in the circle, a determined expression on their faces. Willis knew how to inspire.

"Be the best," he started.

"Beat the best," they answered stoically.

"Let's race," Willis said as he turned for the door, the team falling in behind.

"Who do you think you are, puke-brain?" Willis recognized Chief Administrator Blacc's voice several meters before they entered the door. Blacc wore a perfectly pressed, drab gray uniform, his shoulders sported yellow Alliance officer stripes designating him as Chief Administrator of the station. He stood with finger outstretched, pointing at Stone-zee. Blacc's face flushed crimson as he yelled, and Willis could see the color spread to his scalp underneath is short-cropped hair. "That uniform is the pride and joy of the Alliance. You're privileged to wear it, you little snot-nosed wimp! And you disgrace it with your lack of discipline." Blacc was close enough to Stone-zee's face that Willis believed he saw him spit in the Black Team member's eye.

"Team leader!" Blacc shouted.

"Yes, Chief Administrator!" Creed's spine stiffened.

"I hold you responsible for the discipline of your team. What say you about your teammate's complete lack of respect for the Alliance uniform?"

"No excuses, Chief Administrator." Creed dared to shoot a glace over at Stone-zee's uniform. The sleeves were short as though cut. "I take full responsibility for Black Team."

"In case your sorry backside gets recoded after this race, be sure to tell the doctors to keep this memory in that pea-brain of yours. Next time your team shows up with a member treating the goodness provided to them by our Alliance like it was a Christmas present from their grandma, I'll recode the lot of you for the fun of it. Do you hear me, boy?"

"Yes, Chief Administrator!"

Willis could see the fury on Creed's face. Stone-zee never fit the high-discipline Creed brought to his team and regularly acted out, but this was brazen considering it was a recoding race. His unwashed, black hair flopped to his collar, too long for regulations. His angular face and green eyes presented indifference as though the entire exercise bored him. Creed had long given up trying to correct Stone-zee, so he pressured Stone to keep her twin brother in line as she was the lone person to which Stone-zee would listen. Stone would have to answer for her brother's uniform later. The dampness in Stone's eyes told Willis that she was already thinking about what was coming to her.

Protocol on this track was to begin at the top, racing downward from one level to the next of the cubical structure. The starting gates were located at the beginning of a narrow stretch of floor that extended out to the cube in the middle of the room. Willis had brought his team to the platform in front of the gates at the last second as was his habit, hoping that Blacc's venom had already been dispensed on the other teams. Peering down the line to his right, he could see that he'd done his work.

Each team had lined up shoulder to shoulder, their two-toned racing uniforms creating a rainbow of racers. Beside Creed's red face topping his black and white uniform like a cherry on a sundae, he could see Green Team appearing rather shifty from a tongue lashing Blacc must have given them prior to Willis's arrival. Gold Team, always concerned with appearances, was keeping their plastic smiles on, but Joanne was clearly dwelling on something that was said to her. Blue Team was at the far end of the line, too far for Willis to see their expressions.

He could see Perryn rubbing her neck with her arm, her yellow-banded arm moving back and forth as she tried to calm down. Blacc was never easy on new team leaders. Willis was sure he'd done his worst. What caught his attention, though, was the figure beyond her. Diego's replacement had arrived. From this distance, he could tell he was average sized with not a bad build for a racer, but there appeared to be nothing special about him. Probably another poor sap that thinks he was promoted to the station early because he's exceptional. *Poor kid is going to be recoded before he spends a single night in the dorms.*

"Something about our new bluey of interest to you, boy?" Willis hadn't noticed Blacc move toward him until he was right in his face. That was a mistake. "The Western Alliance's little golden boy thinks he has a new friend down the line. You eyeing the newbie? Is that what you're doing?"

"No, Chief Administrator." Willis snapped his head forward to attention.

"Blue leader, send your baby-faced rookie down the line. Our boy down here has a bit of a man-crush on him already." Willis could see out the corner of his vision the movement of a blue uniform slowly making its way down the line. "Face your new friend, bluey."

He was older than Willis expected. He guessed eighteen. The boy stood before him silent, his brown eyes staring at Willis. His brown hair was short and neat and framed a face that reminded Willis of his father. In fact, Willis and he could have passed for brothers in another life. He was as tall as Willis, but with a little less muscle tone, not having had the benefit of the training at the station.

"So what do you think of your new friend, red leader? Like

the look of him? Wish he was on your team?"

No. You aren't doing this to me. Willis involuntarily clenched his jaw and flared his nostrils. He focused on slowing his breathing, trying not to give Blacc any more clues that this bothered him. Blacc was a master at dividing the teams. Jez had been ready to kill Toad all week, so theirs was a delicate truce.

"How about it, Red Team? Think your fearless leader wants to replace one of you? See how he's all googley-eyed over our new bluey? He's already figuring out which of you to get rid of, so he can have his friend on the team. How about you, big guy?" Blacc was in the face of Kane, but Kane stood silent.

"How about you, worthless piece of dirt?" He stepped over to Toad.

Willis almost chuckled. Toad had been called far worse by the other racers.

"No, I think it's you, little girl." He was in front of Jez now. "Yeah, he doubts you. He'd love nothing more than to see you recoded." At this, Willis heard her stifle a gasp. *When is he going to stop?*

"Jaden."

Willis snapped his head back to the boy in front of him who had spoken. He was waiting for Willis with a hand extended. *Is he crazy? Blacc is going to be all over him.*

"The name is Jaden," the boy repeated, still waiting for a handshake that would never come.

"Look what we have here." Chief Administrator Blacc was suddenly louder so all could hear. "Our bluey thinks he's the new member at the country club. Wants to start getting to know the other members. Fall in line, you lousy, little, good for nothing—"

Blacc's voice faded as he chased Jaden down the line, but not before the boy had raised the corner of his mouth to reveal just enough of a knowing grin to Willis. *He'd done it on purpose. He'd played the part of the ignorant newbie to take the pressure off me. Well played, Jaden.* Too bad for the kid. He would be re-coded for sure today. Willis caught himself rubbing his ear, calmed by the presence of the slight scar.

The air was thick with anticipation. Willis stood ready at his gate, a door-less metal arch. A single green laser line stretched in front of him from one side of the arch to the other. Anyone breaking their laser would be eliminated from the run, almost assuring their team would be recoded. Willis visualized the laser line at the other end of the course turning from red to green as he crossed the finish line. Green meant you hadn't come in last. Green meant you were safe from recoding.

He took a long scan around. Jez's fierce expression was in full bloom as he examined her face. He could see her thinking her way through the first few obstacles. Kane's hands clenched into fists on his left. His breathing had become a deep, steady rhythm to match the intensity of his stare forward. Toad, on the other hand, was fidgety. The kid was all nervous energy, but that was normal before a run. Toad had arrived ready to run today.

Creed's group appeared determined as ever as each thumped the other on the shoulder with the side of their fists. From somewhere beyond, he heard the whispering of Nico's last-minute instructions. The goldies had put down their cameras and were all business. Cleo, Starr, and Lacey had all pulled their hair behind their heads and seemed more like Joanne than before.

It was then that Willis's eye caught a moment among the Blue Team. Facing forward at the line, the teammates on Perryn's team didn't look at each other and missed what happened. Jaden reached a hand over and grab Perryn's hand. She'd been nervously rubbing her fingers together as if the stress of her first run as leader would somehow ignite from the friction and burn away. Jaden never looked at her, even when Perryn gave him a startled glance, but the quick squeeze of his fingers appeared to do the trick. A warmth came to her frightened eyes as she turned to focus on the course in front of her.

"Tone in five seconds," a metallic voice from the speakers echoed off the far wall.

"Elimination run!" Blacc shouted.

"Four—"
"Losing team—"
"Three—"
"—faces recoding!"
"Two—"
"Make the Alliance proud."
"One—"

Chapter Eight

Willis never heard the tone. He'd learned to anticipate it so well that he swore he could feel the hum of the vibration in the air before the sound reached him. His legs were already in motion as the laser disappeared.

The five teams raced the length of the open stretch to the cube. Toad was tiptoeing along the edge and falling behind. Transparent energy fields kept anyone from falling off the side, but the visual of a several story height was enough to give anyone vertigo as they ran on the outside. It was almost impossible to ignore the mind's overwhelming desire for self-preservation.

In front of them the mouth of the run opened, an archway high enough for each of them to pass through, except for Kane who had to slightly duck. A few steps beyond the archway rose a high wall, too high to jump and grab the edge. Each team approached the portion of the wall painted to match their team color. Creed was shouting at his team. Someone on Green Team stumbled as they climbed upon another member's back. Willis's Red Team didn't even whisper as Kane turned at the wall, cupping his hands low for Toad to step into. Toad's foot met its mark perfectly. *Thank God.* Kane's massive body burst from its crouched position as Toad's momentum was transformed from forward to up. Toad caught the edge of the wall and scrambled until one leg was over the wall. Swinging the other leg over, he disappeared down the other side.

An instant later, a buzz came from the wall announcing that Toad had hit a button beyond, and the upper portion compressed and dropped inside the lower third of the wall. Willis waved the other two over first.

He chanced a glance to his right.

Black Team—over. Creed was watching him, measuring their progress in return.

Gold Team—right behind.

Green Team—their runner was hopping off the wall to hit the button beyond.

Blue Team—over. The concept caught Willis as he ran forward, and he stole a second glance behind him to confirm what he saw. Perryn, Dex, and Jaden had joined Amber on the other side of the wall. *That's new.* Willis had time to process little else. Another buzz behind him announced Green Team's hot pursuit over the wall.

Willis caught up and raced ahead of his team. A cube sat above the floor, affixed at one corner to a pole that rose up out of the floor. Covering the cube were a series of levers that moved up and down, nine on each side of the cube. He grabbed the first lever and heard the activation of the energy field behind him that held the rest of the team back.

Each lever, when pulled, moved three other levers. The goal was to move all levers to the up position. It was simply a mathematical problem, and Willis had spent hours the night of their first practice on this track memorizing the solution.

"Come on, Cleo," Joanne shouted to the gold cube.

"I know! I have to start over." Cleo sounded panicked.

"Done in thirty seconds, Creed." Walker was making short order of her cube.

Nico had caught up and was working on their cube. Dex moved furiously around the blue cube shifting levers with confidence. Buzz. Buzz. Willis had finished at the same time as Walker. Buzz. Blue Team was through next. Buzz. Buzz. There were the other two.

Jez flew by Willis as the energy field dropped and started ascending the rope cargo net beyond. No one climbed better than Jez. This is where they would establish their lead. She was halfway up the net, which stretched to the top of the track cube, before others were a meter above the floor. The button at the top of the net released it to fall flat, covering the gap. Willis, Toad, and

Kane leapt onto it as it fell and scrambled across. They met Jez who was dropping from a hanging rope that brought her down to the other side of the gap. Amazingly, Perryn had been the next one down from above the course ahead of the other teams.

Kane threw himself head-first down a chute at the end of level one to begin work on the first part of level two. Toad and Jez were right behind. Willis peeked over as he jumped on to see that Dex had fallen, getting tangled in the ropes. "Sorry, Perryn," Willis whispered as he hurled himself into the chute.

Kane was already making quick work of a lever, pulled back and forth, each yank ratcheting a floor from below into place. By the time Willis was standing next to him, the floor was inches from locking into position.

"Starr, no!" Joanne shouted. Willis glanced in time to see Starr step on to their floor too early. Joanne hadn't quite finished, and the pressure-sensitive floors were rigged to drop until completely raised and locked. Starr disappeared instantly as the floor fell, and he could hear her heavy grunt as the floor stopped several feet below. It wasn't far enough down to seriously injure her, but it would take a minute for her to catch her breath. Her team would have to pull her out before they could start raising the floor.

Click. Snap. Their floor was in place, and the four Red Team members bolted to the other side of the open floor. He could hear the floor of Creed's Black Team click behind him. Blue was ahead of the falling-behind Gold Team. He didn't know about Green.

Up a small flight of stairs, a large gap appeared in the floor. The effect was dizzying as the floor was equipped with screens that projected the bottom of the sphere almost a hundred feet down, making it appear as though they could fall to their deaths. The screens hadn't been active during the training runs, so Willis had to stop to collect himself. Across the span was a rope, which they had tried unsuccessfully to tightrope across in training. In front of the rope, a metal pole rose from floor to ceiling on this level topped with five lights and switches. The lights turned on and off in different sequences, which then had to be remembered and repeated using the switches. Missing even one of the five combinations required starting all over. An expert climber, Jez made quick work of the pole, but she groaned as the lights flashed indicating she'd entered the wrong sequence.

"Hey, Willie-boy. Enjoy getting a new number behind your ear?" Creed's voice shouted out. Willis watched in horror as the Black Team very mechanically crossed the tightrope.

"Ugh. I can't get it, Willis." Jez banged the pole in frustration.

"Get down, let me do it." Willis gripped his scalp in both hands.

Jez came sliding down, looking very angry at herself.

Willis started climbing, his arms burning as he hoisted his weight and held on with one hand, leaving one to work the lights. He could see out of the corner of his eye that every other team had arrived. Amber on the Blue pole slammed her fist on the light switches as she'd obviously made a mistake. Joanne was making quick work of the lights trying to catch her team up. Nico was already sliding down his pole, the puzzle done. *One more combination. One more.*

Buzz. Willis crashed to the floor as a second rope lowered to serve as a hand hold for the crossing. Creed had already disappeared down the chute to floor three. Nico was quickly shoving his teammates down. Willis tried to steady his breathing. He owned floor three. This is where they would have to separate themselves.

Perryn shook her fist as she watched Willis cross the rope. They had a great start until Dex fell on the cargo net. For a minute, she'd believed. Now she stood next to the pole, at the top of which Amber was busy beating her hand against the puzzle in frustration.

Black team—gone.

Green team—reaching the chute.

Red team—right behind.

"Let's go. Let's go!" Joanne shouted as she slid down the pole. The goldies had made up the difference after Starr's fall. *We're in last again. Another recode. I'm not going to make it off this station alive.* She swore the doctors inserted hope into her memory at each recode because its dagger twisted in her heart each time they lost.

Floor three had one obstacle, but it was nothing like Willis had seen on other tracks. The entire floor was a mass of thin metal wires going in all directions. The web spread out throughout the room like a dense metallic rainforest. Each team had to get one player across to hit their button, which would open a trap door in the floor, allowing that team to crawl under the wire system. He could already hear Creed inside the web cursing to himself as he slipped.

Jez grabbed his arm. "You got this, Willis."

Willis approached the wires. They were so thin that he swore they'd cut him if he grabbed them too hard. *Okay, Willis. Right foot over this wire. Duck under that one.* He'd tried to memorize a solution.

Clang.

The bell sound startled Willis, and it was bad news. A bell sound meant the administrators had introduced a change into the course. A sudden pain in his ankle caused him to cry out. He looked down. *How did those wires close on my foot?* Two wires had drawn together and were pressing deep into his skin, not enough to cut, but plenty to hurt.

"Ow!" Lacey cried somewhere in the distance.

"Stupid wires!" Creed was in a rage having lost his lead as he yanked at his arm that was trapped between the wires.

Willis scanned carefully around him. *Was the room moving? No. The wires are moving!* The administrators had waited to reveal that this web wasn't constant. Each wire had a back and forth motion causing the gaps to open and close slowly. He shot a glance at his ankle to see if his theory was right. Sure enough, the two wires had reversed course, and he was soon free. He scrambled forward.

"Willis! You okay, man?" Toad called out.

"It moves! Nothing we practiced is going to work," he called as he quickly pulled himself on all fours through a narrowing gap. "How are the other teams?"

"Creed's right behind you and not happy you're ahead. Nico's somewhere in this mess, but I think he's caught. Lacey is back up and close to Creed. The new guy's running for blue, but I can't see him," Toad reported.

Everyone's here, Willis noted. *Hopefully they're all freaking out over this change too.*

Left, right, under, over. Willis was weaving his way through the mesh, occasionally panicking as a limb would get caught. The most painful was a hole that he misjudged causing the wires to close briefly around his neck. His stomach lurched as the wires pinched around his throat. For a few agonizing seconds, he couldn't breathe, and he had to calm himself to patiently wait for the gap to open. He could hear the other runners working their way through the web, but he didn't dare look. The chaotic movement of the wires was dizzying when scanning around. He learned quickly to focus solely on the next wire.

Falling forward, Willis found himself beyond the web. He stumbled forward and slammed his hand down on the red button. Jez shouted at the team to get into the trap door. Creed had been behind him but was pulling on a wire that had closed on his foot as he tried to climb out.

A flash of gold showed him that Lacey was almost through. Nico had one green and yellow arm reaching into the open air outside the web, but he too, was caught. Willis glanced further at the sound of a *thud* across the room. Amazingly, Jaden had sprung out the end of the web. *Blue can't decide if they want to get recoded or not.*

Perryn's heart leaped when the trap door opened. Jaden had done it. The web was supposed to be Dex's turn, but he fell coming out of the chute. Jaden hadn't hesitated and went running for the web. She called after him to stop him, but it was no use. He was three steps into the web.

Now she was shoving her teammates down into the hole in front of her. *We have a chance.* She jumped in in time to hear the doors for the other three teams open.

The energy field dropped in front of Willis, Jez, and Kane indicating that Toad had made it through the level four 'hamster tunnels,' as he called them, to the other side. The three of them ran underneath the clear plastic tubes that ran above their head over to Toad.

"Stone, don't you dare mess this up!" Creed shouted. Stone jumped and grabbed the first of the hanging rings. She was watching Kane who was a couple of rings ahead.

"You got this, Cleo," a goldie mimicked.

It was going to be close. The bottom floor was an all-out sprint in a shared space. All the teams would be running together through a room with walls that would move suddenly in and out. A second or two lead would keep him from tripping over another team.

"Kane!" Jez screamed. He'd lost his grip and was dangling from a single ring trying to find another close enough. Blue and Green Team had arrived. Perryn was two rings in front of a greenie.

"Be c-c-c-careful, Perr," Dex tried to encourage between heaving breaths.

Buzz. Buzz. Buzz. Red, gold, and black platforms appeared simultaneously, and the teams scampered to the other side. Willis threw himself down the chute head first. The race was won by the first member of each team to cross the line. He didn't need to wait for the others.

The dark chute curved right sharply with a sudden drop. Willis shot out of the chute and landed in a roll, a move he rehearsed many times privately. In one motion, he finished the roll and found his feet to begin running.

"Right behind you, maggot," Creed snarled. Another set of footfalls told him Joanne was there too.

The familiar walls moved in and out, not with smooth predictable movements, but with jerking suddenness. He spun around the first wall on his right and used his arms to bounce off the one to his left. His lungs burned as he pushed his way through the room. Other voices and running steps told him others had arrived, though he didn't know if they were blue, green, or other members of the front three teams.

Crunch. His right shoulder slammed into a wall that protruded from the side in the same spot he'd hit earlier. He'd started to glance back and hadn't noticed it. The weight of Creed's massive body shoved Willis aside. He tried to ignore the growing flame of pain in his shoulder and strained to stay on Creed's heels. They were merely twenty meters from the finish gates.

A half-wall dropped suddenly from the ceiling, striking Creed. "Aaaah!" Creed screamed as he went to the floor. He instantly scrambled to his feet while holding his head, but it was all the break Willis needed.

At full speed, he dropped to his knees and slid beneath the wall right next to Creed. He was on his feet as Creed stood up, but this was his race to win. Creed appeared dazed, still holding his head.

Willis shot across the platform that exited the cube and through the red gate, setting off a tone announcing he'd broken the laser turning it from red to green, meaning his team was safe from recoding. He had done it. He had won. Another tone—Creed was through. A tone at the gold gate let him know Joanne was there.

Willis turned to see who was finishing on the two remaining

teams. The red laser of their unused gates beckoned. One would turn green. The other would remain red and mean recoding. He could see motion through the mouth of the cube, when suddenly a blue and a green uniform emerged. Jaden and Nico were right alongside each other. Sweat glistened off both of their foreheads. Jaden's cheeks were flushed pink with the effort. Nico's darker skin didn't betray his strain, but his expression was all Willis needed to see. It was an expression of fear.

A tone.

The thud of collapsing runners who expended everything they had.

Silence.

The rest of the runners slowed to a walk seeing the race was over. Everyone surveyed each other silently. What was there to say?

Nico stared at the laser at his gate. It was still red.

Chapter Nine

Gasps could be heard escaping from the mouths of several runners, including Perryn, who Willis could see standing on the track with her hand over her mouth and the beginnings of tears appearing in her eyes. The reality of what had taken place was sinking in.

For the first time, Blue Team hadn't lost. The team designed by the Alliance to prevent the truly elite runners from late career recoding had failed to lose.

"This—this can't be right!" Nico stammered. "The sensors must be wrong. I beat you. I had to beat you. I—I—I—"

"Green leader, present your team!" Blacc's voice boomed, breaking the stunned silence.

"Chief Administrator, this can't be right," Nico continued in his stupor.

"On your feet, team leader."

A slight whimper drew Willis's attention over to the rest of the greenies. The other three members of Green Team stood there. A younger girl, whom Nico had recruited quickly after her arrival at the station, tried unsuccessfully to stifle the stream of tears that had begun to pour from her eyes. One of the boys behind her placed a comforting hand on her shoulder, but the tremor in his grip betrayed his own fear. Almost everyone got recoded at some point during the training. Even Creed had voluntarily been recoded after a serious injury rather than put his team in jeopardy. Willis supposed that they'd forgotten what it was like or that the doctors had removed the memory of it. *Or worse, they remember it all too well.*

He'd been too young to remember his own single recoding. What was it like? Did it feel like dying? He massaged the bump behind his ear for assurance. He couldn't allow himself to take his ability for granted. He didn't have to face the obvious horror of recoding.

The other runners retreated when Blacc approached the Green Team as though their coming fate was contagious. Blacc was flanked by several of the station's doctors, all dressed in sterile-looking white lab coats. Willis had seen this sight many times, but this was different. This was not routine.

"Green Team, you are hereby ordered to report to the lab for genetic re-modification." Blacc pointed toward the door. "Team leader, as a top finisher you remain eligible to stay in your current condition should you choose."

The room stared at Nico who nervously tried to keep from locking eyes with anyone. A racer who finished behind the other team winners but ahead of the rest could elect not to be recoded. It was mandatory for everyone else on the team.

Don't do it! Willis screamed in his mind.

"I—I—I—" Nico couldn't manage to form the words.

"Green leader, your decision." Blacc was growing impatient.

"I e-elect not to b-be recoded, Chief Administrator."

There was no response. Blacc simply nodded at the doctors who approached the greenies. The whimpering girl cried openly as the gloved hand of a doctor grabbed her arm.

"No! I don't want to!" she screamed. "We're not supposed to lose. No! Nico, you said we'd never lose. You said we'd be safe. You promised."

Willis watched as Nico hung his head in shame while his teammates were escorted from the track, the girl half-dragged through the doorway to the medical wing. Her shouts could be heard for several moments after the door closed. A tear rolled down to the end of Nico's nose and dripped to the floor.

Blacc stood for a moment staring at the racers who stood as though their feet were glued to the track surface. "All right, you sissy-pants runners. Dismissed. Shower up!"

There were no hugs or high-fives. The runners silently filed out the door to the dorms. Willis watched as the wide-eyed Blue

Team slowly approached Jaden, who was getting up off the floor after diving through his gate. Willis almost expected one of the Blue Team members to reach out to touch Jaden to ensure he was there. As much as the greenies didn't appear to know how to react to losing, the Blue Team seemed even less familiar with failing to lose. Without a word, they joined the flow of sweaty racers leaving the track. Willis was the last to turn to leave when a hand grabbed his arm.

"Your little newbie friend has shaken things up a bit, hasn't he?" Blacc squeezed Willis's arm a second longer, and Willis saw the amused smile on his face. "This should be interesting." Blacc let go of his arm, and Willis tried to walk casually as he hurried to catch his teammates.

"Coward!" Willis could hear Walker's voice before he entered the common room. Normally, the hours after a recoding run were the most relaxed of any on the station. With another recode a month away, much of the competition between the teams was laid aside, if barely for an hour or two. Today would be different. *How is Perryn doing with this?* Willis was surprised his mind drifted to her first.

"I finished in the top five. I don't have to be recoded," Nico complained as he came into Willis's view. He was trying to be tough with Walker standing over his chair, but his eyes betrayed his fear—and his guilt.

"The Chase begins as a team event. Win as a team. Lose as a team," Walker growled.

"But I don't have t—"

"Shut up, traitor. You are no leader. A leader belongs with his team."

"But—" The rest of Nico's words never made it past his lips as Walker shoved her hand over his mouth. With one hand she shoved his face backward while lifting the edge of his chair with the other. The sudden crash caused the room to pause to acknowledge the incident.

"Walker! Discipline yourself." Creed was suddenly there, breaking the silence. Creed had been far worse in his abuse of other runners, but he took pride in seeing his team maintain their discipline. Willis believed he liked to think that he was shaping them to be the perfect runners. Willis waited until Creed and Walker cleared out before approaching Nico.

"You had to know that was coming," Willis said. "Walker believes teams should stick together no matter what. She would have allowed herself to be recoded in a flash if her team lost."

"But—but I didn't have to." Nico was almost whispering.

"No, you didn't. But you can't blame her for having principles." Willis extended his hand, helping Nico to his feet.

"Nico, you all right?" Jaden's voice came from behind Willis.

"What do you want? Come to gloat over your win?" Nico frowned and balled his hands into fists.

"Hey, man. I wanted to make sure you were okay. That's all." At this, Nico moved toward Jaden as if to grab him, but composed himself before doing so.

"Where did you come from anyway, newbie?" Nico meant it as an insult, but Willis secretly hoped he would answer.

Jaden's brow furrowed for a moment, and then his face relaxed. He smiled. "Maybe some other time, friend."

"I'm not your friend, newbie. Stay away from me. Stay away from my team."

"I hear ya. Glad to see you're all right." Jaden turned and walked away to rejoin the Blue Team who sat in uncomfortable silence at their table. They appeared as though they didn't know what to do with themselves. It occurred to Willis that they'd never gotten to join the group in the common room after a recode. They had always been taken away with the doctors.

"Take it easy, Nico." Willis turned his attention to the fuming green leader. "It's not his fault. You were trying to win as much as he was."

"Yeah, but he doesn't have to come over here and rub it my face. Stupid newbie. Where does he get off talking to me?"

"Willis?" Jez called to him. Willis turned to see his team gathering in a pod of cushioned seats. Toad was slouched in his chair with a smirk on his face. Kane sat hunched forward, his elbows on his knees, gripping a hydration bottle. Jez stood and was waving Willis over. The team wanted to talk, or at least Jez did. *Not now.* This was a time for relaxing, and his team already wished to strategize. He took one more peek at the Blue Team. He would give his team a few minutes and go check on Perryn.

"Get a drink, Nico. Try to relax a bit. You survived today." Willis patted his shoulder then turned toward Jez. He hadn't meant it as a blow, but the grimace on Nico's faced showed Willis how much his words crushed him. Nico wasn't much of a leader, but he cared about his team.

Jez didn't even let Willis sit down before she began. "Willis, we need to talk about the newbie."

He settled into a fourth chair in the pod noting that Jez had placed it closer to herself than either of the guys. "I don't see why," Willis replied. "I think Creed is more the issue. He almost had me today. Black Team is getting better, and we can't let them peak in time for the elimination races later this year."

"Will!" Jez glared and dropped her eyebrows. The heat of her stare made him look away. She used the shortened form of his name when she required his attention, and she wanted it now. "Blue Team is supposed to lose. They're supposed to protect the rest of us from recoding."

Willis shot an uncomfortable glance at the table of blueys. *Had they heard that?* "Not so loud, Jez."

"I don't care. This is all wrong. Nico is a waste of a runner, but he's right to be upset. Someone needs to put what's his name in his place."

"Meh," Toad croaked. "Give it another race and things will get set straight. The newbie will get recoded and learn his place. Maybe we're lucky, and he's been recoded ninety-nine times already. That'll take care of him. Anyone catch his coding number?"

"I tried to see it." Jez was suddenly somber, lowering her

voice. Willis noted how serious she appeared. "I saw nothing."
"You mean you couldn't see it," Willis corrected. Kane
looked up. "No, I mean there was nothing to see."
"That's not possible. Everyone in the system gets recoded at
some point. Most are recoded many times before showing up
here. There should at least be a number showing who his parents
are."
"Willis, I swear to you. He has no coding number."

Somewhere, deep in the medical wing of the station where the
screams could not be heard from the common areas, the three
Green Team members endured the house of horrors that made up
the recoding experience. Needles, tissue samples, and the
wrenching pain were nothing compared to the sensation created
when a consciousness was removed from one physical brain and
implanted into the waiting copy nearby. For a split second, every
recoded racer got a good look at their mutilated former body. The
doctors would remove the specific memory of it, but the terror
could never be forgotten. Each would awaken a day later in their
room, in a body with negligible improvements, wondering if they
were even the same person.

Chapter Ten

What am I doing? Willis turned down a hallway he'd never walked. The intermittent blue lights that lined the walls made his uniform appear strange. He was used to his red barracks, but he found himself up earlier than most racers and walking through the Blue Team barracks seeking out Perryn.

He wasn't sure why, but he'd woken with the overwhelming urge to speak with her. Jez hadn't let up for hours the night before. Jaden had done more than send the greenies to the medical wing. The whole station was talking. He guessed some part of him had to know what was being said among the Blue Team.

She's probably not even awake. He stared at the outside of her door. Reaching for the touch pad next to her door, he hesitated.

Schwipp. The door suddenly opened to reveal a bleary-eyed Perryn on the other side. The whites of her eyes burned red and dark patches hung under both eyes. She stared as if gazing at the wall behind him. She was headed somewhere and noticed him when he took a startled step back.

"What? What are you doing here?" Perryn's voice cracked as she spoke.

Had she been up all night? "I-I thought I'd stop by." The response was lame, but he hadn't been prepared to speak. He realized in that instant that he wasn't sure what he intended to say when he came to her door.

"Stop by?" Perryn sounded more annoyed than inquisitive. "You never stop by. Nobody ever stops by, especially in this wing."

"I know," he admitted, glancing at the floor.

"In fact, you've pretty much never talked to me before I made team leader." The accusation was harsh but true.

"Umm—yeah. I know. I—" He stopped. "I thought I'd see if you wanted to talk."

She paused as if to consider if she had the strength to argue with him. "Come in," she sighed. Stepping aside she allowed him to enter. Her room was the same as his and as spartan in its arrangements. The smell was different. It was an antiseptic sort of odor.

"Someone clean in here?"

"They sterilized it after Diego died in recoding," she said coldly. Willis winced when she said "died." He'd never considered it dying. "I guess they thought there'd be another day for the smell to go away before I woke up." She twirled a finger to the space around her. "When Jaden arrived yesterday, I had to move into Diego's room." Perryn dropped her gaze and wrung her hands, seemingly embarrassed.

"So, about Jaden—" Willis hesitated to change the subject, but he saw his opening. "What do you make of the guy?" He sat down and hoped she would do the same. She was content to lean her blue-clad shoulder on the wall by the door. Her brown eyes looked down at her feet as if considering the question.

"So that's why you're here. I thought you wanted to check on me."

Willis straightened instantly. "I—I did. I mean, how are you guys doing after winning—er, not losing? Jaden truly shook things up."

"I didn't sleep if that's what you mean. To be honest, I don't know what to think of him." Her expression darkened. "He showed up late, right before the run. No one knows who he is. No one knows where he came from. Then, there's the race." He noticed her blinking quickly to keep tears from escaping her eyes.

This is a mistake. Perryn must be afraid to say what she was thinking. He'd seen more emotion out of her than most racers, but this might be pushing her too far. "At least you didn't get recoded," was all he could think to say.

"That's it." Her voice rose. "You'd think I'd be happy. All I've fought for was to get on a team that was good enough not to lose so I could survive until I'm too old to race. We're not all like *you*. You'd think I'd be celebrating, but all I feel is guilty!"

"Guilty?"

"Yeah, guilty!" She stood up from the wall and pointed at the door. "You think I didn't hear your little leech of a teammate last night? We're 'supposed to lose,' and we didn't." She took a step forward.

He spotted the same fire in her that he'd noticed a few days ago.

Her gaze pierced him as she threw her arms out to the side. "And what now? Am I supposed to have hope? Am I supposed to think it'll happen again? I'll tell you what will happen. We'll lose. Just like we always do."

Her face got serious as she stooped to meet his eyes. "And you and your privileged friends can go on with your happy life with things back to normal," she whispered. Willis almost wished she was shouting again.

"That's not what I want—" He held both hands up in front of him.

"Shut up. I don't want to hear it." The threat of tears returned to her eyes as the fire in them dimmed. She turned away from him to the wall, swiping at the wetness in her eyes with her hand. "Please leave."

Willis opened his mouth to speak, but he thought the better of it. Standing up, he moved toward the door, pausing for a moment behind Perryn. He stared at the back of her head, noticing the subtle, natural waviness of her long brown hair. He'd never seen it down like this. Normally, she pulled it into a functional ponytail. He started to put a hand on her shoulder and tell her things might get better, but he withdrew it. *She's right. They're built to lose, and I'll never know what that feels like.*

The corridor was far livelier as Willis exited Perryn's quarters. Dex was returning from an early workout. He'd always been an earlier riser, preferring to get time in the gym when he wouldn't have to talk to anyone. "Hi, W-W-Willis," he stuttered, giving Willis an inquisitive look. "What are you up t-to?"

"Congratulating your team leader on a victory for her first time out." Willis supposed it the least objectionable thing he could say.

"Yeah. K-kind of nice to sleep in my own bed last night." Dex smiled and walked on. Dex was a good kid. Willis pitied him. He was transferred so young, and Willis suspected he bore the weight of so many of their losses after critical falls.

He'd be a great racer if he could keep on his feet. He breathed a sigh of relief when he reached the main passageway. No one there. *Good, no more questions about why I'm in the blue barracks.*

The passageway was wide enough for several people to walk shoulder to shoulder with the different colored barracks on either side. The entrance to each side hallway was colored like that of the team living there. Blue and Green were at this end of the corridor, closest to the gym and common room. Red and Gold were at the other end, nearest the track. The middle was occupied by Black Team on the right and an abandoned set of barracks on the left. Orange Team used to sleep there during Willis's first year, but a massive accident had killed two of their members causing the other two to get recoded for the hundredth time.

Rumor had it that the loss of an entire veteran team forced the administrators to rethink the process. Years of investment in training had been lost. While the threat of recoding kept racers training, the Alliance couldn't afford to lose the elite ones. Rather than bring on a new team, they retired everyone on the old Blue Team leaving it ready for four unsuspecting new racers. The Blue Team would serve as a layer of protection. The new blueys brought to the station had no idea what their purpose was until it was too late, and the Orange barracks had been silent ever since. It was a dark reality that Willis tried not to think about when he passed that hallway. If he ever was to get home, questioning the system wouldn't help.

A sound coming from the empty Orange barracks drew Willis's attention. He stepped softly down the passage to the Orange opening, not wanting to announce himself until he figured out what was happening. He peered around the corner.

Casey Stone was up against the wall, tears streaming down her face. Her eyes were full of fear staring straight in front of her, and her hands were wrapped around something. His eyes adjusted to the darkness of the hallway, and that's when he saw that she was pulling on the powerful forearm of Creed, whose fingers were wrapped around her throat.

"Mario, I'm sorry. I'll take care of it. I promise," she whimpered.

"Don't call me by my name." Creed's nostrils flared. "You're not my friend. You are a subordinate. I don't address you as Casey. I think your brother's lazy attitude to our rules is wearing off on you."

"Sorry, Creed." Her voice weakened as she strained at his arm. "I'll get Zeke in line."

"Your brother is going to cost us. I brought him on with the understanding that you'd take care of that slacker. Yesterday's stunt with his uniform brought Blacc's hammer down on our team. I don't *ever* want that to happen again. Got it?"

"Yes, sir. Please, you're hurting me." Stone's tears flowed again.

"Black Team *will* win this year. Make no mistake."

"But what about Red Team? Willis—" Her words were stopped short as the back of Creed's hand found her cheek. He loosened his grip on her airway, and she slumped to the floor holding her face.

"I don't want to hear a word about that pretty boy. We're going to win, and you're going to do whatever I tell you so that we win. Do you hear me? *Whatever* I tell you."

Willis's stomach turned at the scene. Casey was not a friend, but he couldn't stand by to watch this. He hated Creed's style of leadership, but this was beyond intimidation. This was abuse. He stepped out from the edge of the opening. "Pretty boy? Come on,

Creed, I'm not half as good-looking as you are." He smirked, hoping to draw the attention on himself.

"Stay out of this, Willis. I had you beat yesterday. You'd better watch it. We're going to take care of that number behind your ear yet."

"And you'd better watch out for obvious obstacles dropping from the ceiling." He stepped closer, rubbing his ear for a second. Willis breathed a little easier when Creed stepped away from Stone to point a finger in Willis's face.

"You want to start something?" Creed challenged. He wouldn't dare take on Willis here by himself. He was bigger, but any injury Willis delivered could threaten his chances. However, Creed was right. Black Team was threatening every month.

"Nothing I don't intend to finish in first." Willis laughed. He couldn't help it. Creed's face grew wild for a second, before bringing it under control. He shoved Willis to the side and stomped toward the Black barracks.

Pausing in the hallway, Creed spoke without turning. "Watch yourself, reddie. Things happen on the track. Remember which hallway you're standing in." Willis looked around at the orange lights and sighed. Creed meant every word of his threat.

"You okay?" Willis turned to Stone who was curled up on the floor, her eye already pink and swelling.

"He's right, you know." She looked up at him. "He'll stop at nothing to win. You should be careful."

Willis raised his eyebrows and knelt next to her. "You speak from experience?"

"Stay out of it." She waved him off as he held out a hand. "I have to take care of my brother." She blinked hard, and Willis could see the dampness collecting below her eyes.

"Can't your twin care for himself?"

"No, he can't," she shot back, turning her face away.

"Seriously?"

"He'd get eaten alive on another team. He doesn't care about the Chase."

"And that drives Creed crazy." He grabbed her hand and

helped her up despite her earlier dismissal.

"No, it drives him mad—mad at me. Anyway, I've got it covered." She brushed away non-existent dust from her legs and started to walk to the Black Team barracks.

Well, you've got a role as Creed's punching bag covered, anyway. Willis dismissed the joke about her last statement before it escaped his lips. It didn't appear to him like she had it 'covered.' He watched her until she entered her quarters. Then he reentered the main passageway.

"Willis!" Zeke's voice came from behind him. He sounded worried. "Have you seen Casey? She didn't show up at the gym this morning."

"In her room, I think." Willis noticed Zeke failed to shave this morning. Creed would not be happy.

"Thanks." Zeke ran to her door, which was the first on the left, across from Creed's. "What happened to your—" were the few words that escaped his lips when Stone's hand suddenly grabbed Zeke's shirt pulling him inside. Even from here, he could hear the intensity of her tone as she laid into him about yesterday. The voices were too muffled at first, but Zeke obviously didn't get her point. Her voiced raised so that Willis could hear well enough.

"Listen. I know the Alliance forced us to enter race training. Neither of us chose to, but Mom and Dad were too proud for either of us to say anything. I'm trying hard to get out of here, Zeke—to get both of us out of here. We make the Chase, and we're done. We can go home. I know you don't want to be here, but you don't always have to broadcast it."

Forced to train? Willis hadn't heard of anyone being 'forced' to train. As far as he understood, racers were either handed over at an early age by proud parents like he'd been or chose to enter training when they were older. Wrapping his mind around the idea of forced training felt like trying to pick up the entire track sphere. It didn't seem possible.

"So? Let him trade me to another team." Willis imagined Stone-zee standing with his arms held out to the side.

"And what, let you get recoded into nothing? Even if I make the Chase, how could I look our parents in the eye and tell them I couldn't take care of you?"

Willis couldn't be sure, but it sounded like the tears she had held earlier had become too strong to resist.

"Sis, it's no big deal. You don't have to take care of me."

"It's a big deal because every time you mess up, I'm the one who gets punished."

Their voices lowered beyond understanding.

Willis thought better of hanging there much longer. Creed wanted them at breakfast on schedule, so Zeke would be emerging soon. He quickly walked down the corridor and entered the red barracks. The red light brought him comfort. This was where he belonged. This was where he was preparing to represent his Alliance.

Stone's words about her parents stuck with him, though. He'd never reflected on what he would say to his parents after the Chase. He had so many questions. Still, the Alliance couldn't be all bad if his parents were so willing to send him here so young. The idea gave him a flash of comfort. Everything he'd heard about them—everything they said in their occasional one-way communications with him—told him his parents believed in the Alliance. If they did, he would too despite his questions. He sighed heavily. The day wearied him, and it had hardly started.

Chapter Eleven

Sheila stood outside the office of her editor. The frosted glass of the door kept her from seeing inside, but she recognized what awaited her. Chuck wasn't a bad guy, but with the Alliance breathing down his neck constantly, her actions at this year's Chase were going to reap consequences. No matter how hard she tried, it happened that her disdain for the Alliance always seeped through the cracks of her professional exterior.

"You going in there?" Tony walked up behind her, appearing nervous. He placed a hand on her shoulder.

"Better get it over with," Sheila sighed. She glanced at him with a small smile, wanting to wordlessly thank him for his concern.

He squeezed her shoulder and then patted it. "I wonder what my new boss will be like. Hopefully a reporter who appreciates the hard work I do for them." Tony returned to his usual demeanor.

She shook her head. "Shut up, Tony. It's not like much is going to happen. He'll chew me out, and we'll be back to business as usual." She silently hoped that was all that would happen. Had she gone too far this time?

"Dibs on your office." He grinned. "Just in case."

"Thanks a lot."

"Sure thing." Tony winked then walked away.

Sheila sighed, her long breath shuddering slightly. *At least I hope it's not that bad.* She grasped that the day would come when she'd push it too far, but there would be warning signs. He wouldn't take drastic action without some kind of intermediate reprimand. Still, her hand shook as she raised it. *Would he?* Taking a deep breath, she knocked on the door to Chuck's office.

"Enter!" Chuck responded with an unusual level of grit in his voice.

Sheila pushed the panel and waited as the door slid sideways. She expected Chuck to be seated at his desk with his feet up as usual, but it wasn't Chuck at the desk. In his place was a little man in a dark suit. His jet-black hair was pasted to one side, and his overly slender fingers were gripping a file. Sheila gulped as she noticed her picture at the top of the first page.

The man reached up and smoothed the lapels of his coat with both hands. It was then that Sheila saw the Alliance insignia on his coat, two eagles tearing apart a chain on a yellow background. The eagles were meant to represent freedom, a symbol left over from the pre-Collapse world, and the chain was to symbolize the shackles of anarchy. Law and order—The Law—was supposed to bring freedom. The chains were very much still there—polished a little—but still there. She stiffened as he spoke.

"Your employer has been very accommodating in providing all we need to address our concerns about your work, Ms. Kemp." He nodded his greasy head toward the corner where Chuck stood flanked by two uniformed men. They wore the black and yellow uniform of Alliance law-keepers, complete with batons and pistols at their side. Chuck was trying to stand proudly, but his dejected expression told Sheila they'd been grilling him for some time.

"You could have asked me." She threw a frown of concern in Chuck's direction. "I'd have told you all you needed to know."

"I'm sure, Ms. Kemp." The man smiled, revealing a perfect set of teeth. "Yet in the interest of complete disclosure, we believed it best to speak with your supervisor."

"And I'm sure *speaking* with us *requires* guns and batons, Mr—what's your name?"

"Careful, Sheila." Chuck suddenly spoke up, a tremor in his voice. "This man isn't from the Censorship Office."

He smiled again, pleased by Chuck's warning. He folded his hands on the desk in front of him. "Your supervisor is a wise man, Ms. Kemp. You don't need to know who I am, except that I'm your friend."

"My friend?" Sheila huffed. She crossed her arms and

glared.

"Yes, Ms. Kemp. I'm the one standing between you and my two uniformed associates here." He nodded in the direction of the Law-keepers. His warning was not lost on her. "You see, we have enough to arrest you for insubordination and disturbing Alliance harmony. We've worked hard to build a perfect society that remains the best example of the Law throughout the world. It's the Law that protects us all."

"The Law is good," mumbled the two officers without hesitation. Sheila frowned at the automatic response.

He leaned forward. "We can't have people like yourself tarnishing perfection."

"So, if you're not from Censorship, where are you from?" Her heart was pounding hard enough that she could swear he could hear it.

"I am the Administrative Liaison to the Coalition Chairman's Office."

"That's a mouthful." Sheila bit her lip. *Easy, Sheila. Sarcasm isn't going to win points.*

"What that is—is a direct line to Chairman DeGraaf. No representatives. No red tape. I get things done here in the Western Alliance for the chairman."

"Oh, so you do the chairman's dirty work." Sheila blurted the words before she could call them back. She swallowed hard to contain her anger. *A man like this probably made the decision to take my father's business.* Still, her mind screamed at her to stop talking. She was not helping herself.

"What I do," the liaison's voice lowered to an eerie whisper, "is take care of rebellious souls like yourself who seek to unravel the beauty of what our world has created. The chairman isn't happy with your recent reports, which includes your smart little remarks at the Chase. I intend to see that it doesn't happen again, from you or anyone else."

"So much for being my friend."

"I *am* your friend. Instead of locking you up to silence you, we're going to grant you the great privilege of reporting from the front lines of the Chase." His voice sounded hopeful, and Sheila couldn't imagine what he meant. "You'll be relocating to the training station in orbit to report on our young racers. This is a big year for us. Our runners are certain to take the Chase, and you're going to show the world, and others like you, the greatness of the Western Alliance." He paused, waiting to deliver his next words. "You will become a shining example of how reporters should represent our glorious Alliance."

"Gross. You expect me to agree to this?" Sheila leaned forward to show her seriousness. The man simply smiled again and folded his hands on Chuck's desk.

"How is your sister, Ms. Kemp?"

"What does that have to do with anything?" Sheila's heart skipped a beat at this sudden turn.

"How is she feeling in that hospital?"

The image of Audrey lying in a hospital bed in her hometown rose in her mind. Growing up, she had no memories of her older sister in any state other than bedridden. Instead of games of hide-and-seek in the yard after school, Sheila had spent hours entertaining her sister by her bedside. Puppet shows with dolls, impromptu dramas, and long monologues about the cutest boys in school had filled that bedroom with moments that helped them both forget her illness. Nothing, however, brought as big a smile to her sister's face as her little newspaper reporting on the happenings around the home and neighborhood. Even as an eight-year-old girl, she would chase down stories to get the most interesting angle and fill a page with descriptions for Audrey to read. *Keeping up with the Kemps,* she had called her little paper.

"You have a gift, little one," Audrey would often tell Sheila, her tired green eyes twinkling. She was the reason Sheila had pursued journalism in the first place.

After her father's removal, her mother had tried her best to take care of Sheila's ailing sister, but as her condition worsened, she had to be checked into a government hospital. The constant care her sister received was the sole thing keeping her alive. After their mother died, Sheila considered relocating her sister closer to where she lived, but Audrey's condition had progressed. She could never survive relocation.

"I-I don't understand what my sister has to do with any of this."

"Her condition is a sad one, Ms. Kemp." The liaison faked a forlorn expression. "Among other things, the glorious Law provides that we must maintain strict safeguards ensuring that precious resources are not misused. The hospital caring for her is under review this year. It would be a shame for the review board to find something wrong—a reason perhaps to remove the hospital's funding. That would be so unfortunate, wouldn't it? True, the patients could be relocated to other government funded hospitals. Most of them could, anyway."

He smiled again. Checkmate.

Sheila held her breath. He'd left her little choice.

"When do I leave?" Sheila straightened in her chair, not wanting to give away the defeat inside her.

"Ms. Kemp, you've made a good decision. You leave immediately."

Chapter Twelve

"They're here," the man whispered. *He was standing at the end of a window, close enough to see but not be seen from those outside.*
"Here? How did they find out?" The familiar woman's voice held a pleading note.
"I'm not sure."
"What are we going to do? Can we hide him?"
"No, they know he's here. If we ever want to see him again, we'll have to let him go." The man sounded defeated.
"No. No. No!" The woman's tears flowed.
Thump. Thump. Thump. A heavy hand was pounding on the door. "Open up by order of the Alliance Chase Commission." Someone shouted through the door.
"Can't we run?" Panic coated the woman's voice.
"I don't know. I simply don't know." He looked around, his gaze darting from side to side.
Crash. The door was down, and uniformed officers came running in as the woman screamed. Shouts of "Clear!" came from rooms as the officers searched the home. A man in a black suit with the Alliance insignia silently pointed to the man and woman. Both were held at gunpoint.
"No! You can't have him!" The woman struggled, kicking and twisting. Officers pinned her arms from behind. "I won't let you take him. He's our son! You can't have him!"
"Listen, maybe we can talk this out." The father started moving toward the official in the suit. A wave of his finger brought a baton to the father's knee. He collapsed with a scream.
"I love you, Son." The woman was desperate. "We love you. Your mother and father love you so much! Never forget that we love you—Willis."

Sweat beaded on Willis's forehead as he shot up in bed. He checked the clock. It would be hours before anyone else would be up. It'd been weeks since he'd heard Casey Stone discussing her parents, but the idea of seeing his parents again after the Chase hadn't left his thoughts. With it had come the same dream, night after night, a panicked set of parents struggling to keep their child. And then, his name. This woke him at different hours with a sour feeling in his stomach every time. He remembered the day he was handed over to the Chase Commission. He was very young, but he could remember his father's proud expression. His mother had cried, a mix of joy and sadness. Both had hugged him and willingly handed him over to the officials.

So, where did this dream come from? The notion nagged at his mind ceaselessly.

It didn't help that a journalist, someone representing life on the surface—life where his parents lived—had transported to the station after the last race and was interviewing the racers one by one. Each week, she spent time with one of the teams, writing up their backstory and reporting it back home. The Gold Team had eaten up the chance for more publicity. Creed and Walker had, of course, explained their philosophy of discipline and order, challenging the casual nature of the other teams.

"UPSET IN ORBIT: How the Blue Team Changed Everything"—the story happened to be the talk of the entire station. The story of Blue Team's big upset had made major headlines in the Alliance but would be outdone by her story this week, the Red Team.

She said that everyone couldn't wait to meet the hope of the Alliance. It was Willis, the son of two former racers, who was practically bred to win it all for the glory of the Western Alliance. Everyone expected he would win the Chase this year.

"I want the Alliance to see you as more than a Chase runner. I want them to know you're human, where you came from and who you are." Sheila's words had sounded genuine.

70

He didn't know how to tell her that he remembered little of his childhood. And now, he was plagued by these dreams. Sheila had scheduled an appointment with him for later that day, after the team training, so at least he had some time to think.

The gym was quiet at this hour. A good sweat would calm him down, and it didn't hurt that he wouldn't have to work out with the team today. Jez had been so clingy since the last race. She appeared everywhere Willis went, and it bothered him to think of what that might mean about her feelings. The tension about this month's race was thick. Everyone wondered if Blue Team would repeat their non-loss.

Willis walked the corridor studying the other barracks. All these other racers remembered their families. Some even chose to enter training. The idea made him feel very alone. Alone, and different.

To his surprise, the light in the gym was on as he approached. Who else was up at this hour? He walked into the dim overnight lights of the common room and peered to his left. Through the glass wall he could see a loaded barbell rise, again and again. Jaden.

For a moment, he considered returning to his quarters. Jez was so wary of Jaden that he never got to talk to the guy. This might be his first chance. He touched the wall button, causing a glass panel to move aside. He could hear Jaden's labored breaths as the weights rose and fell.

"Can you spot me?" came Jaden's strained voice.

"Me?" Willis pointed to himself, surprised that Jaden would so freely talk to someone outside his team.

"No one else here," Jaden said.

Willis walked over behind the bench and placed his hands under the bar. Jaden was lean, but Willis could see his sinewy muscles flex, betraying a hidden strength. Jaden cranked out a few extra repetitions with the last of his strength and clanged the bar back into place at the end of the bench. "Thanks. I have to cut the reps short when I'm here by myself."

"You're here early." Willis didn't know what else to say.

71

"I'm not the only one, apparently." Jaden smiled.

"Oh, yeah." Willis's face heated. "I guess you can't be accused of being an early riser except by another one."

"Except that you're not an early riser. I never see you in here this early. Dex is usually the next to arrive after me."

"Couldn't sleep," Willis blurted. He feared it might shut down the conversation, but he hoped it didn't. His mind exploded with curiosity, and he scrambled for a way to continue talking. "You mind returning the favor?"

"Sure thing." Jaden hopped off his bench and looked at Willis, inviting him to use the Blue Team's equipment.

Willis glanced over at the red equipment at the end of the gym.

"No point in going over there. This one's all set up. Unless, that is, I'm lifting too much for you." Jaden lifted his brows.

"Way too much." Willis smirked and sat down on the bench. Jaden let out an amused chuckle. Willis didn't know why, but it surprised him to hear Jaden joke like one of the guys. So much mystery had surrounded him since the race that he seemingly became almost inhuman to Willis.

"So, what's got you sleepless, red leader?"

"Don't—know—bad—dreams—I—guess." Willis's words came between breaths.

"Bad dreams?" Jaden's voice was overly dramatic. "The great Willis has nightmares. Call the networks! Better, get that Sheila lady in here. A real human-interest story—the not-so-inhuman hope of the Alliance."

"Whatever." Willis smiled. Jaden did not try to impress Willis, and Willis liked that about him. He also noted that Jaden used the term 'inhuman' in reference to him as well.

"What were they about? Monsters? Things under your bed? Oh wait, I know. It was Chief Administrator Blacc under your bed, right? That'd scare me." Willis couldn't hold it any longer. The gasping laughter burst out of his lungs so quickly that Jaden had to help him secure the bar before he dropped it. "Careful, buddy," Jaden remarked. "I don't want to have to face your team if you get hurt under my watch."

"Yeah, they'd have something to say about that." Willis smiled as he sat up. "You'd make a friend out of Creed, though."

At that, Jaden restarted his fit of laughing, resting his head on the bar. Willis couldn't help but join him. It was the most honest laughter he'd heard in a long time. It occurred to him how little laughter there was on the station. The constant threat of re-coding kept the teams in cutthroat competition. What would it be like if they had the chance to live as friends?

"On second thought, I'll stick to serious business while you're lifting." Jaden sat on the bench next to him. "So seriously, what does the great Willis have nightmares about?"

"First of all, drop the 'great.'" Willis dropped his eyebrows, silently promising he would never apply it to Jaden either. "I don't know. Images of people. Bad things happening."

"Something you remember seeing?"

Willis shook his head. "I don't think so. I guess all this talk about the reporter wanting to know our story has me thinking. Must be messing with me," Willis admitted, pointing to the side of his head.

Jaden raised an eyebrow. "Yeah, I hear you. She wanted to know all about my parents and where I came from. I told her it was a story for another time."

"Seriously? How did she take that?" Recalling Jaden's missing tattoo, Willis hoped he would share more. He waited a long second until Jaden answered.

"She didn't like it. Kept saying she needed to report on more than racing."

"Did you tell her about your ear? About having no number?" Willis bit his tongue, feeling like he'd overreached. He paused hoping Jaden wouldn't be too uncomfortable to discuss it.

"So, you've noticed?" Jaden smiled.

Willis blew out a breath."Talk of the station since the last race."

"Really? Nah, I didn't tell her. Not ready to go there with anyone." Jaden scanned the room, not meeting Willis's gaze.

Willis tried to hide his disappointment. Jaden was more open than most, but it was probably too much to expect he'd have no secrets of his own. Willis moved on before the moment got awkward. "Maybe I should freak her out and tell her my dream," Willis joked. "It's all about the Alliance taking me from my parents by force. Like that would ever happen."

Jaden's face darkened. "Is that how it happened?" In that instant Willis saw something on Jaden's face. Something painful. Perhaps he'd found someone who, like him, had no idea where he came from. Not the time to ask.

"Heck, no. My parents loved and served the Alliance." He threw his hands up in front of him as if to defend an oncoming blow. "They were proud that I would represent it. That's why I've been in training as long as I can remember." Willis considered telling him about how much he hoped to see his parents after the Chase, but that was too much for their first real conversation.

"So, you don't remember leaving them?" He leaned in.

"I sort of do. Images mostly. Good feelings."

Jaden's eyebrows furrowed, and he tilted his head. Confusion filled his face, or was it concern? "So, you're saying your parents turned you over to the Commission at an obscenely young age, and all you had were good feelings about leaving your mom and dad?"

"I don't know. Why?" Where he was going with this?

"Seems odd to me." Jaden looked down at the floor, his lips pulled to one side like he planned to say more but was holding back. "Come, on." Jaden was suddenly more cheerful. "Back on the bench. You're not going to get away with one set this morning."

"Wow. Comedian, therapist, trainer—is there anything you don't do?"

"I can't sing to save my life, so don't ask."

"Noted." With that, Willis and Jaden laughed again. A movement in the shadows of the common room caught Willis's eye. He finished his reps and sat up to breathe. It took him a second to see through the glare of the lights on the glass.

Jez was watching them.

Willis had been distracted the entire rest of his workout. Jaden kept giving him sideways looks, but he hadn't said a thing. Willis showered and changed, to find Jez pacing in front of his door when he returned. Her arms were crossed, and her lips were tight when she stared at him.

"What's up with you?" Willis questioned, bracing himself for the outburst that was coming.

"What's up with me? Oh, great question. Let's talk about me." Her nostrils flared. "I'm not the one laughing it up with the newbie. How about we ask what's up with you?"

Willis shrugged. "Nothing. He was in there when I went in. No big deal." He scrunched his nose in annoyance.

"And you happened to work out on the Blue Team equipment?" She pointed furiously in the gym's direction.

"No rule against it." He sighed loudly, hoping to shut her down.

She pointed at his chest and glared at him. "Willis, that's not done. What if he'd hurt you? What if he'd let you hurt yourself?"

"He wouldn't do that." Willis couldn't believe she was saying this.

"How do you know? How do any of us know anything about him?" She was shouting. "He's one of *them*, Willis. Blue Team. They didn't lose last time. You think they're going to let it happen again? They'll stoop to anything to not get recoded."

"Jez, seriously, you're making this way bigger than it needs to be." His voice grew louder.

"And when he lets the weights drop on your head, and we get recoded because you can't run well, what then?"

Willis's jaw clenched. He reminded himself to keep his cool, but Jez's words infuriated him. "Jez, that's not—"

"I can't lose." Her voice lowered but held its intensity.

"*You* can't lose?" Willis shot back.

She blinked furiously, caught by her words. "I mean, *we* can't lose."

"Come on. Neither of us is in any real danger. I'd hate to get recoded, but a two behind my ear wouldn't be the end of the world, like a ten behind yours wouldn't be either."

"Willis, you have no idea. You don't remember recoding. They—do things to you. Make you think things. Put memories in you that aren't real and take others out. It's bad—and it's not for us. That's why Blue Team exists, so we can be safe, run in the Chase, and get on with our lives." She pulled her black hair behind her ears, something he often noticed her do when her coding number was mentioned.

She was right. He had no idea, but he couldn't help but think she was overreacting. He'd heard that the doctors could insert or delete memories, but he believed they limited it to training memories—ideas that would make them better racers. *They wouldn't mess with people's personal memories, would they? She can't be serious.* Then again, Jez was always serious. His features softened, and he smoothed his voice in an effort to calm the situation.

"Whatever, Jez. It's not going to happen anyway."

"Willis." She grabbed his hand with both her hands and peered up at him. "Promise me you'll stay away from Jaden. I don't trust him."

"You don't trust anyone."

"I trust you." Once again, he noticed that longing look in her eyes.

Stepping backward, he pulled his hand from hers. Not too quickly, so as not to alarm her. That expression was becoming more frequent, and it unnerved him. Did she see him as more than a teammate? Or was it something else?

And why had she singled him out as the lone person on the station she didn't hate?

Jez was wrong about Jaden. That much he knew. He'd enjoyed working out with him. He pondered saying so, but her loyalty worked for their team. Life on the station was all about the Chase, keeping the teams mostly to themselves. Perhaps it didn't have to be that way, but he didn't imagine Jez would ever be able to accept that.

Chapter Thirteen

"Come in." Sheila knew exactly who was at the door. She leaned her forearms on the metal table in front of her. The sparse office the station had given her sported two chairs, the table, and a wall monitor displaying a view out into space. Thankfully, the chairs were cushioned, as she'd spent hours interviewing trainees. The door opened to the side, and Willis stood there inspecting the room like he was unsure he wished to enter.

Make him comfortable.

"Thanks for taking the time to meet with me between training." She gestured to the chair. "My name is Sheila Kemp." She picked up her yellow pad of paper and pulled out a pencil she'd shoved over her left ear.

"Willis." He shook her hand and frowned as she scribbled his name.

"Willis? And your family name?" He winced at the word 'family.' She wanted him to open up, not shut down, so she quickly rephrased it. "Your *full* name?"

"Willis Thomson."

"Mr. Thomson—"

"It's Willis. Last names sound funny around here. Runners don't use them unless you're on Black Team."

"Sounds good to me. First names are better anyway." She smiled. "Less stuffy. How long have you been in training for the Chase?" She leaned forward to encourage his response.

"As long as I can remember."

She pressed her lips together, considering how to rephrase. Most racers were eager to boast about how experienced they were, and his response caught her. "I mean, what age exactly were you when you joined?"

"I don't know."

"You don't know?" she blurted, her eyes wide. She tried to calm the pinch in her eyebrows that must have betrayed her alarm.

"I barely remember life before training."

Silence filled the space between them for the moment. These were not answers she'd expected, and she scrambled for an approach that would get the conversation moving.

"Nothing at all?" Her voice transformed to one of careful concern.

"I was at the Lake Placid Junior Training Center as a child until I came here. That's all I remember."

She tapped her pencil against her teeth. "And when did you transfer to this station for advanced training?"

"Fifteen."

She paused for a second to jot down a few more notes. It was a tactic she'd used many times. Some of her best observations came from the pauses between questions rather than the questions themselves. He looked at her curiously as if he didn't know what she could possibly be writing. When she stopped, she caught him glancing at her notes.

She'd written—*check into W. Thomson background.* She saw his eyes and quickly flipped the page as if she was out of room.

Sheila took a minute to examine the young kid sitting at the table with her. He was nineteen, but with a face that could be mistaken for someone younger. He was above-average height, but the years of training were obvious. He was head-to-toe lean muscle, built for racing. He was slouching in his chair—not like a typical teenager, rather like someone older than his years trying to appear like a teenager.

It was curious to her how the other runners had responded to her presence. The youngest, Dex, had been all positive and kept asking if his parents would see the article. Casey, or Stone as she asked to be called, wouldn't open up. The 'golden girls' had been full of themselves and wanted to know how wide her publication would spread. She even interviewed the new kid, Jaden, who was pleasant, but not very forthcoming about his background. But Willis was different. She longed to know what made him tick. *How could a nineteen-year-old boy possibly carry the hopes of the entire Alliance?* She found herself asking a few obligatory questions about how they became an elite team and what training methods they used. She guessed that beneath that leader exterior had to be something worth probing. She didn't expect it to be his name, but he couldn't hide how he flinched at her question.

Which is why she let him see her notes before she flipped the page.

"Why the pencil and paper?" He waved at her notepad. "Wouldn't a computer be more practical? Be more—this century?"

She smiled at the comment. "Because 'this century' is what we all want to be?" She bit her tongue, knowing sarcasm wasn't needed. She softened. "I guess it's something I picked up from my father. He always made sketches of his new helmets on paper or whatever he could get his hands on prior to designing them digitally. He always had a pencil behind his ear ready to jot down an idea or shape that caught his eye. As a young girl, I would swipe one of his pads of paper and attempt to draw what I saw. The habit didn't leave when I got into journalism."

"Nice." He shifted in his seat to lean forward.

Good. She smiled. *A little personal touch from my side helped. Maybe he'll start to see that I can be trusted.* "So, you're the child of Max and Brenda Thomson?How does it feel to have famous parents?"

"Doesn't make a difference here." He gave her a strange look.

He didn't understand the question. *I suppose it makes no sense asking him about the fame of parents he's never met.*

"Do you ever hear from them?"

He paused, wringing his hands for a moment. "I get a message from them every few months."

"And are they proud of what you've accomplished?" The question wasn't fair considering his hesitancy to talk about his parents, but she wanted to poke and see if she'd found a tender spot. She had a knack with most people about how hard to push them in a line of questioning, but that was when she realized which topic would be sensitive. Family was not a matter she'd been prepared to scrutinize.

"They will be when I win the Chase." His tone was flat. She'd poked too hard. She leaned back to ease the pressure.

"I guess what I mean is, do you feel any extra pressure to win the Chase this year?"

"Probably."

One-word answer. He's shutting down. Careful, Kemp. She chewed her lip for a moment before moving on.

"And how does that make you feel?" Sheila recognized that it was an obviously leading question, but she had to know what was going on beneath the surface. She was called here to report on the potential Chase runners and under orders to keep her opinions to herself, but they couldn't stop her from quoting their prized runner. If he'd give her something to work with.

He watched her, stone-faced, clearly not intending to answer.

She couldn't believe the pressure to uphold the reputation of the Alliance had even found its way here. Either he was not willing to talk about his parents, or he feared repercussions from saying anything negative about the training station. That is, unless the 'glory of the Alliance' is all he'd ever known.

"You said that your parents' names don't make a difference here." Pausing, she jabbed at her chin a couple times with her pencil. "What does make a difference?"

"The track," he responded quickly.

"The track? You mean the one you practice on?" She knew what he meant, but she'd invite whatever he'd say next.

"No one cares who you are off the track. They care about who you are on it."

Grab this thread and pull it, Kemp. She quickly traced a line of questions in her mind and fired them off. She leaned forward and pointed with her pencil.

"And who are you on the track?"

"I'm the one who wins."

No hesitation. She scribbled on her pad. She glanced up without tilting her head up. "Every time?"

"Every time."

Again, no doubt. No scribbling this time. She opted to go for it, lowering her voice to almost a whisper.

"Do you ever worry you'll lose a race?"

Willis stared at the monitor pointing toward the track. They couldn't see it on the screen, but she imagined his eyes penetrating the walls and seeing the sphere. Several moments passed as he must have pondered his answer. She was almost ready to ask the question again when he inhaled.

"Every time," he repeated.

There it is. Sheila suppressed a smile. *There's the chink in the armor.*

Before Sheila sat the best racer in the world, the one who would probably destroy the competition at the next Chase—the same one who was terrified of losing. Compassion flooded her heart as he presently appeared very much like a teenager to her. His body deflated as the weight of expectation must have hit him right in the gut. His face appeared even younger as doubt overtook it. She hated the Chase for what it had done to her father, her mother and sister, and her career. Now she had a new reason to hate the Chase. The evidence of it was sitting in front of her.

He's not allowed to lose. How could she help him with her hands tied by the Alliance and Chairman DeGraaf?

"Willis, if you could say anything to your parents, what would it be?" She asked the question of every racer knowing communications were allowed one-way, but it was usually a simple closing question. She leaned in again knowing that his answer would be different.

What did you say to people you've never met? Willis popped his knuckles one at a time. What would he say to them when he did meet them?

Willis studied the woman's face before he answered. He was tempted to believe that she would never pass on the message, but her eyes said otherwise. Experience told him that he was on his own and that others weren't interested in him unless they wanted something he could offer, yet she had the appearance of someone who was interested in knowing the truth. He almost dismissed her as a reporter searching for a sensational story. He was tempted to give an easy answer that would praise the Alliance and avoid the question, but her eyes held nothing but kindness.

Could she be interested in what he had to say? Willis found himself short of breath as the words bubbled to the surface of his soul. He realized that if he didn't speak them, they would eat him from the inside out.

"I would ask them a question," he said.

"What question would you ask?" She arched a brow.

Willis swallowed hard. "I would ask them if they'd still be proud of me if I lost the Chase."

Chapter Fourteen

He could not believe it. A month of training on this track, and Willis still had no idea how to properly instruct his team. The administrators had thrown a curveball this month with a track unlike any he'd seen in previous months. Willis stood at the entryway to the track, staring at it. He'd dismissed the team early from their last training run with the monthly recoding race tomorrow. Their frustration was reaching a breaking point, and he needed cool heads at the starting tone.

There has to be a combination that will work. He pounded his fists together in frustration while he paced.

The track this month appeared like a large spiral that filled the sphere completely, each floor a gently angled descending surface that curved along the circular walls. The race would begin near the top of the sphere with a finish near the bottom. From the bottom portion of the track, a racer could peer up into the middle of the spiral and see nearly all the action. There were almost no obstacle course elements to this one. It would be a sprint to the end. Starting gates were located at four different sections of the track. Willis had figured that part out almost immediately.

"It's a relay," he'd said to the team.

"You sure? We've never done one of those." Toad had crossed his arms and scowled.

"What's the challenge to a relay?" Disgust dripped from Jez's words.

"It's about figuring out who should run each section," Willis said.

It was one thing to figure out what they should do, but something very different to do it. Blacc was silent on the nature of the different sections of the track. He'd laughed at Willis's questions.

"The surprise at last month's race was so much fun that we thought we'd create a surprise of our own." At least none of the other teams had any idea either. Willis had heard the discussions in the mess hall, common room, and corridors. Everyone was stumped.

The bottom section of the track had nothing interesting about it, a flat surface. The other three sections, though, were unique. Sections one, two, and three had curious metallic lines running the length of the floor, each an inch apart. The team had debated these, but their discussion had ended with Toad making a sarcastic remark. Jez had cursed and taken a swing at Toad. Willis had calmed her down before she'd injured him seriously, and thankfully Toad understood to stay quiet afterward.

He silently took assessment again of each section. Section one was flat, nothing special except the lines in the floor. Two has a series of stairs that went up and down at different heights. How was that supposed to be a challenge? Section three corkscrews as if some giant hand twisted that part of the track over and over. How in the world—?

Willis pounded the floor with his hand. He had no idea how anyone was supposed to race on that, and his mind was exhausted considering the possibilities. They couldn't even practice section three properly. He intended to take this time on the track to think. The secret had to be in the lines on the floor.

What could they be?

Willis stared, hoping the floor would open up and speak to him. He walked the length of the first section to check for variations in the lines. He ran his fingers along them. He even counted them. In frustration, he laid down on his stomach with his hands under his chin to gaze at the lines from floor level.

"What is your secret?" he whispered.

Clang. The bell sounded signaling the end of Red Team's training run. That was it. No time left to figure it out.

"Off the track, reddie." Creed's voice startled him. Black Team was never late to their training runs. "We have the track now."

"Just leaving, Creed." He sighed, not looking at them.

Willis pushed himself up off the track with his hands, the zipper of his jacket tugging gently as he did. He glanced down and noticed that the bottom of his jacket was stuck to the floor.

"Hey, are you deaf? I said off the track." Creed growled.

With his back to Black Team, he knew they hadn't seen. Willis smiled to himself. *The lines are magnetic.*

"All yours, Creed," he said, trying not to sound too cheerful.

"All runners, check in at your starting gates!" Blacc's voice blared over the speakers. He'd given the teams his usual verbal thrashing, but Willis didn't care. The other teams were still talking furiously over breakfast, so there was a good chance that they hadn't figured it out until Blacc revealed it to all moments earlier.

Each team had to declare who was running each section, and then those running the first three sections were presented special shoes. The bottom of each was equipped with similar magnets to the ones in the floor. Willis stood in gate four alongside Walker, Dex, Nico, and Starr. He couldn't bring himself to trust anyone else on the team to anchor the race. He was glad to see Creed was starting his team. Willis didn't trust him, either, after his threats earlier.

Perhaps he'd hoped I would start my team off, so he could do something way up at the top of the sphere. Either way, he was glad he wouldn't have to race with him.

From gate four, he could watch the center of the spiral and had a perfect vantage point to view gates two and three. He recognized the exchange at the gates would be critical to getting an advantage in this race.

"Tone in five seconds," came the familiar voice. Willis tuned out the rest. He didn't have to start at the tone, and he wasn't interested in Blacc's usual "make the Alliance proud" speech. He tried to picture the starting gate. Guessing at the nature of the opening section, Willis had put Kane at the front. He imagined

Kane's snarl as he awaited the tone, his strong grip strangling the baton he was to pass to Jez. Toad would handle the craziness of section three. His smaller size was a perfect fit for the spinning track.

The tone sounded. Immediately the sound of heavy footfalls echoed through the sphere. Kane raced ahead of the pack, his powerful legs fighting the magnetic pull that made their feet stick to the floor. Willis could see him churning his steps and coming short of a run. The others, while working hard, could not keep up with him. Joanne grunted with each step trying not to lose too much ground to Creed. Her eyes widened as Perryn overtook her, the grimace on her face one of determination rather than defeat. Once again, Green Team was in last.

"Not again," Nico whispered to himself, though loud enough for Willis to hear.

Blam. Blam. Blam. Kane's pounding feet marched him around three levels of the spiral track. Each time he came into Willis's view, his lead had lengthened. *We have this one.* Willis dared to believe.

"Come on, Kane," Jez screeched. Anyone could see that Red Team had a commanding lead and might obliterate the others with ease today. Jez contorted her body, reaching behind her starting gate. Her hand twitched, ready to receive the baton. Kane came crashing through his gate, the laser turning from red to green. Snatching the baton, Jez launched herself through the gate.

A scream was the next thing Willis heard, followed by a *thud.*

Willis could see Jez holding her head completely dazed. She must have assumed the magnets on her track were the same. In fact, they'd been reversed so the floor repelled the runner's feet. The effect was that the runner's steps were far more productive than usual. Wanting to compensate for the assumed extra force needed to move, Jez had pushed off too hard and instead shot herself into the air striking the level above with her head.

"Nice move, Jez," Creed called from the gate having passed the baton to Stone.

"Shut up, Creed," Jez spoke through clenched teeth as she tried to stand, her pale skin flushed with anger. Stone launched by her, having seen her mistake, followed by Jaden.

"Get moving, Jez!" Willis cupped his hands around his mouth while shouting. Their early lead was suddenly gone. A greenie was leaving the second gate. Willis was relieved to see her get moving again in step with Lacey from Gold Team.

Within two of the up and down stairs, the runners had all figured out a rhythm. Most realized they could simply launch themselves over each set of steps or to the top of the higher ones.

"Waa-haa-haa!" came a voice, almost laughing.

"Who is that?" Walker questioned, searching for the voice.

Willis let himself smile. Jaden was bounding up one side of each staircase and using his momentum to handspring over the top step. He almost appeared like he was having fun, and he was gaining ground—now even with Stone. Lacey and Jez were right behind. Jez wore a spitting-mad expression as she launched up one stair and down the next.

"Double time, Stone!" Creed hollered.

"You got this, girl!" Starr encouraged.

Nico looked like he was going to be sick watching his team lose again.

Gate three. Jaden and Stone found their teammates together and collapsed breathless. Amber and Stone-zee stepped through their gate reluctantly, appearing unsure what their shoes would do after Jez's mistake. In seconds they realized their feet would hold enough to the track to allow them to run even the upside-down portions of the corkscrew, but it was all the time needed for Jez and Lacey to catch up. Their gates side by side, they were locked at the shoulder as they ran, their black and blonde ponytails almost synchronous in their back and forth motion.

"Cleo, reach!" Lacey cried as she lifted her baton. So close to Jez, her left hand momentarily hooked Jez's right forearm, who reacted with a jerk of her arm. Willis watched Lacey's jaw crunch under Jez's elbow. The grunt was loud enough for Willis to hear, even two floors down. Stone-zee, Amber, and Toad were careening through the corkscrew trusting every step to the shoes, but everyone in gate four hardly noticed.

Lacey's feet tangled, throwing her to the side, her hand barely grabbing the edge of the track as she fell off the side. *Why aren't the protective walls on?* Willis instinctively reached out a hand and stared, unable to peel his eyes from the scene above.

"Somebody help me!" Lacey half squealed, half screamed. She was holding on by one hand and quickly losing her grip. "Somebody!" Somewhere below, the gold team baton clattered as it hit the floor below.

Starr gasped as Lacey's hand let go of the track. An eternal breathless moment passed as Willis saw Lacey free fall, destined to land horribly at the bottom of the sphere, but she didn't fall. Willis shook his head to clear the images of his mind's eye. Lacey was dangling mid-air. Willis followed her hand to the two hands clasping it, followed by two forearms, to the red-faced Jaden trying his best not to get pulled over the side.

"Serves you right, you little princess!" Jez taunted trackside. She glowered down at Lacey, offering no help. "Go ahead and fall."

"Please don't drop me," Lacey pled, her face streaked with tears and mascara.

"A little help here," Jaden grunted, slipping slowly forward.

Willis stood in disbelief as Jez continued her insults as the others rushed to grab Jaden.

"Hello? Anyone paying attention?" Amber's voice broke the silent tension. The runners in gate four snapped their faces in her direction. *The race is still on!* Willis screamed in his head. *Wake up, Willis!*

Toad had nearly caught Amber as the two emerged from the last upside-down portion of their track. Stone-zee was right behind.

Crashing through the gate, the three passed off their batons. Blue—Red—Black, all neck and neck. Dex took off, his blazing speed showing its colors. Willis's legs burned as he tried to keep up. He knew that Walker couldn't beat him, but Dex had a second's lead.

Watch him, Willis. He will fall. He always falls.
His teeth clenched as Willis prepared to leap.
He falls. I trip. Black Team wins. Watch for the fall.
Around the spiral the three of them chased each other with nothing but a footrace to decide the final outcome.
He will fall. He always falls.
The gate drew nearer. Willis's legs screamed at him. He could hear the wheezing breaths of Walker who was trying to outrun her normal pace.
He's not falling.
Willis drove his legs to pass Dex.
Tone. Tone. Tone.
He didn't fall. I lost. Willis shook his head trying to clear it. The words didn't even make sense in his mind.

Willis turned his attention to Dex who was on all fours, his lungs heaving breaths too slow for the demand of his muscles. Willis's eyes were wide as he took in what had happened. Blue Team won the recoding race.
Tone.
The fourth runner passed the gate. Elimination was decided. Turning his head, Willis turned to the fourth runner. Nico stood there, his hands on his knees trying to catch his breath.
Nico won? How did he ever overcome the lead Gold Team had?
Then, the idea occurred to him. Willis turned around. Peering up a few floors, he could see Jaden lying on the side of the track catching his breath. Next to him were two gold runners crying in an embrace. Cleo stayed to help her teammate. Starr was still at gate four. Gold Team lost.

"All runners will report to the staging area," Chief Administrator Blacc's voice had blared over the speakers. The anger in his voice echoed against the walls of the spherical room.
Willis sat against the wall where Blacc usually made his pre-race

inspections. He peered up at the window from where the administrators would observe. The rather statue-like figures that normally stood in the window were in a flurry of activity. Monitors were being watched. Debate appeared heated between administrators. Blacc stood by the door awaiting their decision. Perryn leaned in toward Willis. "What are they doing?" "They're deciding who gets recoded," Willis said flatly. Jez placed both hands on her hips. "Deciding? How can they do that? Gold Team lost."

"Because you pushed Lacey over the side." Joanne stood to her feet. Both of her hands balled into fists, and she appeared ready to knock Jez unconscious. Lacey sat in the corner still in tears. Cleo and Starr clutched her, their tears and running makeup creating a distorted version of the three goldies that Willis had never seen.

"Because she can't keep to herself." Jez shot the words back and rose to her feet. She moved toward Joanne who braced her feet.

Willis moved in to restrain his teammate.

Schwipp! The doors to the staging area opened, freezing all the runners. Chief Administrator Blacc and the medical team entered, Blacc staring down Jez and Joanne. Both girls took a step away from each other.

"Alliance trainees, at attention!" Blacc shouted. Their training kicked into gear and all the runners quickly found themselves lined up in front of Blacc. "The Chase Commission Administrators have come to a consensus. The altercation at gate three has been ruled incidental. By refusing to run the final two legs of the track, Gold Team is forfeit and will be recoded."

"No!" Lacey screamed through her tears.

"It's not fair, Chief Administrator!" Joanne protested.

"Silence, gold leader." Chief Administrator snapped. "Present your team for recoding."

Joanne shot a look of death at Jez, who crossed her arms and grinned smugly next to Willis.

He couldn't help but lean away from her, not wanting to associate with what had happened. Still, he was glad she wasn't in trouble. A suspension would have been devastating for the team. Joanne turned to gather her teammates. Lacey's legs failed her, and she collapsed to the floor sobbing. Cleo and Starr placed their arms under hers and started the walk toward the medical wing.

"I'm sorry. I'm so sorry," Lacey whimpered.

A moment later, the door panels shut leaving the room silent.

"Red Team leader." Blacc's tone had quieted.

"Yes, Chief Administrator." Willis kept his voice neutral—somber.

"I expect better discipline from your team. Today was a poor showing of the pride of the Alliance."

Somewhere Creed snickered.

"Yes, Chief Administrator." His heart raced as he exhaled long and slow, feeling both anxious and relieved.

"Blue Team leader." Blacc said, more animated.

"Yes, Chief Administrator." Perryn seemed almost fearful to be addressed after all that had happened.

"The Alliance may make a team out of you yet." Blacc smirked. "Congratulations on your first win. It was an ugly dog of a win, but still a win." With that Blacc turned on his heels and disappeared behind the medical wing door.

Silence. Then, a "Whoop!" from the Blue Team.

Perryn ran and wrapped her arms around Dex, who still looked astonished at his win. Jaden and Amber gathered around them, wrapping their own arms around their teammates. The other teams stood still, watching Blue Team celebrate their victory.

Willis studied Perryn's face as she cried and shouted with her teammates. He'd never seen her smile, and he liked how she smiled with her entire face. Her eyes caught his, and in that moment, he saw the light return to them. The fire, of which he'd seen glimpses, was back at an intensity he'd never seen. She smiled at him, and he found himself returning her smile.

She was sweaty, her brown hair knotted from her exertion, her face red and streaked with tears. Willis saw none of it.

She has a beautiful smile, was all he could think. He hoped he'd see more of it.

Chapter Fifteen

All four teams were in the gym that morning. Willis guessed that the outcome at the track had inspired everyone to get an early start. Gold Team wouldn't return from recoding until later, but everyone else was there. He could hear Creed's grunts as he pushed the weights skyward with Walker spotting him. Nico had his team doing various cardio workouts. Willis was supposed to be leading his team through a workout this morning, but he was distracted.

Blue Team had an energy that he'd never seen.

"So you didn't know that you'd won?" Perryn's face was bright after a night's sleep. She held out her hands under the weight bar that Jaden was lifting with slow, deliberate movements.

"N-n-not at all," Dex's excitement aggravated his stutter. "I th-th-thought W-W-Willis had w-w-won. We passed the g-g-gate almost at the same t-t-time."

"I know. But I couldn't help but think it was hilarious to see Jez fume over losing." Amber smirked.

"Quiet, Amber," Perryn interrupted. "Let's not talk like that. Not here anyway." She couldn't fully hide her smile.

Willis could hear the Blue Team's conversation clear across the gym. He chuckled as they tried to keep their words in low tones, but in their excitement, their voices kept carrying. Perryn had looked over at him nervously when Amber made her comment. He smiled at her, producing the slightest laugh out of Perryn.

Amber had been right. Jez had put on quite a show the prior night. She threw a chair in the common room in her rage. He'd never known that she was so sensitive to losing. Willis had never lost a race, and the experience had unsettled him. Yet, he couldn't help but laugh as Jez lost it. It was so sorry a display that it was comical.

The laughter had been momentary as his thoughts about the race had kept him awake most of the night. *We lost.* The thought repeated itself over and over. *How could we have lost?* He could think of nothing else until his eyes had met Perryn's. Her smile had surfaced for a second, and it calmed his spirit. At least something good came out of that race.

"Man, the blueys win their first and can't shut up about it." Toad's lip curled.

"Mmm." Willis and Toad shot surprised glances at Kane, who rarely spoke. Willis wasn't sure if he was agreeing with Toad or simply expelling air while lifting the weight bar.

"Let them have their fun, Toad." Willis turned to him. "Don't you remember what it was like to win your first?"

"I beat a sorry junior team's butt for my first," Toad said.

"Yeah, well they beat our sorry butts," Willis retorted. "So, let them have a little pride." Toad's face darkened at Willis's comment, but he could swear he saw a small smile flicker across Kane's face. "You guys know where Jez is?"

"Probably doesn't want to show her face after she went psycho last night." Toad chuckled, his usual demeanor returning.

"Back off you little—" Jez's voice crackled through the air on cue. Willis turned to see her shove Amber who must have made a smug remark judging by her expression. "I'll break your face if you don't shut it."

"Amber, seriously we don't need to be like that." Jaden's voice was serious but soft. He wrapped his arm around her shoulder and guided her back to the group.

Jez looked like she'd rolled out of bed. Usually, her raven hair was straight and well-kept, but its slight tangle betrayed a lack of attention. Her cheeks were red with anger, and her eyes shot daggers around the room. Her demeanor seemed to dare anyone to say something about the prior night and give her reason to explode.

"So the little drama queen decided to join us this morning." Toad laughed. He inhaled for another comment, but Jez's right fist cut him short.

"Shut up, you little snot." She screamed and lunged for a second strike. Willis grabbed her arms from behind below the shoulders to hold her in place. "I'll beat you so badly they'll have to recode you to heal you."

Kane replaced the weights and silently stood up from the bench, his size offering a barrier between Jez and Toad. Jez continued to strain against Willis's grip.

"Calm down, Jez." Willis spoke into her ear.

"We lost, Willis, and this little rat wants to tell jokes." The words came out in a snarl.

"Jez. Jez!" Willis turned her around to look in her eyes. Her fierce glare met his own. For an instant, he believed she wanted to kill him, but her expression slowly softened. "Jez? You can't lose it like this."

"No, Willis. *We* can't lose it—not ever again." Jez whispered at a level only Willis could hear, her eyes showing a glimmer of fear. "Selection runs will start in a few months, and we can't lose those. We can't have that happen ever again—or we'll never survive this place." Her frightened appearance startled Willis. He couldn't believe this moment of vulnerability.

"It's okay, Jez." He leaned closer and whispered. "I've got it covered." With that, he felt her muscles relax, and her expression transformed to one of trust.

"You have to stay focused, Will. You *have* to get me—us—to the Chase."

Jez brought her hands up to grab his arms, changing his hold on her into an embrace. His face grew hot as he realized how they must appear, but the silence of the watching room kept him from reacting. She wouldn't like it if he pulled away, and he had her calm for the time being.

"Let's get back to work," he said a little louder. "A good sweat will do us all good."

The rest of the workout had been mostly uneventful. Blue Team had continued their hushed excitement prompting several dagger-type looks from Jez, especially at Amber. Toad kept cracking jokes at the expense of other racers which kept the mood from getting too dark. Willis had worked them harder and longer than the rest of the teams mostly because he had no desire to see what would happen if Jez had to pass Amber again. *What does that girl have on Jez that gets under her skin so much?*

He cleaned up, changed, and returned to the common room. He'd never had to coach a team after a loss, and his mind was conflicted with an urge to rehearse what went wrong and a desire to move on to the next race. He went over his notes as he waited for his team to arrive.

"Bwahahahahaha!" Dex's laughter suddenly filled the air. Willis glanced over to see all four members of the Blue Team doubled over in laughter. Jaden was sitting in the corner facing the rest of the room. He sat on the back of the chair with his feet on the seat. Willis presumed he'd been talking with the rest of the team when Perryn had muttered a joke—she wore the amused smile of the joke's architect. The joke had obviously been at Jaden's expense—he broke into a laugh with an embarrassed blush. Amber's hand was at her mouth muffling a small giggle, but Dex hadn't restrained himself. He hung off the side of the chair almost falling to the floor in his stupor.

"Nice one, Perr." Jaden playfully shoved her with one hand.

"You're the one making it easy with your ridiculous analogies." Perryn giggled.

"All I'm trying to say is that Dex has some serious speed, more than he lets on."

"So why didn't you say it like that?"

"Because that wouldn't be half as fun." Dex laughed again.

"For real? You try to pay a guy a compliment." Jaden feigned offense. With that, the team burst into laughter again.

It was then that Perryn's eyes met Willis's. He hadn't realized he was watching them so long until she spotted him. They silently communicated their wordless mutual admiration. Perryn is a genius, Willis realized. Jaden had a natural magnetism that made others want to follow. Perryn was team leader, but she led the team by letting them follow Jaden. He was fully engaged in his pep talk to Dex, building up the insecure kid. Most team leaders were too insecure to allow another to assume that role, but it was working for her. He found himself nodding at her with a smile.

"What the heck is that about?" Jez snarled suddenly behind him. Willis wondered how long she'd been watching. "Why are you staring at them? At her?"

"I'm not staring," Willis said relaxing his face to hide how much she'd startled him.

"She was definitely staring at you."

"Chill out, Jez." Willis couldn't contain his annoyance. He stopped his next words, surprised at his defensiveness.

"Whatever," she moved on. "Seriously, look at him."

"Who?"

"The newbie." Jez pointed an angry finger over his shoulder, seeming not to care who noticed.

Willis frowned. "His name is Jaden."

"I don't care what his name is. I don't like him."

"You don't know him."

Jez turned and stood in his face. "Good. I don't want to, and you shouldn't either." He could feel the warmth of her breath she was so close. He stepped backward.

"Seems like a nice guy. Also appears to be good at pulling his team together."

"Willis." She was suddenly louder. "Don't you see it?"

"See what?"

Her eyes were on fire with an air of alarm and hatred. "He's dangerous." Her voice lowered to a deadly whisper.

"Dangerous? Yeah, sure Jez." His sarcasm was thick.

"I'm not kidding, Willis." She grabbed his arm. "Ever since he got here, nothing has been right. Everything has changed.

They are our protection. *They* are not supposed to win—ever."

"It's no big deal." Willis said the words but didn't believe them himself. He picked at the bump on his ear. "We'll take them in the next race."

"No big deal?" Her eyebrows raised with the words. "Tell that to the greenies and goldies."

"One win doesn't make them a threat. They ran a good race. Our concern is still more with Creed and his team." He opened his hand in front of himself to silently tell her to quiet down. She didn't appear to notice.

"Willis, promise me you'll stay away from him—from all of them. He has them believing they can win. Look at him talking to Dex like he's the best racer here." She jabbed a finger at Blue Team again. "The last thing they need is confidence. The last thing we need is to give him a chance to get in our heads. If you ask me, someone needs to do—something."

"What do you mean by 'something'?" Willis narrowed his eyes.

"Never mind. Let's say I wouldn't have cried if *he* had fallen off the track." She crossed her arms and settled into the chair as if to enjoy the image of Jaden falling to the floor of the sphere.

"Whatever, Jez." Her comment bothered Willis, but he couldn't let it show. "It's not like I plan on hanging out with him."

If she believed she wouldn't get caught... Jaden had better watch his back.

Things had changed. She was right about that much. Willis saw it. Jaden had Blue Team believing, and Perryn was letting him do it. Meanwhile, his team was distracted by it all. He needed to find something to focus them.

"Guys. You need to come now." Toad interrupted.

"What is it?" Willis raised his eyebrows.

"It's Kane. They're arresting him."

His jaw clenched as he shook his head. *This isn't what we need.* The three ran for the door.

Chapter Sixteen

Willis wasn't sure which way they should run until he heard the commotion coming from the red barracks. Wheeling around the corner, the three of them slid to a stop. Kane was lying on the ground with four officers holding him face down. Even then, they were having trouble keeping him contained. Beads of sweat dripped from Kane's dark skin as he struggled to keep them from cuffing his wrists behind him. Chief Administrator Blacc stood by watching.

"What is going on?" Willis demanded.

"Ah, our fearless Red Leader wants to know why we'd treat his superhuman specimen of a teammate this way." Blacc's lips twisted in a mocking leer.

Willis ignored the look. "Something like that."

Jez and Toad stood silent taking it all in.

"There has never been an incident on this station during my oversight like the one that occurred yesterday. A young, beautiful girl nearly lost her life because someone took it upon themselves to sabotage the protective walls on the track about one hour before the race. It brought shame to our great Alliance, and leadership wants answers. Frankly, I think there's exactly one."

"Kane?" Willis couldn't believe what he was hearing.

"Do you know any other convicted murderers on this station, Red Leader?"

So that was the secret. He'd known that Kane had a checkered past and that the Alliance had pulled him from prison to race. He had heard the rumors but never considered them serious. He crouched down in front of his teammate who had fallen still as Blacc had revealed his past.

"Is that true, Kane?" Willis whispered, leaning in so Kane

alone could hear.

The giant laying in front of him dropped his head and stared at the floor. He nodded almost imperceptibly. Here before Willis lay the strongest human being he'd ever seen, but his face wore the appearance of defeat.

Shame. Compassion flooded Willis. *He feels shame for what he did.* The expression didn't look like that of a hardened criminal who was bent on repeating his evil. Kane looked like a man who had done something desperate and regretted it every day that followed.

"So you see, Red Leader," Blacc continued, "we can't have a murderer up to his old tricks here. I was certain the Alliance had overlooked something when he was sent here, for they couldn't possibly want a murderer representing them. I liked it even less when you came out of nowhere to select him for your team. Those who love the Law shouldn't be made to associate with those who profane it. How would it appear for the Alliance's greatest hope to be standing next to the scum that threatens to undo our great society?"

Kane looked up at Willis when Blacc mentioned his selection to Red Team. Willis's breaths came rapidly. He wanted to unleash a torrent of curses at Blacc. Instead, he could merely gaze at Kane silently.

"Red Leader, don't you go getting upset. I'm sure you'll have your choice of replacements." Blacc elbowed one of the other officers who snickered. "Maybe you can even bring your bluey friend aboard. I'm sure little missy here would love that. Would you, Red team member?"

Willis didn't have to see to feel Jez's anger as her feet shifted behind him. It was as if Blacc heard the conversation they'd had in the common room.

"You want to keep running with us, teammate?" Willis furrowed his brow in concern.

Kane's tiny nod came once again.

"Didn't you hear me, Red Leader?" Blacc's voice rose. "This boy's a felon. Once a criminal, always a criminal. Aren't I right?"

With that, he tapped his boot on Kane's ribs, but the runner kept staring at Willis's face. His expression was almost hopeful.

"Chief Administrator, my teammate didn't sabotage the walls." Willis kept his eyes locked on Kane.

"What do you mean?" The question was posed slowly as if Blacc was using the pauses between words to guess what Willis might say next.

"I mean, you said the walls were deactivated about one hour before the race." He turned to Blacc and pointed at the air with a finger as though he were seeing their previous conversation.

"That's right."

Willis shook his head. "There was no way Kane was able to do that."

"And why's that?" Blacc's eyes narrowed, his fists resting on his hips.

"He was with me."

Willis held his breath after the words. It was a stretch to say they were together. Willis had been in his quarters alone the hour prior to the race, but Kane never left his quarters right before a run. He lived right next door to Willis, so they were in the same place *in a way*. He believed Kane had been there, and he hoped his face didn't give away his doubt.

"Are you saying you can vouch for the whereabouts of this runner, Red Leader?" Blacc stepped forward to meet Willis's eyes as he stood up.

"Yes. Yes, I can."

Blacc stepped backward appearing rather frustrated. He muttered a couple of curses to himself and then blurted, "All right, let him go."

The officers climbed off Kane and removed the cuffs. Kane slowly rose to his feet and rubbed his wrists. He was still watching Willis.

"Red Leader, I hold you responsible for this runner. If I hear someone sneeze too loud and find out he has something to do with it, it's you I'm coming after. Do we have an understanding?"

"Yes, Chief Administrator."

With that, Blacc and the officers made their way to the administrators' offices. Everyone stood silent enough for Willis to hear their steady breathing above the constant drone of the station.

"That was nuts," Toad said.

"That was close." Jez nodded.

Willis put a hand up on his runner's massive shoulder. He didn't care what Kane had done in the past. He trusted that his teammate wasn't the man Blacc assumed he was. Kane hadn't moved his gaze from him the entire time.

"You okay, Kane?"

Kane searched Willis's face.

"We've got to take care of each other if we're going to get out of here. Don't we? Besides, you'd do the same for me, I'm sure." Willis smiled and meant what he said. Kane had been nothing but the most dedicated and hard-working member of his team since he'd arrived on the station. The idea that he'd risk that for a random act of violence seemed ridiculous to Willis. "Wouldn't you?"

Kane nodded. Willis believed he could almost see him smile.

Chapter Seventeen

Months had passed since the Blue Team's win. Providing Kane an alibi had unhinged Blacc, who went on a rampage to uncover the truth, screaming all along about protecting the 'greatest alliance in the world.' Teams were endlessly frustrated as runners were pulled in the middle of training exercises to be questioned. Even Willis had to leave his team on the track to answer questions. He simply told them that he couldn't see why any racer would risk running that track without the invisible fields.

Then, as suddenly as the interviews had started, they stopped. Life returned to normal. At least, it returned to the new normal.

Willis worked his team extra hard following Dex's win, and they resumed their winning streak. Blue Team, however, hadn't resumed their place as the monthly recoded team. That burden had fallen largely to Nico and his greenies, but others had taken their turn. Two months ago, Creed had broken an ankle attempting to short cut an obstacle. He volunteered to be recoded to avoid the lingering effects the injury. Walker had insisted the whole team join him. The week prior, the goldies had lost again. Jaden's encouragement had the Blue Team running with desperation and threatening every race, and Willis had barely edged him out this run.

The pressure to win was increasing. He had to win. He had to represent the Alliance in the Chase. It was expected of him. It was what he'd worked for all his life.

Willis stood frozen in place when the haggard looking woman

appeared in the corridor. He'd been the last of his team to clean up and head for the common room. He wouldn't have even noticed her had he not forgotten his coaching notes. Returning to his quarters, he saw her half hidden in the shadow of one of the curved beams that lined both sides of the corridors.

"Who are you?" Willis stopped in his tracks.

Silence. The red glow of the lights in his team barracks cast dark crimson shadows around her eyes. Her skin was dry and aged. Her greying hair was loosely pulled out of her face with several wavy strands hanging, unevenly framing her face. Her eyes, which appeared grey in the light, gazed up at him coldly.

"You okay?" He reached out a hand to offer help.

Still no answer. He stepped closer. She wore a dark jumpsuit that was tattered on the edges of the sleeves. A tear was visible above one knee, and both elbows were worn out. He guessed she'd worn the uniform, if that's what it was, every day for years.

"Ma'am, you must be new on the station." His voice shook. She must be a recent arrival as he'd never seen her, but her appearance said otherwise. "Can I help you find your way?"

She reached up her thin hand slowly and laid it on his chest. It was her gentle touch that finally convinced him that she was real. She straightened the collar of his red jacket as a mother would a son.

"We live," she whispered. Her voice sounded like it was rarely used. With that, she turned slowly and walked down the hallway. Willis watched her in stunned silence until she entered the mess hall. He shook his head to clear his focus.

"Wait a minute." he called after her. "Who are you?"

He raced up the hallway and burst into the mess hall. It was empty.

Willis stood outside Blacc's office and hesitated as he reached to touch the panel to announce himself. He'd visited this office once. It was the day he'd been made the leader of Red Team.

Blacc had congratulated him and grilled him on the importance of representing the Alliance. His final words had been, "Red Leader, the Alliance is counting on you. In a couple of years, it will be your time. You come by here if you need anything."

He never took that offer seriously, and his success never required anything different, but for three days, the appearance of the woman in the hallway had bothered him. He'd contemplated who she could be, but with so little to go on, it simply amounted to lost sleep.

His weariness finally had showed up on the track when he stumbled uncharacteristically on an easy obstacle during practice. Jez had flipped out and insisted that his obsession with Jaden and the Blue Team was the reason.

"You're not yourself this week." She blurted the words, showing both her concern and frustration. "You seem like you're somewhere else."

He'd told the team about the woman. Toad had laughed thinking he was making a joke. Kane, of course, said nothing. Jez had told him to "forget about it" while stepping away from him slowly. It was his confidence that had originally won over Jez, and he'd showed his uncertainty for the first time. Willis understood he couldn't lose her unquestioned trust and chose not to mention it further. Sweaty and still in his training clothes, he stood at Blacc's door. The metal door was no different from the many that lined the plain hallway, except for the emblazoned star inside a diamond, the symbol of Blacc's rank in the Alliance.

"Enter," Blacc announced.

"Chief Administrator, may I speak to you?" Willis entered the spartan office. Other than a desk, at which Blacc sat, the office contained a couple of chairs. Hanging next to him, the lone decoration was a plaque, indicating Blacc's promotion to Chief Administrator.

"The pride of our Alliance wants an audience with me?" Blacc smirked. "I'm honored."

"Sir, I wanted to ask you a question."

"Ask, and I shall impart my wisdom, trainee."

"Sir, is there anyone else on this station?"

Blacc glanced up from his computer. "What do you mean, 'anyone else'?"

"What I mean, sir, is—" Willis counted off the types of station residents on his fingers—"besides the trainees, administrators, and doctors—is anyone else aboard this space station?"

Blacc leaned in his chair, the hinges squeaking slightly. "Of course, there's that reporter who has been telling the entire Alliance of your exploits. The people are ready for you to deliver this year."

"Yes, of course, sir. Besides her?"

Blacc's face darkened. "Why do you ask?" He straightened in his chair.

"I saw someone."

"Who?" Blacc was suddenly very serious.

"I don't know who she was. She was in the shadows of the hallway—in my barracks—and I saw—" Willis started.

"It's nothing," Blacc interrupted. He stood and pretended to admire the plaque. "You're seeing things. Must have been your exhaustion after a training run. You guys have been working hard on the track this month. Blue Team have you nervous?"

The change in subject was obvious. He would get nothing from Blacc. Who could he turn to? Right then, his station schedule card chirped a reminder. Glancing down, his eyes ignited as he read the words 'Interview with Ms. Kemp' on the card.

Willis sat at the table gazing at Sheila Kemp. "I need your help," Willis started before she could even ask her first question. Sheila didn't flinch. In fact, he believed he saw a smile tug at the corner of her mouth as she slid her notepad to the side. Good. At least he was getting further than he did with Blacc. "I need your help."

"You said that already." Sheila's expression reflected genuine interest.

His eyes darted left and right, not wanting to meet her eyes.

"I saw something. I saw some*one*."

"Who?" She leaned forward and folded her hands on the desk.

"I don't know, but my team thinks I'm crazy, and Blacc won't talk to me."

"So why do you think I'm going to help?"

His eyes locked on hers. "Because this might be the story you're searching for."

Sheila sat as though mesmerized as he retold the story of the encounter with the woman. Though in a private room, Willis kept glancing at the door expecting someone to burst in having heard the whole story. She pressed him for as many details as could be remembered. Willis tried to tell her everything he could recall, from the color of her eyes to the condition of her uniform to where she'd been standing outside his quarters. Her surprise appeared to center more on Willis's reaction than the presence of the woman.

"And you've never seen her before?" Sheila continued her questioning.

"No. Never."

"Willis. . . how do you think they run this place?"

"What do you mean?"

"I mean, how do you think this huge station operates?"

"Operates?" Willis furrowed his brow. *What is she getting at?*

"Food. Clothes. The track for crying out loud!" Her voice rose as she spoke. "Who do you think does all of that?"

He stared. He watched her take a long, deep breath as if she was trying to calm herself. He'd hit upon a subject she was obviously passionate about, but the pieces were still coming together in his head. He was unsure what she was saying.

"Every morning you wake up and open that panel in your room to find a clean, neatly-pressed uniform for the day." She paused until he nodded. "Later, you'll find your jumpsuit for the track in there." She spoke slowly as if to allow him to drink in each word. "Who does that?"

"That's automated." He spoke as if it was obvious, but she pressed her lips together like she meant to correct him, then seemed to relax. "Three times a day you enter the mess hall and find a hot, perfectly balanced meal."

He hadn't considered that. "I'm sure the doctors have something to say about what we eat."

"And the track you find completely torn down and rebuilt each month?" she paused getting frustrated. "Who does that? The administrators who stand all day behind a glass barrier observing you?"

Willis didn't like where she was going. He wanted to call her crazy and storm out of the room. What she was proposing was— too much. If there were others on this station, why keep them hidden?

"Willis, do you understand what I'm telling you?"

"You mean this station is full of—"

"Slaves." Sheila filled in the word, letting it hang in the air for a long moment.

"Slaves?" He repeated as if it were a question. "You're saying there are slaves operating the Western Alliance training station."

She folded her arms on the table and leaned in to whisper. "Slaves are the underbelly of the entire World Coalition."

"But in the *Western Alliance*—"

"Especially in the Western Alliance. It's far easier to prosper when you have a workforce of slaves." Willis flinched at her repeated use of the word. "Oh, they don't call them that. That would tarnish the image they've worked so hard to show to the other alliances. They call them 'rehabilitation candidates.' Anyone caught breaking the Law, or even more, showing anything less than complete allegiance to the Alliance, forfeits their freedom."

"Forfeits?"

"The powers at work would tell you they're given the choice between prison and rehabilitation, but those who are willing to watch with a more objective eye are quick to notice there's little difference. No one is ever rehabilitated. No one exits the program."

Willis sat in stunned silence. He was the son of two of the greatest runners in Alliance history. He was the pride of the entire Western Alliance. Surely, his parents wouldn't have supported a place like she was describing by handing their son over to it. It was this thought that pushed one question to the front of his mind. One question he wasn't sure he trusted Sheila to answer.

"And how have I been in the Alliance system so long without ever knowing this? How could the other runners? You sit here slandering the name of the Alliance that my parents represented." The words came out in a low growl. Willis shook his head before jabbing a finger at her. "What are you saying? My parents loved the Alliance! Don't you think they would have known? Don't you think I would have noticed?"

"That's what I've been trying to figure out." She spoke calmly, placing a hand on Willis's. He stood and gripped the corners of the table. "The other racers are easy to figure out. But you—"

Willis's breathing slowed. "What about me?"

"Any racer who uncovers this fact might question the integrity of the Alliance. They could cause a lot of trouble for the Alliance's future. I'm guessing what you do and do not know about the Alliance is carefully monitored." Sheila stopped and scanned the desk in front of her. She looked up at him. "Truth about how the Alliance runs could cause a rebellion among the racers who are taught solely the glory of the Western Alliance. Managing to win the Chase every few years keeps the WA among the elite. It's one of the advantages of training in space. They control every bit of the environment—including your perception of it.

"When that perception is challenged"—she waved a hand in the air—"the answer is easy. They recode you. Recoding allows the doctors to mess with memory. They can take things out. They can plant suggestions. They can tell you how to perceive your surroundings. Keeping this knowledge secret would be easy, even with someone like me aboard who knows the truth. There's one problem."

"What is that?" Willis was listening intently.

"You."

"Me?"

"You are the best racer in the world. You never lose. You're never recoded. Recoding is meant to improve your ability to race, but the genetic breakdown is unavoidable. Those with high recoding numbers are prone to emotional instability, lessening their reliability as a racer."

Sheila waited until he nodded. She took a deep breath.

"Willis, you're the long-awaited hope of the Alliance. Your win has been expected for years. The Alliance has no desire to recode you, not even one more time. Any stage of the recoding can begin the breakdown."

"And now I know." Willis completed the line of reasoning.

"Now you know. I've told you." She paused. "If Blacc suspects you know, the Alliance both loves you and hates you. And we're both in danger."

"If it was so dangerous, why tell me? If everyone but the trainees know, there isn't much story here for the media. Why are you telling me this?"

Sheila studied his eyes for a long time as if trying to read his soul. Her lips parted slowly as she breathed the words. "My father was rehabilitated, many years ago. As a girl, I watched them take him away, and for a long time believed he would eventually be released. I never saw him again. I noticed right away when I got to the station what they're doing, but I've stayed quiet to protect you all. You seeing the woman changed everything. She's living my father's fate. She deserves that I speak the truth."

Willis's chest ached with the familiar pang that comes with thoughts of lost family. In a strange way, he connected to Sheila in that moment. "I'm sorry," was all he could say. "About your father, I mean."

"You have to be careful, Willis. No more asking around. No more talking to other racers. You have to pretend that you've given up the idea of figuring this out. Blacc knows you saw her and will be watching for any sign that you're causing trouble."

"They can't randomly recode me. Everyone would wonder why."

"It's not hard to create an excuse, Willis. Accidents happen."

"Accidents? Sure, but—"

"Yes, accidents like the collision on the track between Jez and Lacey. Accidents like the Gold Team being moved to the outside lane of the track at the last minute creating that scenario. Accidents like," she hesitated and looked at the floor as her final words struggled to pass her lips, "like the protective walls mysteriously lowering on that section of the track."

It took a second for Willis to understand what she was saying. His eyes widened in fear as it dawned on him. She was referring to Jez.

Willis returned to his quarters instead of going to the mess hall for dinner. His appetite was gone, anyway. He sat on the edge of his bed processing what Sheila had told him.

Could it be true? Would the Alliance engineer an "accident" because Lacey had seen something?

His mind wandered to Jez. Sheila had confirmed his thoughts before he left her office. Willis knew Jez was capable of being nasty, but would she risk committing murder for the Alliance? Even that was beyond her. What could the Alliance possibly have on her to make her want to do that?

He didn't feel like being around his teammates and had feigned a stomachache. With luck, they would assume his illness was the reason for his poor performance on the track.

Willis pushed the panel on the wall and removed the sleepwear inside. Picking up his uniform from that day, he placed it inside where his sleepwear had been. Examining the red and black mass of cloth, he carefully grabbed the sleeve and tugged at the seam. A slight tear, almost imperceptible, appeared in the armpit of the shirt.

He had to know if the woman had been real—if all that Sheila said had been real. He turned out the light and went to bed, expecting that sleep would be unlikely that night.

Morning. Willis sat on the edge of his bed examining the fresh, clean uniform. The stitches under the arm, obviously done by hand, stared back at him. Suddenly, the uniform felt heavy in his hands, and his fake stomachache from the night before became real.

Chapter Eighteen

"Willis?" Jez spoke in a hushed tone.

Willis realized that he'd stopped in the middle of a sentence as he coached the team. He had called a meeting in the common room first thing that morning. No more speeches about winning for the Alliance. No more being inspired to be the best. Willis had a new reason to win. The idea that the doctors might take his memory, even a memory of a nameless woman, disturbed him and filled him with an urgency to win.

The team had immediately taken to the fresh seriousness he brought to the meeting. Jez had spent much of the morning smiling after seeing his focus. *If only she knew why.* He didn't want to think about the fury of anger she would unleash if she learned the encounter with the woman still haunted him.

All of that was on hold for the moment, though, as most had paused their discussion to listen to the commotion on the other side of the space.

"One second, Jez," Willis responded.

"Ignore him," she pleaded.

Nearby, Creed was growling through his teeth at Stone. Stone-zee had failed to buckle the strap on his training helmet, causing it to slip when he fell during a training run. The resulting injury had landed Stone-zee in recoding, costing the Black Team the remainder of the week of training without him. He'd grabbed Stone the instant she entered the common room, his frustration causing him to forget there were others present. Walker sat there with a cold expression, watching.

"I'm done with that undisciplined little brother of yours," Creed spat at Stone.

"Creed, please. I'll work extra with him to catch him up after

he returns. Please don't trade him to another team." Stone pleaded with him through her tears.

"You think any of the other teams want a loser like him?"
Creed shot back. "The Alliance will be forced to trade him to another alliance. Heck, they might have to give him away."

"Please, no!" Stone's knees buckled. She reached out to grab
Creed, but his sharp look made her hesitate. He grabbed her wrist
and forced her down into her chair.

Anger burned inside of Willis. Creed's threat disgusted him.
It was a new level of cruel, even for Creed. He would have no
problem replacing Stone-zee's spot from another team on the station. At the very least, any member of Green Team would happi-
ly abandon the role of being recoded so often. Getting cut from a
team never sat well with the administrators, who generally responded by bringing up a runner from the junior training centers
rather than rehabilitate the problem runner. Stone-zee would likely be traded to another alliance for one of their racers, and that
would mean a permanent change in his citizenship. He could
never return home to the Western Alliance—or to Stone.

"Don't get involved," Jez whispered. She'd placed her hand
on his forearm. The touch sent shivers up his spine. He still
wasn't sure she had done what Sheila had suggested, but the notion bothered him. "Creed would find any reason to hurt you.
Elimination races are coming up, and we need you. I need you."

Jez was right. The final elimination runs were right around
the corner, the races that would decide the team headed to the
Chase. He couldn't afford injury as recoding would be the way to
speed recovery and minimize training time loss. The doctors
could not be allowed to change his memories.

He peeked over at Blue Team, who had been having their
own meeting in the other corner where he'd first noticed Perryn
holding her armband. She appeared nervous as she tried to keep
her team's attention. Normally, Jaden did much of the coaching,
but he wasn't even watching Perryn. His eyes were firmly fixed
on Creed, and his anger wasn't hard to spot.

"Don't worry, Jez." Willis squeezed her hand on his forearm

before pulling away. "I'm not going anywhere."

Her sigh of relief was immediate. Willis turned slightly away from Creed and explained their strategy for the track that week. Kane's huge size was causing a problem with a small space he needed to squeeze through. Willis explained the solution that he'd rehearsed, but a portion of his attention remained across the room.

He could see the forearm muscles in Jaden's arms tensing and relaxing, as if he were talking himself into and out of intervening. Perryn had given up on him and was trying to explain something to Amber.

"Jaden, no! Don't." Willis heard the hushed whispers of the Blue Team as Jaden stood. Willis could see their fear as he walked toward Creed.

Don't do it, Jaden. He'd love to hurt you. Everyone had gone silent.

"What seems to be the problem?" Jaden kept his voice calm.

Creed paused, running his tongue along his lower lip as if to contemplate which part of Jaden to take a bite out of first.

"Out of my face, bluey," Creed snapped.

"Oh, no worries, Mario. I wanted to talk to Casey anyway."

Creed flinched. Willis wasn't sure if Jaden meant it to disrespect him, but he was sure that's how Creed took it.

"She's busy," Creed straightened in front of Jaden, his size dwarfing Jaden's frame. Tears continued to stream down Stone's face, but Willis could see she was holding her breath. He did the same, not wanting to rip the delicate tension in the air.

Jaden frowned. "Oh, come on. She's got to have a minute."

"Like I said"—Creed spoke slowly through clenched teeth—"she's occupied. We have some team business to take care of."

"Team business." Jaden let out a hard breath. He shook his head.

"And no concern of yours. Go away."

Walk away, Jaden. Walk away. You made your point. You interrupted him. That might be enough, Willis pled silently.

"Team business," Jaden repeated, quietly looking down. "I

don't think so."

He turned to Stone.

"Casey, you don't have to listen to this guy—"

"What are you doing?" Creed screeched.

"—He's full of it anyway. Walk away from him when he's like this."

"Back off!" Creed shouted as he grabbed Jaden's shoulder. Jaden straightened and delivered a dagger look at Creed. Reaching up, he removed Creed's hand from his shoulder.

"Casey, why don't we take a walk to Chief Administrator Blacc's office." Jaden spoke calmly, extending a hand to her. Stone glanced at Creed, who continued to seethe, and slowly took Jaden's hand. She stood, her knees shaking. The room was so still, the flames in Creed's eyes could almost be heard. "Come on. Let's go."

"That's it!" Creed exploded. Stepping forward, he grabbed their wrists, yanking them apart. With his left hand, he pushed Jaden. His right hand grabbed Stone's face like it was a ball. She cried out.

For a half a second, Creed glared into her fearful eyes peeking out between his huge fingers. With a great shove, he launched Stone backward. Her momentum carried her over the chair she'd been in, toppling her over. Moving swiftly, Creed grabbed her arms, and practically lifting her, threw her into the wall. Her head smacked hard enough that Willis, who'd stood up, could hear it clearly.

Before Willis could move, Jaden composed himself and threw his body at Creed's midsection. The two fell to the floor, Creed striking his head on the corner of a table. It was all the advantage Jaden needed as he rained down blows upon Creed.

"You stay away from her!" Jaden shouted.

Creed swung at Jaden, connecting with his jaw and hurling him backward. Willis finally found his feet and moved with speed he normally reserved for the track. Jaden reached for a chair. As he raised it above his head, Willis stepped between the two racers with arms extended.

"Jaden, calm down." Willis braced himself for a blow.

A long moment hung thickly in the air, Jaden's heaving breaths the remaining sound. Willis watched a tear escape the corner of Jaden's eye as he cautiously lowered the chair. Movement caught Willis's attention, and he turned to see Perryn move toward Stone who had begun to stir.

"That's right, pretty boy. Step up in time to be the hero." Creed stood. His black uniform glistened where blood from his mouth and nose had soaked it. Willis shot him a glance that reminded him he was outnumbered.

"Perryn, she's going to need a doctor." Willis nodded toward Stone. She was whimpering, hiding her face in Perryn's arms.

"I'm not sure she can move yet." Perryn shot him a glance. "Better to bring the doctors to her."

"All trainees will remain where they are until further instructed," came the mechanical announcement over the speakers.

Willis smirked, and he made sure Creed saw it. Creed was going to get his. The administrators must have been watching the altercation on the cameras and would see Creed's actions as a clear violation of station rules. Creed's shuffling feet told Willis he must have come to the same conclusion.

Not a minute later, the doors to the common room slid open to reveal Chief Administrator Blacc, two uniformed Alliance officers, and several doctors. Blacc stormed toward Willis and the rest of the group.

"What in the name of all that is stupid is going on here?" Blacc shouted.

Willis parted his lips to say something but shut them quickly under Blacc's heated glare.The question wasn't waiting for an answer.

"Black leader," Blacc said, "how is it that you and yet another teammate find yourselves injured?"

"Just a disagreement, Chief Administrator." Creed lowered his gaze like a dog before its master. The doctors were prying Stone from Perryn's arms and placing her on a wheeled stretcher.

"Disagreement? Disagreements use words. Disagreements

do not land half your team in the infirmary."

"Yes, Chief Administrator." Creed's voice shook a little.

"The Alliance is shamed by this disgraceful display. We can't have it repeated. And so, as a consequence—"

"Chief Administrator, please." Fear appeared in Creed's eyes. Extending a hand, he took a half-step forward.

"Silence, Black Leader." Blacc glared at Creed, his frenzied gaze halting Creed's steps.

Creed retreated. "Yes, Chief Administrator."

"As much as your actions are disgraceful here today, it is the opinion of the administrators that you were operating within the allowances of a team leader until provoked by a challenge to your authority."

Willis stood stunned. That couldn't be. Creed attacked first.

"Blue team trainee," Blacc turned to Jaden, "you are hereby under arrest and will spend the remainder of the month isolated to your quarters. You're to have no contact with any trainee aside from team leaders."

"No!" Perryn shouted as the officers moved to flank Jaden, tears appearing in her eyes. "He was trying to defend her."

"Blue Leader, you would do well to hold your tongue," Blacc snapped. "Your team member deliberately involved himself in a private team matter with intent to create an opportunity to injure members of that team. Any further outburst from you and your visitation privileges will be revoked. Good luck preparing for the next race while having no contact with your team member at all."

"Chief Administrator, is there any way—" Willis started.

"No there isn't, Red Leader. You will silence yourself as well unless you want your team to feel the pain of training without a team member."

"You're right, Chief Administrator," Jez stated calmly, suddenly at Willis's side. "Our team has no wish to associate ourselves with these kinds of actions."

Blacc smiled and winked at Willis. "You can thank your little teammate, here."

Willis shot a look at Jez.

"She warned us this newbie was causing friction between team members. If we hadn't been watching him, you might have gotten more involved than you did before we stopped it. You wouldn't want to get injured, would you? It would be a shame to be—recoded."

Sheila's warning about 'accidents' shot through Willis. Jez's fingers suddenly felt like icy claws on his arm.

The officers stowed their batons and grabbed Jaden's arms. He stared at Willis trying to communicate as they spun him around to walk out. Perryn was crying. Creed was smiling to himself. Jez squeezed Willis's arm.

Willis hadn't missed Blacc's raised eyebrow on the word 'recoded'—a clear warning. They were watching him.

Chapter Nineteen

It was a crushing blow for Blue Team. Rumors spread that Perryn, Amber, and Dex fell apart in practice without Jaden. With the elimination races next month, Willis figured the administrators had decided it was time for the teams to resume their traditional places in the pecking order.

Willis sat in the mess hall, picking at his food. He couldn't help but stare over at the blue table where Amber and Dex ate in silence. Jaden was still confined to quarters. But where was Perryn?

Creed and Walker sat in equal silence not interacting with Stone-zee who sat next to them. In fact, they pretended like he wasn't there. After Stone had been sent to recoding for her injury, Blacc had frozen all team rosters. No changes could be made. Creed had made a grand speech to Stone-zee about the benefits of team discipline, citing his sister as an example. He'd meant it to shame Zeke, but it served to infuriate him. Willis couldn't help but wonder what was going through Zeke's mind.

The silence in the mess hall had sucked away his appetite, so Willis elected to leave. Nodding at his team and reminding them of their meeting later that morning, he pushed away from the table as the mess hall doors opened. The entire room was staring behind Willis. Turning around, he saw Stone, returning from recoding. She walked awkwardly, still getting used to her new feet. Her hand raised to her mouth and tears filled her eyes.

She rushed forward. Stone-zee could hardly get up from his chair before she embraced him, her sobs emanating without shame.

"I thought you'd be gone." Her muffled voice came from his shoulder.

"It's okay, Sis. I'm not going anywhere," Zeke stroked her hair as he whispered in her ear.

The two sat in chairs next to each other as if the width of the table would have been too much separation.

"Don't think you're off the hook," Creed whispered. The volume of his voice in the silence couldn't disguise his words.

Stone nodded, gazing at the floor. On her other side, Zeke's hand balled into a fist. Anger appeared ready to burst from him like a valve reaching its maximum pressure, but he said nothing.

Creed had better watch out. Willis held his breath until Creed pushed away from the table and stormed from the room.

Willis walked out the mess hall door. With everyone else eating, the barracks and hallways were as quiet as he'd ever seen them. The hollow drone that was ever present in the background on the station echoed until another noise caught his attention. He paused and waited for it to return.

It came again. A quiet, sniffing noise faintly caught his ear. Glancing around, he couldn't see the source until he neared his quarters. In the shadows next to the doorway to his quarters, sat Perryn. Her face was tear streaked. Her hair, still braided from sleep, was frizzing and coming apart. Trembling hands clutched her knees pulled up in front of her. Her inner fire was gone again. She sat by his doorway broken, moving when a shudder caused her to inhale quickly, making the noise he'd heard.

He hadn't seen her like this since the day Diego had died, and a heaviness descended on his chest.

"I can't do this," she sobbed looking up at him. He squatted down next to her. "I didn't know who else who to turn to. No one else talks to me outside of my team."

Willis glanced around to see if there was anyone watching. He nodded toward his door and helped her up. Entering his quarters, they sat on the edge of his bed.

"Everyone says that you guys aren't practicing well." He

waited a long moment for her to answer.

"We're not practicing at all."

"Not at all?"

"We tried the first couple of days, but it was horrible. Dex is falling all over himself. His confidence is gone. And Amber, she keeps talking about our next recoding."

"At least it would be the last recoding of the year. Elimination runs next month. No more races until after the Chase."

"But it won't be our last recoding, will it?" She pounded a fist on the bed frame not waiting for an answer. Willis sat silently. "We'll lose our elimination race without Jaden, be recoded, and be stuck here another year."

"Yeah, probably."

"He had us believing, Willis." Her voice grew louder. "He changed our whole team in a way not even Diego was able to."

"Hey, you're the leader."

"Not really. I may wear this armband"—she tore it off her arm and balled it into her fist—"but I can't inspire this team. Dex and Amber ran for Jaden. He picked them up when they fell. He built them up when they succeeded. I-I stay out of his way."

"So what's the worst that could happen? You stay here another year? You'll have Jaden back and kick some butt. So what if you get recoded a few times? You'll be out in a couple years, even if you don't make the Chase."

Perryn hid her face in her hands and silently cried again. He put his arm around her, feeling awkward as he did so. He contemplated removing it, but he didn't want to upset her more. He breathed a little easier when she relaxed into his embrace.

"Do you think I'll last a couple more years?" she whispered after a quiet moment passed.

"What do you mean?"

She pulled away from his shoulder and turned her head toward the far wall. With one finger, she pulled her ear forward.

He caught his breath. Staring him in the face was the number 96.

She turned toward him and looked him in the eyes. "I get

recoded more than three more times, and I'll no longer need to worry about the Chase. Blacc has it out for Jaden. He won't let us win next year, and I'm as good as dead. So, I hope you don't think me a wimp if I shed a few tears before we've even lost."

"I'm sorry." It was all he could think to say as he reached to his own ear, the familiar bump filling him with guilt. "I'm so sorry."

The two of them sat in silence for several minutes, the dampness on his shoulders where she'd wet it with her tears reminding him of the moment they'd shared. He already missed her warmth as she leaned on him. For the first time in a long time, life on the station didn't feel cold and metallic. His insides melted with compassion, a compassion what was easily slipping into fondness. He missed her smile. He wanted her fire to return. He longed to honor the trust she'd shown him.

He broke the silence. "Well, that leaves one thing you can do then."

"What is that?" She straightened and wiped her eyes.

"You'll have to not lose your elimination run next month."

"Shut up."

"I'm serious! I don't know how, but I know who would be able to figure that out. When are you next allowed to go and see Jaden?"

"Later today. Why?"

"Let's go see him—together."

They agreed to approach Jaden separately. Willis had made a joke about Jez seeing them going there together and flipping out, and he'd received a brief laugh from Perryn as a reward. He loved how she lowered her head and looked up at him when she laughed like she wasn't sure if her laughter was appropriate.

After lunch, Willis left the mess hall early again, bringing protests from Jez, which he chose to ignore. Making his way to the blue barracks, he placed his thumb on the panel outside

Jaden's door to confirm that he was a team leader and entered. He was surprised to find that Perryn hadn't arrived.

"Hey, man, come in!" Jaden smiled. Jaden appeared a little weak. A half-eaten soggy lump of meat lay next to stringy, over-cooked vegetables on Jaden's meal tray. "Yeah, you don't get the same food when you're confined to quarters. As hungry as I am, it's hard to eat."

"Maybe I should wait for Perryn?" Willis hovered awkwardly by the doorway. "She and I were supposed to meet here at the same time."

"Not at all. Sit down." Jaden waved him into the room. "What is going on?"

He bit his lip, wondering where to start. "She can tell you most of it, but your team isn't doing well."

Jaden sighed heavily. "I wondered. They have so much ability. They don't see it."

"Perryn is terrified they won't win their first elimination run without you."

"I feel horrible about that." He studied Willis with misted eyes. "I promised Perryn I would do everything I could to get her out of here and look at me."

"She can't stay here next year."

"She showed you her number?" Jaden dropped his gaze.

"Yeah. This morning. And Blacc has frozen the rosters, so there's nothing I can do about it." Willis paused. "She'll die if she has to stay."

Jaden stared at his hands. "Willis, can I ask you a question?"

"Sure."

"What are you going to do after the Chase?" He looked up.

Willis cocked his head to the side. "Go home, I guess. Why?"

"No, I mean what law will you pass?"

The question caught Willis. He sat in silence, Jaden's hopeful eyes eagerly waiting him out, and realized that he had no idea. He'd never stopped to think about *after* the Chase. All his efforts to date had been to get to the race. It unsettled him that he was no more prepared to answer that question than the young girl had at the last Chase.

"Not sure. I have to win first. I guess I haven't given it much thought yet."

"But then you plan on going home? To your parents?"

"Yeah. I barely know them, but that's the plan. I've been thinking of them a lot lately. I have a ton of questions." He paused. "What's with all the questions? How do I know it won't be you on that stage passing a law?"

Jaden suddenly became quite serious. His head dropped. "I hope so. I have to get there someday."

"Have to? You go home either way you know. Once you go to the Chase you're out of racing."

"I know. And no. I won't go home. Not if I win. Not if I pass a law."

"What are you talking about?"

"I won't be able to go home."

Willis contemplated asking more, but the door opened revealing Perryn. Jaden's face lit up, and Willis saw he wasn't going to talk about himself any longer. Perryn looked at Willis and Jaden as if unsure how to handle the two of them together.

"Perr, how are you?" Jaden stood, waving her in.

"I take it Willis filled you in?" Perryn gestured to Willis as she stepped inside. Her eyes glanced anywhere but at Jaden.

"He was letting me know how badly you want to win." Jaden caught her eyes and smiled, producing one from her in return. "Come in. Sit down."

"It's more than that, Jaden. I can't do this." The tears returned to her eyes.

"Do you remember what I called you that day I first arrived, right before the race?"

"You said, 'So you're our fearless leader, our rock.'" Perryn made a big show out of imitating Jaden, deepening her voice and standing in a confident pose. Willis couldn't help but chuckle, which produced laughter from the other two.

"Yeah, something like that," he said, blushing. He leaned

forward in his seat, giving her a slight shove like a brother teasing his kid sister. "I meant what I said."

"Which part?"

"All of it. You're the rock of this team."

She shook her head. "No, I'm not. You are."

"Hardly. I can get the team jazzed up, but you're the one who's been with them through all of this." Jaden leaned forward, placing a hand on Perryn's shoulder. "You're the one who stuck it out, even through the losing and recodings. It's easy to lead when you're winning, but they turn to you when they're hopeless, not me."

"I may have been around, but I'm not fearless like you." Her voice lowered to a whisper. "I'm terrified."

"Fearless doesn't mean you aren't afraid sometimes. I'm afraid every time I step on the track. I was telling Willis, here, about something that scares me."

Perryn looked curiously at Willis. Willis found himself trying to put the pieces of what Jaden had started to say together in his head.

"Fearless means that fear doesn't control you. It doesn't get to cripple you. Fearless means you look at fear and push forward anyway."

"But—" she protested.

"—but you've never stopped pushing forward, have you?" he interrupted. "Perr, you were born for this. Yeah, I can't run with you until after next month's race, but you can do this."

"I don't know."

"That's okay. I do. And so does Willis. Don't you, friend?"

Willis smiled and nodded. Her eyes were showing the glimmer of hope again. He realized, then, what Jaden had done for his team. He hadn't made them better runners. He made them become the runners they were already destined to be.

"He's right," Willis reached over and grabbed Perryn's hand. "You're stronger than you realize." She let him take it. Jaden smiled approvingly.

"That does it. If you can win over this guy," he pointed,

smiling at Willis, "you're far more talented than I even realized. Come on. Let's get a plan together." He nodded toward a sketch he'd made of the track on the table.

Perryn would not let go of Willis's hand as they approached the table, and something in his chest leapt.

Chapter Twenty

"Stone, to the right. Walker, go left. Stone-zee, stay right here." Creed's commanding voice barked orders to his team. "Hold on. We're going for another ride."

Willis stood in the observation booth watching the races between the other teams. Final standings had been released that morning, and Willis's Red Team had done what was expected of them. They were first in points for the year allowing them to wait to see which team would get to challenge them for a chance at the Chase. The other four teams had been seeded according to their standings. Blue Team had shocked everyone by pulling out fourth overall in the standings, so they were paired with the third place Gold Team next. Currently, Creed was busy making short work of Nico's Green Team. Green Team had the unfortunate distinction of coming in last in the standings.

Willis marveled at the administrators' creation for this race. None of the teams had been allowed to see the rotation of the track until the actual race. Since he wouldn't have to race this track, Blacc had invited him as team leader to observe with the administrators. The quiet tapping on screens as they manipulated the track and followed the progress of the players served as a backdrop to the movement going on outside.

The track was a massive sideways cylinder, which slowly rolled in place as the teams raced from one end to the other of the interior. Obstacles of all sizes made of what appeared like large blocks littered the inside. Some of these blocks were constructed to resemble pyramids or diamond shapes. Others were simply irregular shapes. This made the gaps between the blocks unpredictable, some requiring runners to squeeze through or even lay down to pass by them. Rather than smooth edges, the blocks were rimmed with handles, which the runners could hang from as the rotation gently turned their section of the track upside-down.

"Come on, guys, we have to catch up!" Panic filled Nico's voice. Willis shook his head as the greenies struggled with every rotation. They didn't have the strength of the Black Team and would simply hang as they helplessly watched Creed and his squad monkey-bar their way forward.

"No miracle run for the greenies, huh?" Blacc said somberly behind Willis.

"Doesn't seem like it," Willis replied, trying not to convey his disappointment. Perryn's team had a chance against the Gold Team, but he didn't know how they would ever match Creed, Walker, Stone, and Stone-zee the following week. "Looks like Nico is going to have to come up with a new plan for his team next year."

"It won't be his team next year."

"What do you mean, Chief Administrator?" Willis turned to Blacc, stunned at the comment. Blacc remained stone-faced at the window.

"Things are going to change, Red Leader. The Alliance is about order, and your bluey friend has fooled with that order. It has cost our elite runners too many recodings."

"So you mean—"

"I mean," he interrupted, "that your friend will be made Green Leader to get them winning again. That should give us three strong teams to truly compete these next few years. Nico, well, he'll become a bluey."

"But why wouldn't you—" Willis hesitated, knowing he was on dangerous ground to challenge Blacc.

"Leave things the way they are?" Blacc raised an eyebrow. "Because it's becoming too hard to predict the outcome of the training runs. Your newbie friend is to thank for that. We need three teams consistently improving while maintaining some threat of recoding to motivate them. His removal will see to it that Blue Team serves its proper role again. Things can go back to the way they were—to order."

Willis shuddered at what that meant for Perryn. Without Jaden, she wouldn't make it more than a couple months the following year.

"Chief Administrator, why do *I* get to know about this?"

"Because, Red Leader, I want one thing to be clear." He turned to Willis and lowered his eyebrows. "I want you to be clear that you serve the Alliance. We all do. Our personal feelings do not matter in the face of our duty.

"As soon as both teams are eliminated from this year's Chase team, the announcement will be made. And—I don't want your soft spot for the blueys to cloud your judgment. The wisdom of the Alliance is that Blue Team is there to push the other teams to become better, not to compete for the Chase. The Alliance leads us, and we must accept their guidance."

Willis couldn't take a full breath. The image of Perryn's recoding number crystalized in his mind.

"Chief Administrator, they can't." He stepped toward Blacc. He could feel his heart beating wildly, and he wanted to shove Blacc through the window or race from the room. Maybe both.

"Already did." Blacc remained stone-faced as he spoke. "And you're not to speak another word about it. Have I made myself clear?"

Willis retreated. "Yes, Chief Administrator."

Willis turned to the window to see Creed standing over an exhausted Nico, laughing. The entire Black Team had finished before Nico ever crossed the line. The race had not even been close. Nico hid his face to conceal his tears as the doctors took the green uniformed runners away.

Minutes later, Blacc exited the observation booth to give his usual pre-race speech to the next set of runners. Willis rested his head on the glass trying to process what he'd been told.

What am I going to do? The words raced through his mind. His entire life to this point had been about serving the Alliance. Everything was about this year. This was his year to win the Chase and benefit everyone in the Alliance. Winning the Chase wouldn't save Perryn. *Winning isn't going to change that I serve an Alliance that uses slaves. Winning doesn't change anything. Not really.*

Down below, Perryn walked through the doorway. She had a renewed energy about her. Even from the booth, he could see her determination. She had her hands on the shoulders of Dex and Amber, drawing them into a small huddle to offer last minute instructions. Short a team member, he guessed she was reminding them that exactly one had to cross the finish for the whole team to move on. She was leading. She had hope again. She planned to win.

"It doesn't matter," he whispered to himself. He knew she might win today, but Creed would never allow it, and even if a miracle happened, he couldn't ask his team to lose for her sake.

Down on the sphere's floor, Perryn peeked up at the observation booth. She could see Willis standing there staring down at her. He didn't look good.

"What's up with Willis?" Dex followed her gaze.

"I don't know, but that's not important. You guys clear on what we're going to do?"

"Yeah." Amber nodded.

"Gotcha," Dex said smiling.

At least I've got him in a good mood. It's going to take more than that to win, though.

She turned to watch as the doors opened to reveal the Gold Team. For a split second, she didn't recognize any of them besides Joanne. Lacey, Starr, and Cleo stood shoulder to shoulder talking about the track without looking at each other. No nail polish. No make-up. They'd each pulled their hair back tightly into a bun to match Joanne's.

"What is up with the goldies?" Amber muttered.

Dex shrugged. "I guess a couple of recodings changes you."

"They didn't come to lose today, that's for sure." Perryn looked back at the observation booth to see if Willis had noticed the Gold Team.

Willis didn't like the Gold Team's appearance. Their obsession with themselves, which had always been their handicap, was gone. Joanne had finally won over her team, and they came ready to win.

"Stay focused, Perryn," he whispered.

Blacc made his usual rounds harassing the runners and finished with his speech about the pride of the Alliance. The runners took their places at the gate, and the tone sounded. Both teams took off into the cylinder which slowly turned. Joanne directed her team over the closest pyramid of blocks trying to draw as straight a line as possible along the deceptively short track. Perryn, Dex, and Amber were climbing through a hole on the nearest side of the opening. It would slow them down, but Willis smiled as he realized it'd also maximize their time before the track turned them upside-down. The early lead of the goldies was erased as they were forced to hang on with their hands while Perryn and her team had extra moments on their feet. Joanne moved the girls slowly forward, encouraging them not to lose their grip. A fall would surely injure any runner enough to remove them from the race.

Having seen the first two teams, he wasn't surprised this time at how slow the teams made progress. They had seconds on their feet until they were hanging on again. Willis's nerves turned his stomach sour as he watched Perryn catch her team up to then lose ground as they hung in the air.

She needs a different plan. She's using the same approach as the goldies, and they're out performing her. He closed his eyes and breathed out a long, slow breath to will his thoughts to Perryn. When he opened them, he stared. Perryn, Dex, and Amber were hanging on the upside of the track without moving forward.

"What are you doing?" he shouted, pounding on the glass. He hadn't meant to say that out loud, but he couldn't contain it. "Don't break down!"

"Perryn, we can't beat them this way," Amber cried out.

"She's r-right. They're gaining ground on us with each r-rotation." Dex grunted as he strained not to lose his grip.

Perryn panted as she tried not to fall. Her racing heart was sinking inside. *We're not going to lose. Not again. Not now.*

She watched as the Gold Team slowly moved forward. Motion in the corner of her eye caused her to glance at the opening of the cylinder. It was Willis. He was shouting something, his arms pounding at the window.

"Perryn, what do we do?" Dex pleaded. "They're getting f-further away. I c-c-can't hold on much longer anyway. This is getting harder each t-time we go around."

Everything blurred in Perryn's vision. She realized it was tears starting to seep out of her eyes. Blinking them away, she heard Dex repeat, "can't—hold—on."

"So don't." Her order received puzzled looks from her teammates. Her mind raced through the idea. *It might work.* "Next pass, Dex, run. Run against the turn of the cylinder. Stay on the ground moving sideways through the obstacles."

"But what if I get caught?" he said. "What if I fall?"

"Amber and I will keep going this way, but you're fast. Dex, maybe you can outrun them."

"You sure?"

"No. I'm not, but if anyone has the speed to do it, it's you."

As soon as they came to the near side, Dex split off of the group, running as if on a treadmill uphill against the turn of the cylinder. His legs churned as his speed kept him in pace with the moving track. Perryn's heart leapt as an opening big enough came, and Dex jumped sideways through it.

Perryn and Amber continued to move straight forward, directly chasing the Gold Team. Joanne and her team appeared exhausted, barely able to hold on until back on their feet. Dex was expending a lot of energy, but he was steadily gaining on the others.

That's it, Dex! Perryn chanced a look away from the handle she was reaching for to see if the Gold Team had noticed Dex.

"Joanne, what's he doing?" Cleo readjusted her grip on her handle. Joanne looked down, horror crossing her face. Dex was right below them, darting sideways anytime he saw an opportunity to move forward.

"As soon as we get down again, do what he's doing." Joanne said between heavy breaths.

"Dex, look out!" Perryn shouted. Starr leapt too early on the rotation, falling next to Dex. Her knees crumpled with her momentum, and the track movement flipped her over backward. Her head smacked one of the blocks, and she sat confused for a moment.

Once her feet were under her, Perryn scaled to the top of a pile of blocks and saw that Joanne and the others were copying their plan. She thrust her spent legs forward, knowing Dex's tiny lead was their one hope. She and Amber could never catch up.

Please let him make it, she begged silently.

As she and Amber squeezed through the next small opening, she caught a glimpse of Joanne, who ran practically even with Dex.

"Run, Dex!" Perryn's voice squeaked, unable to conjure enough breath to voice her words. Amber tripped and stepped on Perryn while trying to recover. Perryn's ankle buckled, causing her whole body to fall forward. Their momentum and the added rotation sent both crashing into a block pillar and sliding sideways on the floor. Dazed, Perryn tried to clear her vision.

Tone.

The cylinder shuddered to a halt. The race was over. Someone had won. *But who?* She started to climb to her feet to see over the last several meters of obstacles.

Willis held his breath. From his view out the window he could see the starting gate and most of the inside of the cylinder. The slight downward angle prevented him from seeing the end of the track or the finish gate. Someone had finished first, and everything in him longed to peek over the administrators' shoulders to peek at the monitors.

Instead, he closed his eyes. *Please let it be Dex. Please,* he repeated to himself.

"Do we have confirmation?" Blacc watched the administrators for an answer.

"All monitors and gate sensors read the same," came the voice of a man in a laboratory coat. "They won."

Who are 'they?' Willis tried unsuccessfully to control his rapid breathing.

Blacc stood motionless. He had one hand at his chin as if contemplating his next move. Willis saw the corners of his mouth turn upward and his shoulders shrug as he let out a single breath of laughter.

"All right, Red Leader." He slowly nodded once to Willis. "Your little blue friends get to race another day. Remember to keep your mouth shut about the Alliance's plans. I'd hate to have to come up with a reason why they'd need to forfeit this win."

For a moment, Willis didn't care about the Alliance's plans. As long as Blue Team wasn't eliminated, he had time to figure it out. Presently, all he could think about was reaching Perryn. He knew she would be wearing the smile he loved so much.

Chapter Twenty-One

The quiet of the barracks' hallways pressed in like a tomb that afternoon with both Green and Gold teams in recoding. Willis could hardly stand the wait outside Perryn's quarters. The three members of Blue Team had celebrated briefly before Blacc ushered them off the track. Willis had missed her, and she'd retreated to her room to clean up. Now he stared at the doorway unable to stand still as he waited for her to emerge.

Schwipp. The door opened, and Perryn took a step back, a startled expression crossing her face. She smiled at him.

Willis hadn't pondered what he would do when she came out of the room. Seeing her smile, he wanted to lift her in his arms and spin her in the air. Instead, he managed a quiet, "Hey." To his surprise, she leapt forward and wrapped her arms around his neck.

"Thank you," she whispered.

"For what?" He pulled back enough to give her a puzzled look.

"For not letting me give up."

"I didn't—"

"No, I mean it." She stepped backward. "Without your help, I think I would have crumbled into pieces at the starting line today."

"Don't go falling apart on me. Besides, it wasn't me who came up with the brilliant plan to have Dex outrun the track. I hear that was all you."

"I suppose." Perryn glanced down at the floor, a faint blush appearing on her cheeks. She paused, taking a second to move a stray lock of hair behind her ear.

"Does Jaden know yet?"

"No, I guess I should go tell him."

"Seriously? The guy's probably climbing the walls wanting to know what happened!"

"Yeah, well...he isn't the one I wanted to see first."

"Come on." He took her hand and led her to Jaden's doorway down the hall. It was when they got to his door that he realized what she'd said. "Wait! Were you coming to see me?"

Schwipp! Jaden's doorway opened. He stood there smiling, obviously glad for some company.

"Hey, guys. How'd it go?" Jaden's eyes darted back and forth between them. The quiet corridor quickly became awkward as Perryn stared at Willis. The corners of her mouth turned upward shyly, answering his question. Jaden noticed their joined hands and smirked. "I'd say that I don't want to interrupt, but I believe you came to my door."

The joke broke into the moment, and both Willis and Perryn let out embarrassed laughs.

"Seriously, I've been in here for a half an hour since I heard you guys return." Jaden put his hands on his hips like a scolding mother. "A guy needs to know what happened. Please tell me you come with good news."

"Let's just say you're not done racing this season," Perryn said.

"Yes!" Jaden leapt in the air and pumped his fists. He grabbed each of them on one shoulder and pulled them toward his room. "Come inside. I want every detail."

"You'd have been unbelievably proud of her, Jaden." Willis smiled and patted Perryn on the shoulder. "She was incredible out there. And that decision to have Dex start running—"

"That was nothing, really." Perryn waved him off.

"Hardly." Jaden's ear-to-ear smile hadn't left since they'd told him the news.

They'd been talking for an hour recounting every move of

the race. Perryn told Jaden about the Gold Team's appearance, the cylindrical track, and her fear when she and Amber had fallen. Willis wouldn't let her get away without telling Jaden about her leadership.

"All I did was make a quick decision. I had no idea what to do."

"But that's leadership, Perr." Jaden leaned forward.

Willis nodded his approval. "Don't sell yourself short."

"Whatever." She looked down and ran a hand through her hair, a slight flush appearing on her cheeks.

"Seriously, friend," Jaden responded soberly. "You are made to lead. I think you're going to do something great one day."

"Gotta get out of this place first."

"Yeah." Jaden whispered loudly as he pretended to lean in to tell a secret. "But we can't discuss our top-secret plans to win it all with the opposing team present."

Willis sat up straight trying to appear as serious as possible, which was difficult with the laughter welling up inside him. "If I'm not welcome here, I'll leave."

Jaden snorted, not quite stifling a laugh.

"Speaking of getting out of here." Perryn suddenly sat up straight. "When are you free to leave your quarters?"

"I'm a free man." Jaden smiled. "With the elimination race done, the month is officially over. Lunch anyone?"

"Yes. I'm starving." Perryn held her stomach in both hands.

"Me too." The tension of the race gone, Willis realized how hungry he was. "I need to stop by my room for my notes, though."

"Do you ever stop training?" Jaden softened the question with a smile.

"You see, there's this new upstart team threatening to win it all."

Willis smiled. Perryn started to giggle. Jaden snorted again before a fit of laughter overtook him.

"I'll be minute if you want to wait here," Willis said. They were in the main corridor near the mess hall. Willis moved toward the red barracks.

"Nah. We'll walk with you," Jaden offered. "Besides, it's not every day that I get to peer into the quarters of the *red leader.*" At this he waved his hands next to his head as if in awe.

"I'm sure your life will be forever changed," Willis shot back, smiling.

Willis walked ahead of the other two down the hallway. The red lights appeared unfriendly to him after their time in Jaden's quarters, and Willis was momentarily saddened that his home was separated from theirs. He was about to say something to that effect when he saw her.

The woman stood in the same shadows she'd been in before. She was wearing the same ragged uniform, and her hair was falling out as if she'd been working for hours. In fact, her appearance could have been a memory had Willis not noticed the healing wound on her left temple.

Willis's feet froze as she stepped into the light. She looked him in the eye with a note of longing in her gaze. It was when her eyes shifted to glance behind him that Willis remembered that Jaden and Perryn were still with him.

"Who are you?" Perryn's voice was barely audible. She placed her hand on Willis's shoulder.

The woman didn't answer. Her eyes studied Perryn's face and moved to Perryn's hand. She turned once more, this time to look at Jaden who had stepped forward to Willis's other side.

"And here I was thinking she'd end up with you, Son," she whispered, her voice sounding tired.

Son? Willis repeated to himself. He glanced at Jaden who wore a warm expression on his face as he looked at the woman.

"Mother, you need to be more careful. You shouldn't be out here."

Mother? Willis's mind raced. *This is Jaden's—mother?*

"My boy," her gaze softened, "you told me these were the two people on the station that you trusted."

"I do." He smiled. "Someone else could come by at any moment. But—it's good to see you, Mom." Jaden stepped forward and embraced the woman. She appeared so small next to the much taller Jaden.

"I got your message. Did you get mine?" She cocked her head to the side. Willis realized she was addressing him.

"Message?" He pointed to himself.

"Wait, you've met her?" Perryn's eyes widened.

Willis nodded. "Once. I'm not sure I can say we met. What did you mean by 'message'?" He turned back to the woman.

"The tear in your uniform. It was in a place that wouldn't casually tear. That journalist told you about us, and you wanted to know if she was imagining it all."

Willis brushed the repair on his uniform with a finger. "And so, you answered."

"We are here, Willis. We're all over the station."

"We?" Perryn was still catching up. "All over the station. What are you talking about? How many people?" She placed her hands on the side of her head as if to contain the thought.

"Workers—slaves," Jaden said flatly. "The station is operated by hundreds of them."

"Slaves? Since when?" Perryn stepped backward as though threatened.

"Since forever."

"Sheila says the entire Alliance depends upon them," Willis added.

The woman nodded slowly and frowned. The wrinkles on her face deepened with sadness.

"Mom, that was too big a risk, repairing Willis's uniform like that." Jaden placed a hand on his mother's shoulder. "If the administrators found out, they would—after last time—" His voice choked for a moment. Willis saw him holding back tears.

"Son, what they did to me after the last time I showed myself," she responded, fingering the wound on her head, "cannot change my hope. This young man could change everything." She motioned to Willis. "They don't want to recode him lest they risk ruining him and their near guarantee at winning, so he's one of the few who gets to keep his memories. He can remember we exist."

"Willis, what is she talking about? Who's 'we?' Someone please explain this to me." Perryn scanned the group with furrowed eyebrows. Willis understood. She'd been recoded almost the full one-hundred times. Who she was currently, or had been in her past, was at the mercy of doctors by this point. Any knowledge she had of slavery was gone.

"Perr, I'll explain later," Jaden said. "For now, Mom, you have to leave the hallway."

"I will. I wished for him to see me one more time. Willis, you're the hope of the Alliance, but not for the reasons *they* think you are. If my boy doesn't make it to the Chase, you're the one who can help us."

Willis tilted his head. "But how?"

She gave no answer but instead stepped closer to Jaden. Bringing his face down to hers, she kissed him on the forehead. "Take care, my son." With that, she walked to the shadows and disappeared into an opening that shut behind her, leaving no trace that there was ever a door.

It all made sense to Willis in that moment. Jaden's unknown background. His tattooless ear with no sign of countless recodings from the junior training center or even of his parentage. The burden he carried about law-passing if he won the Chase. Even the plan Blacc had shared with him. It all came together. Jaden was the son of a slave. Jaden was the unknown boy of a nameless mother, and he hadn't grown up like the rest of the runners on the station. Whether he lied about himself to enter Chase training or was strangely recruited late by the Alliance, Willis didn't know. What he did know is that Jaden could destroy everything the Alliance had built.

And if he could not, his mother hoped Willis would.

The three stood in the hallway for a minute before disappearing into Willis's quarters. At the mouth of the hallway, near the mess hall doors, Jez stepped out of the shadows into the red light. She clenched her teeth and glared at Willis's door.

They hadn't seen her standing there. Coming out of the mess hall to look for Willis when he'd been late, she had seen and heard everything.

Chapter Twenty-Two

"I can't do it," the woman whimpered.

"It's the only way we can save him. They'll take him away as soon as he's walking," a male voice nearby pleaded.

Something was different in the dream this time. Usually the images were fuzzy and appeared distant. This time, Willis was eerily conscious of the dream.

The woman dabbed at her eyes but couldn't quell the steady stream of tears. "What if he hates us for it?"

Who is she? I have to see her face clearly. He strained to see her features.

"He won't. Not when he's old enough to understand," the man caressed her face with one hand. *"Here, you hold him. I'll take care of it. You don't have to watch."*

Willis waited for the jolt of imagined pain that would wake him from his sleep, but instead one more image appeared. *The man stepped into his field of vision. He had strong features and appeared strikingly similar to Willis. His hair was the same color brown with some grey patches, and his body was well toned like that of a racer.*

Yet, despite his obvious strength, he had tears welling in his eyes. He took his large hands and placed them around Willis's leg, one above the knee and the other below. The hands looked huge and powerful compared to the leg. The man's tear-streaked face gazed at his.

"I love you, Son. Please forgive me for this."

Dad?

"We love you, little one," came the woman's voice behind him.

Mom? Willis silently panicked.

With that, the man's hands jerked his leg in opposite directions at once.

Pain. Excruciating pain.

"Dad, no!" Willis screamed as his body shot upright in bed. His violently shaking hands lost their grip as he tried to turn to the edge of the bed, and his sweat-soaked body slammed to the floor. He winced with the pain and slowly hoisted himself up to his hands and knees. It was then the weeping started.

His body quaked as the swells of sobs came like waves during a violent storm. Lowering his head to the cold floor, he allowed the bitter truth of his recurring dream to overcome him. The emotion poured out of him with each tear dampening the floor with his rediscovered reality.

Willis wasn't the prodigy of two proud parents who longed to serve the Alliance by offering up their son to the Chase. He was the kidnapped child of parents who had attempted to rescue him from the same nightmare they had lived. With their own hands, they tried to cripple him to save him.

It was the silent secret of his one recoding. The Alliance had forcefully taken him from his home before the damage was permanent and recoded him to alter his memory of his parents. They wanted him to believe the tale of his parents' willing sacrifice, so he would never question the Alliance.

Jaden's mother had changed all that. He'd fallen asleep questioning everything, including what he believed he remembered about his parents.

It must have been those questions that allowed him to remember more of the dream.He hated using the word dream because it was not. Memory. It was a memory. What he'd been told—the messages he'd received from his parents urging him to serve the Alliance—they were all fake. But this—this was memory. His memory. Another memory he'd lose if they recode him.

It would be hours until it was time to get up. He lay on the icy floor, one arm draped across his eyes. With his other hand, he rubbed furiously at the number behind his ear. It was no longer a source of comfort but a symbol of what was taken from him.

"You okay, Willis?" Jaden approached the table.

Willis looked up from his untouched morning plate. He'd spent the entire meal picking at his food without eating it. Normally, Jez would have nervously tried to get him talking, but she too seemed lost in her own thoughts. Her eyes had kept darting angrily left and right as if she was attempting to decide between two unlikable options. Thankfully, Toad had caught the idea, and the team had said nothing during breakfast. Presently, the mess hall was empty except for the two of them. The others had all finished and left.

"Didn't sleep well." Willis looked down at his plate.

"Yeah, that was pretty intense last night." Jaden sat down at the table. Willis glanced up and caught Jaden studying his face. "Listen, Willis. About my mother—"

"Don't worry." He placed a finger at his lips. "I'm not saying a word."

"Thank you." Jaden glanced away for a moment pausing. "Last time she showed herself to you, the administrators weren't kind to her. If they found out she'd done it again—" He stopped, his eyebrows furrowing as his voice trailed.

"They'd hurt her and recode all of us." Willis bit his lip.

"Probably."

Both sighed and allowed quiet to fill the room. They picked at their food.

Willis sighed, breaking the silence. "What's it like?"

"What is what like?"

"Knowing your parents."

Jaden was slow to respond. "My father died a long time ago. That's how my mother ended up a slave. She couldn't care for us all alone, but she's a good mom." He stared beyond Willis like he was viewing the memory in the distance. "When she could no longer afford our basic needs, the Alliance took my brothers and sisters to work elsewhere. I was younger, so I stayed with my mother. When Blacc came on a trip to the surface, he saw me running with a load of supplies my mother had forgotten for her work and must have liked what he saw. He followed me to see where I was going. A day later, he arrived with officers and told my mother I must be the luckiest rehabilitation child in the Alliance."

"So that's how you ended up here?" Willis pointed at the table with his fork as the blanks on Jaden's story filled in.

"Yes. I guess Blacc thought I'd lose that race on my first day and give him the excuse to have the doctors recode me. And when I didn't, he couldn't recode me without reason. It would raise too many questions."

"And how did your mother get here?"

"She traded in a lot of favors to get transferred here to the station when I came here. I wasn't sure it was the right choice, but she insisted. Willis, don't you know your parents?"

Willis paused and sat silently. "I thought I did."

"And?"

"That all changed last night. Something happened to me. Something about meeting your mother." He stopped, considering his words. "It helped me remember."

"Remember what?" Jaden probed quietly.

"That my parents weren't proud citizens wanting to serve their Alliance. That I was taken. That they never wanted to give me up. That they did the unthinkable to try to save me. That everything I believed about them was a lie that the Alliance crammed into my head robbing me of who I really am." He spat these whispered words through his teeth as his eyes filled with tears, Willis shoved his tray of food, causing it to fly nearly halfway across the mess hall. He buried his head in his hands. "I want to know them. I want to go home."

Hearing his own words, Willis realized that everything was

different. He had always been about winning. He served the Alliance. He would win to live up to his parents' expectations. He would win because it was what he was made to do. None of that mattered any more. Now, winning was about his family. He had to go home. He couldn't allow himself to get recoded, or they'd rob him of his memories again.

Jaden sat silently, his eyes showing limitless compassion. Turmoil began to well up inside Willis. If he planned to keep his memory, he had to win. If Blue Team made it to the final elimination run, Willis's win would send Jaden—and Perryn—to recoding. Saving himself would be condemning them. The conflict tore at his soul.

"She's right you know." Jaden broke the silence.

"Who?"

"My mother. You are the hope for the Alliance, the *real* Alliance."

"But you would—and Perryn—you would both—"

"Willis, that doesn't matter. There's a bigger picture here. No one is more likely to win than you, and the law you pass could change everything, now that you know. Perryn wouldn't tell you any differently."

Willis couldn't believe the permission Jaden was giving him, but he was right. No one was more likely to win than he.

"A message?" Sheila stammered. She stood in the doorway of her office, preventing him from entering. Willis remained in the hallway, determination washing over his face.

"I want you to send my parents a message." Willis repeated the words again, making sure to speak each one distinctly.

"Why? How?" Sheila stepped back as if afraid to be too close to Willis. Then, she waved him inside. Peering up and down the hallway, she closed the door.

"I don't know, but you're the only one who can help me."

"Willis, you don't know what you're asking. If I'm caught—

I—my sister—" She flopped down in her chair, resting her head in her hands.

"Look, I can imagine what will happen to you if they catch you, but I need to find something out. I need to know if this is all going to be worth it."

Sheila straightened at the desk in her quarters. Her hands were trembling as she reached for a pen.

"Okay. I might be able to send a coded text to them when I transmit my next article, but the message would have to be incredibly short to go unnoticed. It's still no guarantee they'll get it. Willis, we need to be very careful. It's one thing to talk face-to-face like we have, but I'm on a very short leash with the Alliance. I have no doubt they're monitoring my transmissions."

"I don't want to get anyone hurt."

"What's the message?"

Willis stood there thinking. He wanted to give her the shortest, vaguest message possible that would communicate what he meant to say.

"Tell them, 'I remember,'" he said finally.

Sheila sighed and nodded. "I'll let you know if anything happens. I'll be transmitting later tonight."

Willis jolted at the sound of someone at the door to his quarters. The clock revealed it was the middle of the night. He rubbed his eyes and made his way to the entrance to his quarters.

He opened the door. No one was there.

All that he saw in the empty hallway was a torn corner of yellow, lined paper on the floor by his feet. He picked it up, remembering Sheila's yellow notepad. A tear escaped the corner of his eye as he read the two-word response to his message, 'COME HOME.'

Chapter Twenty-Three

Willis stood with his mouth agape staring at the track. The administrators had outdone themselves with the design this time. He craned his neck backward to see the top of the six-sided column that rose to the top of the ten-story sphere. Covered in small platforms, hand holds, and ropes, it was a climber's dream course—and a non-climber's nightmare. The column was broken into eight levels, each offering six different means of reaching the next stage. A platform ringed the column at each interval, allowing racers to move around the column to reach their desired obstacle.

"Why couldn't we get this track?" Jez shook her head. "I'd wipe the floor with all of them."

Willis nodded. "Maybe that's why, Jez. Or maybe it's because it greatly favors Creed's stronger team."

"What do you mean?" Toad questioned.

"I mean that Blue Team has never been great at climbing. Jaden is the only one who will be able to keep up with Creed and Walker."

"And you think—" Jez looked at Willis.

"I think that the administrators want to see the best two teams compete in the final elimination. That's all."

Red Team had been invited as a team to view the race. The four of them stood near the starting gate. Willis gazed at the Blue Team. The four of them were huddled together. Jaden's face was intense without masking its usual friendliness. He drew with his finger in the air explaining something to the team.

Willis's eyes met Perryn's, who he hadn't realized was watching him. Her hair was pulled into a ponytail, and her lips were tight together as if deep in thought. Her eyes blazed with fire. *She came to win today.* He couldn't help but feel anxious for her. He allowed the corners of his mouth to turn up slightly into a smile, perceptible enough for her to see. Her eyes brightened, and she took a deep breath, turning back to Jaden.

He longed to run over to her and tell her she could do this, but they were here as observers. Blacc had given explicit instructions that they couldn't interact with either team, no matter what they heard or saw. Besides, he knew Jez would hate it.

"Willie and Perryn sitting in a tree," Toad muttered snickering.

"Shut up, Toad!" Jez snapped. Her eyes knifed at Toad's smirk.

"Whatever." Toad snickered. "You said yourself, Jez, that they were spending a lot of time together. Now they're making eyes at each other."

"Shut your trap, you little rodent," Jez snarled. "Willis wants nothing to do with her that way." Her voice was forceful, but Willis couldn't help but feel she was trying to convince herself. He'd better pay attention to the Black Team for a while.

"Look," Creed stabbed a finger at the air, "the newbie is the real threat from the blueys. You see your opportunity, you take it."

"Yes, Creed," Walker responded.

"Sure," Stone-zee sighed.

Casey Stone looked at the floor.

"Stone, have I made myself clear to you? You know what to do when the time comes." Creed stepped forward bowing his head to catch her gaze. She raised her head a little to look at him.

"Yes, Creed." Stone's face fell.

"We'll see. You'll answer for it if you don't." Creed glared at her for a long moment. He stepped away pulling Walker into a private discussion.

Zeke grabbed his sister's arm and pulled her aside. He whispered, "What was that about? What are you supposed to 'know to do?'"

"Nothing." Her voice rasped in a hoarse whisper, and she once again stared at the floor.

"You sure, Sis?"

"Zeke, leave me alone. I've got it."

Willis could see Zeke's hands ball into fists again as he glared at Creed. He appeared ready to pounce, but he restrained himself.

"Blue Team! Black Team! Enter your starting gate." Blacc's voice boomed. The teams lined up. Jaden wrapped one arm around Perryn and whispered in her ear, no doubt giving her some last-minute encouragement. Amber and Dex lined up behind them. Creed and Walker stood at the front of their team.

"Here we go," Willis said to his team.

"Runners, this is a vertical track. You are reminded that there are no protective barriers extending from the floor's edge as usual so you may pass from one level to the next. The safety of your teammates is your responsibility. Do not waste the investment of your alliance by slipping. You want a crack at Red Team over there, you gotta get through this track first. First team to advance a runner to the line wins the chance to compete to represent the greatest Alliance at the Chase."

Tone.

Both teams crashed through their gate and bolted for the track. Blue Team elected to start at a set of small platforms, each high enough to require the help of another team member to scale onto it. Perryn put her hands together to give a boost to Jaden, who scrambled up and reached down to begin lifting team members.

One section to the right, Creed and his team grabbed a rope and climbed hand-over-hand to the next level. It was the most direct way to the common platform that ringed the next level of the structure.

"Come on, guys," Amber shouted scrambling over Jaden to help Perryn to the next level. "They're already getting ahead of us!" Indeed, Black Team was already at the top of their ropes and moving along the narrow platform to their next obstacle.

"She's right, Perr." Jaden slapped the platform above his head. "These platforms are too slow. We're going to have to climb."

"Okay, let's use the hand holds to the right at the next level." Perryn nodded.

Willis was impressed to see her taking command so quickly.

Dex pointed upward at the Black Team. "Are you suggesting we out-climb C-Creed?"

"Do we have a choice?" Amber shook her head.

Jaden waved a hand to urged them on. "Just climb, guys."

Willis cringed as the teams ascended the second and third levels. Creed's team gained a slight lead at each platform, and even from here, he could see that Perryn and the others were starting to tire. Jaden climbed frantically as the single Blue Team member with any gas left. At Perryn's request, he'd charged ahead to try to catch the Black Team, who had split up, giving Walker and Stone-zee an opportunity to move ahead as they climbed the wall.

"Aaaa!" Walker shrieked as her feet lost their grip on a hold. Jaden, seeing a chance to gain some ground, doubled his efforts. Recovering, Walker finished her climb and turned to help Stone-zee. One section over, Creed and Stone were nearing the top of their rope. Jaden ran along the fourth platform intending to climb the same rope. Willis could see the two Black Team members talking, and Stone was shaking her head.

"He's gaining on us. Take care of him." Creed thrust a finger in Jaden's direction.

"I can't do it." Tears streamed down Stone's face.

"We had a plan," he whispered. He grabbed her arm, twisting her to meet his face. "You pretend to slip and be sure your foot connects with him. He falls. We win. Your brother stays."

"No, Creed. I won't."

Jaden was beginning to climb the rope.

"Then, say goodbye to your brother." Releasing her arm, he didn't even look back as he climbed up to the platform.

"Please, Mario." She stretched her hand to grab the edge of the platform.

"I told you," he muttered, suddenly calm, "don't call me Mario." With that, his foot moved imperceptibly to the left and came down with crushing force on her fingers.

Casey screamed as her fingers of her right hand instinctively pulled away from the edge of the platform. Willis watched in horror as her left hand failed to maintain a tight grip on the rope and her body nearly free fell.

"Casey!" Zeke shouted as he ran across the fifth platform, which he'd reached.

Though it was a few feet, it seemed like an eternity as Casey slipped down the rope. Finally, her hand likely burned from the friction, she let go above Jaden, who was already reaching for her.

Jez's nails pierced the skin of Willis's arm as she grabbed him. The pain startled him and broke his gaze. Returning his attention, he gasped as he saw that Jaden had miraculously grabbed Casey's arm, dragging his own hand down the length of the rope. Their joint momentum carried them downward with Jaden's grip barely keeping them from plummeting five stories to the ground.

For an instant, the room was frozen, with Zeke's footfalls running to the rope and Jaden's strained grunting as he held on the only sounds. With a thud, the two crashed to the platform at the base of the rope, and Casey twisted, slipping over the edge. Willis could hear Jaden's cry under Casey's shriek as he tightened his grip to keep both of them from being carried over the edge.

A second later, they stopped. Casey's feet dangled freely in the air as Jaden, twisted awkwardly, held on to both her and the rope. The doors behind Willis opened as two officers raced in only to stare helplessly upward. They could never intervene in time.

Willis allowed himself to exhale as Jaden slowly pulled her up to the platform, but his attention was drawn to the sound of Creed's voice above.

"You've got to be kidding me," Creed snarled, crouching over the edge of the platform.

"Casey! Casey!" Zeke screamed as he slid into place next to Creed.

"Creed, did you—" Walker pointed at Stone. Zeke shot a glance at her.

"Silence, subordinate." Creed slapped his teammate. "Come on, let's move before he recovers."

"What?" Zeke searched their faces for answers.

"Nothing." He turned to resume climbing. Zeke alternated between glancing at his sister and at Creed.

"Nothing? Nothing?" Zeke fumed, shoving Creed into the wall with both hands. Creed pushed off the wall and turned to him. He straightened up to show his full size to Zeke. Walker stepped back stiffly, nearly immobile in shock.

"I don't think you want to go there, Stone-zee," Creed growled.

"I'll go anywhere if it's between you and my sister."

Zeke's fists tightened as he glared at Creed. Creed looked at Zeke's hands and chuckled. "Right. Like you could ever match me." Creed's fist came with blinding speed toward Zeke's jaw, but he was ready for it. Stepping to the side, Zeke pressed himself against the column allowing the strike to fly harmlessly by.

Creed had committed his whole body to the punch. Without Zeke to stop his momentum, his body twisted toward the open air and then spun around to face Zeke. His hands flailed and grabbed at Zeke's sleeve, catching it with one hand and tearing it at the seam, which held enough to catch his weight.

"Mario," Zeke said stoically. Creed's face contorted in anger at the use of his first name but shifted to fear as the sleeve began to tear. "You're never going to touch my sister again." Zeke lifted his arm, shifting the angle so Creed's body weight pulled directly at the seam of the uniform. The sleeve tore free with ease.

Creed stared at the piece of cloth in his hand as he tumbled backward.

Screams from Jez and Walker filled Willis's ears as Creed toppled head over feet in the air. Seconds later, Willis closed his eyes, sickened by the crunch of Creed's body slamming into the floor.

Chapter Twenty-Four

Several moments passed before he dared to look. He didn't allow his gaze to linger long on Creed's lifeless mess. Turning his gaze upward, he could see Casey clinging to Jaden, who was doing his best to comfort the sobbing girl while tending to his bleeding hand. Walker slid down the wall to a seated position, her feet dangling over the edge of the platform. Zeke was making his way down the rope to reach his sister.

"Did that happen?" Toad was the first to break the silence.

"I'm going to be sick." Jez grimaced.

Willis scanned the column. He found Dex first—he was on his hands and knees peering pale-faced over the edge of a platform staring at Creed's mangled form. He appeared fixed to his spot. Amber, seemingly oblivious to the events, was still climbing toward the summit. Perryn was hurriedly making her way to Jaden and Casey. Even from the floor, Willis could see her tears.

Schwipp! Doors behind Willis opened revealing Chief Administrator Blacc and a team of officers and doctors. The doctors raced over to Creed. Blacc stopped feet away from Willis and scanned the room, his hands on his hips. A shake of a doctor's head confirmed that Creed was dead.

"What a glorious, God-forsaken mess we have," Blacc muttered to himself. "Officers, I want that snot of a boy in custody the second his feet hit the floor. I want to review the footage before I decide what to do with him." He pointed at Zeke.

"Chief Administrator, I saw what happened," Willis blurted.

"*We* will tell you what you saw, Red Leader!" Blacc's nostrils flared. "You may be this year's hope for the Alliance, but Creed was our best bet for repeating next year. Now years of training and preparation is wasted in a heap over there. Even recoding can't save a dead man. Of all the things I've seen in my time serving our Alliance, this is the most disgusting display possible."

Willis couldn't help but feel sickened that Blacc acted concerned about the dishonor brought to the Alliance when a young man lay dead yards away, even if it that man was Creed.

Tone.

"At least someone remembered why we're here." Blacc tapped the side of his head looking up at Amber who had reached the top. "Guess you'll be facing your blue buddies in the final after all."

Willis looked up at Perryn. She was busy examining Jaden's hand. Her face was streaked with tears. Jaden appeared exhausted and rested his head on the wall behind him. Casey sobbed in Zeke's arms, who gently brushed her hair with his hand.

"He can't hurt you anymore, Sis." Zeke's soft assurances carried through the silent room.

Willis turned to his team. Jez stared at Creed's body. Her lips trembled, in anger or sadness, he couldn't tell. Kane stood and stared straight ahead. Toad gazed at his own shifting feet.

Willis turned to leave without a word. His team followed silently.

A week passed before the teams were permitted to practice on the track again. The administrators had shut down the sphere to investigate the death. Zeke hadn't been seen since the day of the race, and Willis assumed they'd shipped him off to another alliance. Casey spent most days in her quarters. When she did emerge, her eyes were bloodshot and her face full of worry.

"Track opens tomorrow, team. We've got to refocus. This is the final run," Willis waved to gather the team. Jez sat in her usual place next to him. Kane sat opposite him with Toad to his left.

"We're racing the blueys." Toad chuckled. "What's there to prepare for?"

"We have to be ready. They aren't going to come wanting to lose."

"What about you?" Jez snapped suddenly. Her lips pulled tight, and she stared forward instead of at Willis.

"What do you mean?" Willis shot back.

"Are you looking to lose?" Her head bobbled with the mocking words.

"What makes you say that?"

"You promised me you'd stay away from Jaden." She pounded the arms of the chair, finally turning to him.

"And?"

"Will, bad things happen around him. Remember what happened to Creed."

"Creed was psychotic. He died trying to kill Jaden." Willis was livid. He rose from his chair. He couldn't believe her callousness. For a moment, he had a mind to throw her off the team.

She rose to meet him and pointed at her head. "Exactly, he got in Creed's head. Made him crazy."

"Crazier," Toad corrected.

"Shut up, Toad." Jez shook a fist, looking down at him.

Toad withered under her gaze.

She turned to Willis. "All I'm saying is how do we know he isn't in *your* head?"

"What?" Willis scowled and took a step backward.

"Will, you haven't been yourself since he arrived on this station. Until he came, you were focused. You wanted to win. Now—" She hesitated to finish her sentence.

"What?"

"You seem focused on—other things."

"Let me make one thing clear, Jez." He tried unsuccessfully not to sound angry. "I have every intention of going to the Chase. I plan to win the finals next week."

Jez sat back in her chair, her arms folded. She shook her head. "I hate Jaden. I wish he'd fallen too."

Willis stared at Jez. How could she hate someone that much?

"That's sick, Jez. As if Creed dying wasn't enough, you're

wishing for more death. Don't you realize that he would have fallen if Casey pulled him over? So you want three people dead?" "I don't care. That's my point. *You* care too much—about them. *He* made you care. You should care about me—about us— about winning. Nothing else."

"Not that it's going to happen but losing isn't the end of the world." Willis spoke calmly trying to diffuse Jez's fury.

She leaned forward in her chair, her eyes glaring into his. "I will not lose." She spoke slowly and deliberately. Standing up, she stormed out of the common room.

"I have to say," Toad snickered, brushing his red hair to one side with his hand, "team meetings have been way more interesting since the newbie came."

Willis ignored Toad's remark. He stared at the corridor entrance that had swallowed Jez. He realized that he didn't trust her. She'd do anything to win.

Chapter Twenty-Five

Sheila sat at the desk in Blacc's office. Once again, she found herself staring at the greasy little man she knew to be the Administrative Liaison to the Coalition Chairman's Office. He sat examining her face for several minutes without saying a word. The silence was killing her, but she had no intention of talking about anything he didn't bring up himself.

"Ms. Kemp." He sighed. "Do you know why I'm here?"

"You got exiled here too?" She laughed and smiled at her own smart remark. It wasn't wise to provoke him, but she couldn't help it.

"There is no need for that tone. Being on this station is a great privilege, not exile, as you call it. I've often longed to have the joy of seeing our racers up close, and you've had the honor for months."

"So you're here for pleasure, not business," she scoffed. She folded her arms and looked away from him, annoyed. Out the corner of her eye, she could see him lean forward in his chair to rest his elbows on the desk.

"Hardly. I wish I could be here under more positive circumstances."

"Something bad happen to you?" She still refused to turn in his direction.

"Not exactly. Let's say Chairman DeGraaf saw your latest article."

He slid a copy of the paper across the table. She didn't need to glance at it to know the headline. At the top of the page were the words, *Tragedy Visits the Alliance Runners*. She hadn't been able to keep quiet about Creed's death.

"You told me to 'report on the young racers,'" she quoted.

"I believe I also told you to show us all the 'greatness of the Alliance.'"

The liaison picked up the paper, clearing his throat. His eyes momentarily met hers over the edge of the paper as if to communicate he couldn't believe he was about to dignify her words with his own voice.

He read. "'Mario Creed, the imposing 19-year old Western Alliance racer, fell in a tragic accident during an exercise aboard the orbiting training center last week. While authorities are investigating the nature of the tragedy, the remaining runners struggle to find meaning in the highly anticipated final elimination run next week, the race that will determine who represents the Alliance in this year's Chase. The loss of Mario Creed, a potential favorite in next year's Chase, strikes a severe blow at the Western Alliance's dominance and inevitably casts a shadow over the whole training program. Time will tell what long-term effects this will have on the Alliance's chances in this and future Chase events.'"

He stopped reading, allowing the paper to float silently to the table. His stare filled the room for several moments of uncomfortable silence.

Finally, Sheila could take it no longer. "And?" she said exasperated. She looked him in the eye to stand by her work.

"The last thing the citizens of the Alliance need is worry that their chances in the Chase are lessened." He barked the words, standing from his chair to lean over the desk. "Ms. Kemp, the perfection we enjoy in the Western Alliance is a delicate balance. The chairman has long been happy that we support the Chase. Our voice speaks loudly in the Coalition, even when other lesser alliances want to challenge the system."

"So there are alliances who dislike the Chase?" She gave him her best 'gotcha' look.

"There are alliances whose opinions are irrelevant as long as the strongest remain in full support. None more than ours, Ms. Kemp."

She hated how he attempted to belittle her by repeating her

name so often. She wanted to vomit every time he spoke it.

"Our people need to believe, Ms. Kemp." He returned to his seat. "They need to continually believe they're part of the greatest piece of that balance, that every choice they make has a profound impact on preserving the glory that we all enjoy in the Coalition. To cast doubt on that glory causes people to question."

"What is so bad about questioning?" She arched a brow.

"People are not responsible enough to question." He slammed his hands down on the desk. "Those of us who are informed know how to interpret and carry out the Law. It is the role of the uninformed masses to follow."

Sheila slumped into her chair. "Sounds like control."

"It is order. And your little stunts are calling that order into question." He leaned forward in his chair, his face red, and whispered, his voice menacing. "You're going to issue a complete retraction of your story."

"Really? And why would I do that?" She smiled.

The liaison reclined slowly and breathed a long breath. His lips curled, baring his teeth as he spoke. "Because the order to cease funding your sister's hospital has already been sent."

Her eyes grew large as she digested what he had said. She saw the corners of his mouth turn upward. He had her, and he knew it. She hated him for that.

He frowned and tried to appear pitiful. "It'd be a real shame if I forgot to make a call for them to ignore that order."

"When do you want the retraction?" Her chin quivered as she examined the floor. She despised herself for giving in, but she couldn't see harm come to her sister.

"You can give it to me personally when I leave in an hour." He held a hand toward the door, dismissing her. "Thank you for serving this great Alliance."

She got up to leave.

"Oh, and Ms. Kemp?"

"Yes?"

"I'm afraid I don't have time in my schedule to return to this wonderful space station, so make sure I won't have to retract another funding order, all right? I'm afraid it wouldn't happen in time."

She nodded. The message was clear. She could not take any more chances.

"Sheila?" came the weak voice over the computer speaker.

"It's me, Audrey." Sheila's voice caught as she spoke her sister's name.

"I can't believe you're calling me. I heard you were on the station reporting on the racers there. Didn't I always tell you that you'd have a glamorous reporting job one day?"

"Yeah." Sheila laughed for the camera, while her insides ached from sorrow. "Somehow you always knew I'd be a journalist."

"So why is my famous sister calling me from outer space?" Audrey chuckled, unable to laugh without coughing.

"I had to know you were okay, Sis." Sheila remembered the retraction she'd handed to the Liaison. If he kept his word, the funding order would be rescinded within the hour. Tears welled in her eyes as she considered what would have happened if she hadn't obeyed.

"Are you kidding?" Audrey's voice held a sweetness that always warmed Sheila. "Didn't you know? I'll be dancing bed-side in no time."

The joke was meant to lighten the mood, but it tore at Sheila's heart. "That's so good to hear," she said, unable to disguise her tears this time.

Her sister suddenly grew serious on the screen. "What's wrong, sweetie? Are you okay? Has something happened?"

"No, not yet anyway." She looked away, uncomfortable with the half-truth. "I needed to hear your voice. I needed to know I'm doing the right thing up here."

"Listen to me." Audrey had a way of commanding Sheila's attention with a tone like their mother's. "Do you remember what I told you when you left to chase your dream of becoming a journalist?"

"Yes. I do."

"And?"

"You told me to tell it like it is—to tell the world what I see, the way I see it."

"And to never give in to anyone who made you think otherwise." Audrey held a hand out to touch the screen. "After what happened to Dad, we can't let the world push us around."

If she knew. What would Audrey think when she saw the retraction printed later that day?

"I feel like I'm not taking good enough care of you. I feel so far away up here," Sheila said.

"Hey, who's the big sister here?" Audrey's voice conveyed her smile. "It's my job to take care of you, Sis. Don't you worry about me. You hear me? Don't you *ever* worry about me."

"I hear you."

"Sheila, I'm so proud of you."

"You sound like Mom." Sheila swallowed hard to prevent from breaking down. "You were always the brave one like her."

"I love you, Sis. You take care of yourself up there. Okay?"

"I will. I love you too." Sheila ended the call and placed her head on the desk in front of her. There in the sterile office on the station, she allowed her tough exterior to melt. The tears flowed freely, and shame flooded her for becoming the pawn of the Alliance. Audrey would never allow it if she found out.

One day. She promised herself. *One day soon.*

Chapter Twenty-Six

Willis zipped the last couple inches of his racing uniform as he stepped into the corridor. Chief Administrator Blacc had called him to an unexpected meeting prior to their final training run. He quietly muttered his frustration to himself. The final run was tomorrow, and he hoped that Blacc's blabbing wouldn't eat too far into their track time.

It had been two weeks since Jez had stormed out of the common room. She'd barely spoken a word to Willis since. He wanted to try to patch things up with her this afternoon. He still didn't trust her, but he needed her to bring her best to the run tomorrow.

He rounded the various twisting hallways to the administrative branch of the station. He so rarely came this way that he had to stop a couple times to remind himself of the direction of Blacc's office. Coming around the corner, the flash of blue uniforms startled him as Jaden and Perryn were both outside Blacc's door as well.

"Willis?" Perryn appeared as startled as he was.

"What are you guys doing here?" Willis searched both of their faces for answers.

"Blacc called us to a meeting," Jaden said. "Aren't you supposed to be training?"

"Supposed to be." Willis gestured with a thumb over his shoulder.

Perryn arched a brow. "What do you think this is about?"

"No idea, Perryn." Willis shrugged.

"One way to find out I guess." Jaden sighed and turned to the door.

Jaden touched the pad next to the door to announce their

arrival. *Schwipp!* Blacc's door opened suddenly, giving all three of them a view inside. Blacc sat behind his desk, his elbows resting on the surface. His hands were clasped one over the other, so he could rest his chin on them. His grave appearance matched the drab grey of his uniform.

It was not Blacc, however, that kept Willis's attention. In the chair to the left sat Jez. Her jet-black hair hung loosely rather than its usual place behind her ears, hiding her averted face. She simply stared at the wall in front of her, arms crossed. Willis tried to piece together what it all meant.

"Have a seat, you three." Blacc broke the silence.

"Chief Administrator, what is this—" Willis started.

"Sit down!" Blacc barked. He pointed to the closest empty seat.

The three traded silent glances as they took the other chairs in the room. Jez never turned her head. *What has she done?* Willis worked to catch her eye.

"Forgive my momentary outburst, trainees." Blacc sighed. "But I've received some disturbing news."

Willis, Perryn, and Jaden froze to their chairs.

"Your teammate here, Red Leader"—he motioned toward Jez—"has informed me that she observed you three being accosted by a rather disagreeable character in the corridor several weeks ago—a woman with gray hair."

Willis shot a glance at Jez who appeared furious, the red in her face nearly matching her uniform.

Jaden sucked in his breath.

Perryn's eyes widened as the truth came together in her mind.

"What did you do, Jez?" Willis whispered.

Blacc reclined in his chair. "What she did was think of the good of the Alliance." He stood and paced, his hands clasped behind his back. "That woman was a renegade—a traitor who slipped onto this station to undo the glorious work we're doing here."

Willis could hear Jaden's breathing quicken. "I'm not sure I would call her a—" Willis started.

"She is a traitor and a fraud!" Blacc shouted, jabbing a finger at him. "By showing herself to you, she threatens to undermine the entire process of preparing you all to represent this Alliance in the Chase. Red Leader, of all our trainees, you should have reported her appearance immediately. The damage she has done—"

"What damage?" Perryn interrupted.

Blacc nodded to Jez. "Your teammate tells me she observed quite a lengthy conversation between you all. In the weeks since, she says that Red Leader has been quite—oh, how should we say it? Distracted."

"I'm not distracted." Willis stopped himself from rising from his chair.

Jez huffed. It was the first sound she'd made since they arrived.

"Do you have something to say to me?" Willis allowed the contempt to drip from his words. He didn't want to believe she'd done this, but he knew her better. She didn't answer. She didn't even look at him.

"Your team leader has asked you a direct question." Blacc jumped in when she failed to respond. He sat, crossing his arms.

Jez finally turned to look at Willis. Her eyes were dark with anger and appeared to burn him with their glare. She stared him down.

"You. Are. A. Liar." Each word thrust like a knife.

He answered with an expression of disbelief.

"That's right, I said you're a liar."

"Where do you get off saying that?" Willis threw his arms open.

"Where do I get off?" She pointed at herself, her voice rising. "I call you a liar because that's what you are. For months, I couldn't understand your sick fascination with the blueys. I told myself you were stressed, that losing that race threw you off. I convinced myself that you'd pull yourself together and return us to nothing but winning. You—promised—you—would.

"But now I know you're a liar. You've been working against us ever since you met that woman." She stood and placed her hands on Willis's chair to lean over him. "I don't know if it was that woman or these two insects next to you, but someone has gotten in your head. I told you I wouldn't lose, so if you won't pull yourself together, I'll do it for you."

"You're crazy," was all Willis could think to say.

"No, you're confused," she shouted, furious and out of control. "*They* have confused you. The newbie has brainwashed you. *We* are your team, Willis. *We* are your friends. Not them."

"I'm not sure you have any idea what it means to be a friend." He couldn't keep the disgust from lacing his words.

"What I'm sure of is that I—we had a plan. We were going to win, you and me. We were supposed to go to the Chase and win together. I won't let them take you away from me."

Jez's eyes narrowed as she glanced over Willis's shoulder at Perryn. His stomach turned as he realized she meant she had feelings for him, and he looked around to see if the others were connecting the dots. They were.

Blacc tried to hide a chuckle "Well, since we're all over-informed, what do we do with all this?"

Jez flopped in her chair, her face even redder, the realization of what she'd given away dawning on her.

"Chief Administrator, I beg you," Jaden said. His voice was unlike Willis had ever heard it, shaky and uncertain. For the first time, Willis heard joyless fear come from Jaden.

"Quiet, Blue runner," Blacc interrupted. "Your mother made her choice the instant she emerged. You can be certain that her punishment has already begun."

"No!" Jaden's breaths came rapidly, and he gripped the edge of the desk in front him. His hands trembled as his knuckles whitened.

"Yes. You made your choice too, and you can lie down tonight knowing that her fate is partly your responsibility."

At these words, Jaden slumped out of his chair to the floor. Falling to his knees, he covered his head with his hands and curled into a ball. The room was silent enough to hear his tears quietly patting the floor, interrupted by occasional whimpers of "No" and "I'm sorry, Mom," escaping his lips.

Jez's lips curled into a smile as she watched Jaden, and it all came together for Willis. Jaden was breaking before their eyes. *This is what she wanted.*

"Hear me," Blacc continued, his tone even and flat. "I would see all of you recoded to put this matter to rest once and for all, but I can't very well do that the night before the final race. We need to submit our Chase team to the Coalition, and there is no time.

"The way I see it, tomorrow's race will lead to recoding for one team and removal from this station for the other. Knowledge of what has taken place dies here if you all keep your mouths shut. If I catch even one hint that this is getting out, I'll recode all four of you and ship the rest of the trainees to the Chase. Do you hear me?"

"Yes, Chief Administrator." Jez straightened, suddenly alert to the realization that she could be recoded for having knowledge of the woman.

"Yes, Chief Administrator," Perryn sniffed between silent tears.

Jaden was slower to respond but did in a weak voice. "Yes, Chief Administrator."

"And you, Red Leader?" Blacc's gaze shifted to Willis.

Willis hadn't realized that he was glaring at Blacc. He slowed his breathing and unclenched his jaw.

"Yes—Chief Administrator," Willis managed.

The meeting had ended with a few more words about the glory of the Alliance from Blacc, who dismissed Willis with a sneer. "Enjoy your training, Red Leader."

Perryn had retreated with a tearful Jaden to the blue barracks.

Willis led his team through a rather wooden practice run and left to clean up. Not a word passed between Jez and him with the threat of recoding fresh in his mind. If Toad and Kane noticed, they hadn't mentioned it. He had an idea, but he needed to move quickly.

Emerging from his quarters, the red glow of the lights reminded him of his new hatred for his teammate. He couldn't believe what Jez had done. She must have heard who the woman was. What kind of person could do that, even to someone they hate? Then, almost as if she sensed he was thinking of her, the door to Toad's quarters opened, and Jez emerged. Willis retreated into the shadows by his own door and watched.

"So are we clear, Toad?" Jez spoke in a whisper.

"Yeah, I got you." He gave her a cocky smile. "It's about time you saw how valuable I am to the team."

She glanced around, her expression nervous. "Shut up, weasel, and lower your voice. I came to you because I know you're the only one slimy enough to want in on this. Not a word until the race tomorrow. I'm not going to lose, and he's the real threat to that."

"Sure thing." Toad appeared smug.

With that, she retreated to her own door farther down the corridor. Peering around one more time, she went inside.

Willis stepped out into the light again. He could not believe what he'd heard. He'd have to warn Jaden that Jez and Toad were plotting to sabotage him, but he had time to do that.

First, he needed to find the person who might be able to help him. He started walking toward the office of Sheila Kemp.

"What are you doing here, Willis?" Sheila stood at the doorway, not permitting him inside her office this time.

"I need your help again." He recognized he was asking a lot of her, but he had to.

"Shh. Keep your voice down. I can't." She waved a hand to quiet him.

"But—"

"No, Willis, I can't help you."

Willis tried to step inside, but Sheila moved to block him. "You don't understand. They found out about *her.*"

"That's not all they've found out about. Please, you have to go." Her eyes scanned the hallway nervously.

"What do you mean?"

She let out a frustrated breath and grabbed his arm, pulling him inside the office. "Listen.There are others with something at stake here too. I nearly paid for opening my mouth a little too much. If they discovered I've been telling you things or passing messages—let's say I'm not willing to pay that price."

"But I thought you cared about telling the real story." Willis frowned.

"I did when I was the one going to get hurt. Willis, trust me, the Alliance has a lot of power, but the Coalition chairman has even more. And I have him breathing down my neck."

"So that's it? They've bought your silence."

She sighed, shame washing over her face.

Seeing her expression, Willis regretted his comment. "I'm sorry—I shouldn't have—"

"No, they haven't bought me." She glanced up at him. "I have to be silent for now. I feel for the woman you met. She's not the first to suffer for the Alliance's abuse, and she won't be the last. When the time is right, someone is going to have to tell the truth, but my hands are tied while I'm here. That won't last forever, though. I've been instructed to travel with the winning team to the Chase. As soon as I can, after the race, I plan to get my sister somewhere safe."

"And then?"

"Then, the gloves come off. I promise."

Chapter Twenty-Seven

The muscles in Willis's legs trembled as he waited for the tone. The starting gate stood at the end of a cold, metal platform that created a long, narrow ramp into the final track Willis hoped he would ever run at the station. The ramp ended at a square opening centered on one side of a solid cubical structure. During training, Willis had done his best to memorize the inside of the cube, which contained a labyrinth of passages. Each passage had obstructions jutting out in all directions and openings to force the runners to climb up or drop down to different levels. It was very disorienting to be inside. Despite their practice time, Willis mistrusted the solution he'd memorized.

Jez's accusation had become self-fulfilling. His mind was distracted with the knowledge of her intentions. He'd visited Jaden's quarters and warned him that Jez and Toad were up to something, but Jaden acted too distraught to care. He wore the same lost expression when he'd arrived at the morning meal.

Willis was sure nothing had changed, though he couldn't see Jaden, as Blue team's ramp was on the other side of the cube. He'd tried to encourage Perryn when she arrived for the run, but her face told him all he needed to know about her nerves.

He shifted his thoughts to the one thing that would focus him. *One more race, and I can be with my parents. One more, and I'm going home.*

"Red Team. Blue Team." Blacc's voice blared over the speakers from the administrators' window. "Welcome to the final run to determine the team that will represent our glorious Alliance in the Chase. This is the day for which you've been preparing. May your service to the Alliance today be remembered by all who follow."

Here it came. Willis crouched, ready to spring out of the gate.

Clang.

It wasn't the tone. Willis couldn't believe his ears as he realized the administrators were introducing a new feature to this track.

Whirrrr! The entire room around him moved with dizzying effect. Looking to his right, he realized the sphere wasn't moving, but rather the cube maze in front of him. The entire track structure was turning counter clockwise.

"Anyone else seeing this?" Toad tapped Willis on the shoulder.

"Oh—my—" Jez's voice trailed off.

Toad turned to Willis. "So much for everything we practiced. What are we going to do?"

"Split up." Jez spoke before Willis could even open his mouth. "It's the only way. We need to cover more ground. I'll go with Toad."

"No," Willis blurted without thinking. He couldn't allow them to both be out of his sight. "Jez, you stick with me. Toad, you work with Kane." At least this way, he could watch Jez.

"Fine," Jez responded, turning away from him. Willis shook as the confidence in his team withered inside of him. He wondered how Perryn was faring on the other side of the cube.

"Jaden, what should we do?" Amber's gaze was riveted on the moving track.

"I—I'm not sure." His voice lacked its usual confidence.

"J-J-Jaden, you okay?" Dex's stutter gave way to his nerves.

"He's fine, Dex. Run your hearts out, guys." Perryn tried to sound confident. "This is messing Red Team up as much as it is us."

At least, I hope it is.

Tone.

Willis sprang through the gate and raced up the platform. The cube had been rotating the entire countdown and for the moment was frozen in place. He had tried to track the number of rotations to adjust the map in his mind, but he'd lost count.

"Jez and I will go left," he yelled to the team, taking his best guess.

"Gotcha." Toad gave a small salute.

Kane nodded.

Darting through the cube's opening, he turned left immediately and ran the length of the passage. Moving from the light of the room to the relative dark passage of the cube required a second to adjust, but he could not risk slowing down. Rounding the corner at full speed, he guessed the passage doubled back on itself. Instead, the corner revealed an unexpected opening in the floor. He fell to his backside to slow himself, but he couldn't stop his momentum. Grabbing for the edge, his fingers caught their grip right as his feet and body fell in the open air and then slammed into the side of the opening. Jez was a few steps behind and managed to slide to a stop. He hung there catching his breath.

"Yikes. Wasn't expecting that," he said.

"Looks like there's a raised portion of the floor below you," she said. "You can drop down onto it."

Glancing down, he saw what she meant and let go of the wall. It was a bigger drop than he was comfortable with, but he managed to land without injury. Jez hung herself over the side of the hole and landed next to him.

"Lefts and rights might now be ups and downs," he said. Indeed, the floors, walls, and ceilings all appeared the same. There was no way to tell which part of the passage had been the original floor of the track.

Jez nodded. "I think we should take it slower."

Whirrr! The passage shifted, and the two of them slammed into each other as the metal wall suddenly became the floor. Willis sucked in a deep breath trying to refill his lungs after the air was forced from his chest. Jez rubbed at her knee which had hit the floor next to him.

"Definitely slower." Willis frowned. The two of them recovered and moved in a direction they hoped was forward.

"You okay?" Jaden gawked at Perryn who was holding her side. They'd barely entered their part of the cube, taking a cautious approach, when the maze had moved.

"I'm not sure." She emitted a soft groan. The last shift had moved their left turn upward causing her to fall backward into an obstacle in the middle of the floor. Jaden leaned over and gently pressed her ribs.

"Nothing seems broken as best I can tell. Probably badly bruised." He helped Perryn to her feet, opting for the passage to their right that was currently level.

"Yeah, but that doesn't stop it from hurting with every step. Go on ahead." She couldn't hide her frustrated tears.

"No way," he said as he put his arm around her for support. "There's no way you'll be able to climb without help, and if this thing shifts again, climbing may be the way to keep from falling."

"Jaden, come on. You're not thinking straight."

"Yes, I am. I don't know what has happened to my mother, so I don't intend to go to the Chase without you. I leave you here, and you'll get tossed around like a rag doll in these hallways. Besides, maybe Dex and Amber are already way ahead of everyone."

"Fine, but don't slow down." She winced as she raised her arm to stretch out the spot. *At least taking care of me has focused him a bit.*

"We're not going to let you idiots follow us." Jez glowered at the hallway's other occupants.

Willis had been the first to hear Amber and Dex coming, and he'd tried to steer clear of them to keep moving. Presently, all four of them were in a standoff, not making any progress.

"Can't stop us," Amber said. The two sets of partners stared at each other at a crossroads. As best as Willis could tell, they were near the center of the cube.

"Amber, l-l-let's g-go left." Dex pointed with a trembling finger.

"But I'm pretty sure the way out is to the right."

"That's why you're not going that way." Jez squared her shoulders.

"Everyone, listen!" Willis shouted over them. "This thing keeps turning. None of us knows the way out. Jez, let them go that way. We'll take the other hallway."

Amber and Jez circled the center of the intersection, not willing to turn their backs on each other. Jez slowly backed down the passage Willis indicated. Amber suddenly turned, and grabbing Dex's sleeve, dragged him into the passage and around the corner.

Whirrr! The way that Amber and Dex had gone started to lower beneath them. Willis turned and threw himself toward the corner that was quickly becoming the edge of a drop-off. Hauling himself up to the top, he clasped Jez's hand and pulled her to safety. The two of them knelt at the edge looking down the drop.

"That's it," Jaden encouraged, "a little higher." Perryn grimaced as she reached her arms for Jaden's hand. A moment ago, this had been a simple right turn near a barrier that jutted out from the left wall. She stood on her toes atop the barrier to reach Jaden who had managed to get over the edge before the turn was completed.

"How about next time you get hurt, and I'll help you." She allowed herself a small smile. She let out a grunt as her hands found Jaden's, and he hauled her up.

"Deal," he said between breaths.

"Perryn?" came a new voice. It was Willis. They looked up at him standing at the corner of two passages. From behind him came Jez, whose eyes narrowed at the sight of them.

This is it. Willis froze. Whatever she was planning, this would be the time to do it. He moved to his left, so he could see Jez out of the corner of his eye. His hands trembled with the adrenaline coursing through him. He would have to move quickly.

"Stay out of our way." Jez balled her hands into fists.

"Not sure we're in your way, Jez." Perryn's voice creaked. "I'm pretty sure the way we came isn't the way out."

"All the same, you stay there until we move out of here."

Willis chanced a glance at Jez, but he didn't see her usual look of hatred. *She's nervous.* Her dark eyes were riveted on the other two. Her hands gripped the sides of her uniform, and her weight shifted backward as if her feet intended to take flight. She didn't have the appearance of someone about to do something horrible. Maybe separating her from Toad unraveled all her plans.

It was then that Willis noticed the strange silence in the passage. Jaden hadn't spoken, which wasn't like him. Glancing over, he understood Jez's hesitation. His eyes were filled with a righteous anger that filled the space between him and Jez. If she'd wanted to do anything to Jaden, his expression was enough to make her think twice.

"Okay. There's a passage to the right and left here." Willis gestured in both directions. "Which way were you going?"

"Does either of them have any climbing?" grunted Perryn. She winced as Jaden helped her to her feet, clasping her arm.

"You all right?"

"Not stopping if that's what you mean." Her comment hurt him. He was genuine in his concern, but in that instant, they weren't on the same side. He chose to let it go. She was the one in pain, after all.

"I'll tell you what. We'll go right, which climbs up a level. Left looks flat at least until the corner."

"Got it."

"We need to go, Will," Jez said softly. She started to inch forward to the passage on the right, never taking her eyes off Jaden. Jaden's gaze never wavered, and Willis hoped he'd never hurt anyone in a way that earned such intense anger.

"See you at the finish line, Willis." Perryn tried to smile.

"The finish line. See you there."

This track was so unlike anything they'd experienced. The slow pace and the surprise encounters with other teams had Willis forgetting he was racing. He was used to the breathless running and climbing of the other tracks. This race was as much in the head as it was the body. He breathed a sigh of relief that Jez hadn't followed through on her plans with Jaden. For the first time since the starting tone, he could focus.

Whirr! The track rotated right as they climbed to the next level. He braced himself against the wall until the rotation was complete. Brushing floor dust off his uniform, he studied his surroundings. It was then that something clicked in his mind.

"Jez, I got it!" Willis blurted.

"Got what?" Jez glanced behind her where Jaden had gone.

"I've been here. This looks familiar. The track must be upright again."

"Where do we go?"

"A couple turns from now is a junction where several possible passages converge. From there you go up one level and to the left. Any other direction returns you where you came from. We'd better move. I bet we run into others there."

"Show me." She was suddenly serious. They took off at a jog.

Willis was himself again. He could see the solution clearly in his mind. Right. Left. Down one level. Right again. He prayed the track wouldn't rotate.

"The junction is right around this corner," Willis said, excited. "This thing is almost over, Jez." He turned to see her reaction, which he hoped was more positive. They were going to win this thing, and that had to lift her spirits. "I bet you thought we'd be lost in here for—"

He searched the passage for Jez, but all that met him was the cold steel reflection of the low lights.

"Jez?"

Nothing.

"Jez, you there?"

"How could you betray me, Will?" Jez's voice sounded like a distant echo. Willis couldn't tell where it was coming from. He made his way back the way they'd come.

"What do you mean? Where are you?"

His feet froze to the floor as he turned the corner. Jez was standing there. Toad was next to her.

"Toad, where'd you come from?" Willis pointed at him.

"I ditched Kane way at the beginning. He's too big for these passages anyway. That dufus is probably stuck somewhere." He chuckled at his own joke. "I've been shadowing you guys the whole time."

"But why?" Willis's mind raced as he contemplated the scenario. It didn't make sense. Why would Toad leave Kane? Why would Jez stop when they were so close to finishing? She missed her chance with Jaden, so why not finish the race?

"Why?" Jez said hatefully. "Because he sees what I see."

"What are you talking about?"

"You, Willis. You aren't for us anymore." She looked at Toad, and he nodded in agreement. "You're for them. You want them to win."

Willis held his hands up in surrender. "If you think I—"

"Shut up!" she snapped. She stepped forward. "I've seen how you look at her. I know what is going through your mind. You're going to win this thing and take them instead of us. You are going to betray us and leave us to rot on this station."

"I never—Jez, the finish line—" Willis stammered. He pointed toward the exit, which was so close.

Willis stepped backward. Something about all this made him uneasy. Maybe it was the almost calm demeanor of Jez's face that never wavered, even when she screamed at him. Maybe it was how Toad had slowly inched down the passage and was working his way behind him. Maybe it was the realization that Jez was with the person she'd plotted with, and he alone was the recipient of that plot.

"Don't talk to me about the finish. Amber and Dex are imbeciles, who couldn't figure this track out if they had a map. Perryn is hurt, so there's no way she and the newbie have moved as fast as us."

"So we're going to stand here and chat? About what?" Willis scoffed.

"No, Will. I'm going to win this race—but not with you."

He watched as she reached her hand into the left sleeve of her uniform. With a tug, she produced something that appeared to Willis like a small roll of plastic. The light reflected off the glossy surface. She unrolled it silently as she walked toward him. Toad was behind him.

"Toad may be a weasel, but he has his talents." She smiled, unnerving Willis.

"Thanks, Jez," Toad said smugly.

"He swiped this from your newbie friend's tray last night. He was so upset about his poor mommy that he never noticed it missing, fingerprints and all."

The roll of plastic reached its end and the glint of metal caught Willis's eye. Gripped in her fingers, the handle still wrapped in plastic, was the sharp blade of a dinner knife like they'd used the night before. She was a couple feet away from him.

She tightened her grip on the knife. "I told you I wouldn't lose."

Chapter Twenty-Eight

As Willis saw the twitch in Jez's arm, he was acutely aware that he had two choices. Toad was behind him, so he was sure backing up would be met with resistance. He could duck to the left or to the right. One way would save him. The other would help plunge the knife further into his body. He chose and moved.

Whirr! For a moment, it didn't register what was happening. Jez had anticipated his leftward movement, and Willis could see the knife headed straight for his abdomen when its path suddenly curved upward and to the side catching his shoulder as it swung wildly. Jez cried out as she fell backward, the rotation of the moving track throwing her against the far wall. Having thrown his weight against the direction of the rotation, Willis's feet held their place a critical second longer than Jez's.

His head smacked the new floor beneath him. He grabbed at the side of his skull, wincing at the pain as he scrambled to a seated position. Jez was on her hands and knees and swung wildly with the blade. Willis pushed backward with his feet, barely dodging the knife. The warm sensation of another human body was suddenly behind him, and Willis realized he'd pushed himself right toward Toad. In an instant, Toad had thrown an arm around his neck, choking the air from his lungs. Jez, seeing his capture, slowly stood to her feet.

"J-Jez." Willis choked. "You don't have to. P-please."

"Willis, you disappoint me." Her words came out on as a snarl. "I didn't take you for a beggar."

Willis strained at Toad's grip. He was much smaller than Willis, but he'd locked his hands together. Spots started to appear in Willis's vision as the lack of blood to his head took its toll.

Jez was going to kill him here where no one could see.

Jaden would get the blame.

No one would know about the slaves, and he would never see his parents.

Jez switched the grip on the knife for a downward blow and raised her arm to bring her entire weight down with the strike.

"Goodbye, Will," she said flatly. With that, her arm descended.

Willis squashed his eyelids together and waited for the searing pain of the knife entering his chest cavity. It never came. It was when he heard Jez's grunt that he dared open his eyes.

A huge, dark hand wrapped around Jez's still raised arm. She pulled against it, unable to move as she turned and looked into Kane's forceful eyes. He stared down at her, the pressure of his grip causing her to drop the blade.

Her eyes filled with fear as Kane's lip curled. In one motion, he twisted her arm and threw her entire body into the corner of the wall. The sound of the bone breaking in her arm could be heard an instant before her scream filled the passage.

Kane ripped Toad's arm away from Willis's throat, and he rolled over gasping for air. With two powerful hands, Kane lifted him to his feet and met his eyes inches away.

"Go. Win. They won't touch you. We've got to take care of each other if we're going to make the Chase." Kane whispered Willis's words from months ago to him. It was the first he'd ever heard him truly speak.

Willis staggered as Kane let go of him. Metal scraped as Toad picked up the knife, glaring at Kane with wild eyes.

"Go!" Kane shouted as he lunged at Toad.

Willis saw the glint of the swinging blade and Kane's huge mass come together. He turned and stumbled toward the passage junction. A couple of turns later, Willis saw the brighter light of the station reflected off the passage wall ahead, broadcasting the exit from the cube.

The bright lights of the sphere blinded him as he emerged onto a downward ramp. His feet tangled as he adjusted to the decline of the track, and his body tumbled forward. Somersaulting twice, Willis caught himself, scrambling on all fours until he could get his feet beneath him again.

Running in a panicked fury, he crashed through the finish gate and fell to the floor. The tone sounded, announcing the end of the race, and Willis pressed his forehead to the cold floor. He jerked at the sudden presence of a hand on his shoulder.

"Welcome to the winner's circle, Red Leader," Blacc announced, bending over him. His smile vanished as he saw the tears in Willis's eyes. "What's going on?"

Willis turned his gaze to the cube. Emerging from the exit were several figures. Perryn and Jaden had stopped as they realized Willis was already through the gate. Their attention was turned to the blackness of the passage behind them. Kane's giant outline took shape as he stepped into the light. His enormous hands were wrapped around Jez and Toad's necks, who he half-dragged to the finish line.

"What's going on?" came Amber's voice as she and Dex emerged from the exit.

"I don't know." Jaden's soft reply could barely be heard.

They were the lone words in the vast silence of the room as Kane brought his two prisoners to the finish. Willis could see the wetness of blood on his red uniform from where Toad's blade had done what little it could before Kane overwhelmed him. Jez was clasping her shattered arm and crying. Toad was barely conscious, his face already swelling from the beating he'd received.

"What is the meaning of this?" Blacc barked sharply.

"Chief Administrator," Willis stammered, "it's not his fault!"

"You mean to tell me that two of your teammates can hardly stand because of the beating they've taken, and it's not the responsibility of the injuring party?"

"Chief Administrator—"

Schwipp! The door behind Blacc opened revealing four uniformed officers and another administrator who raced to Blacc and whispered in his ear.

"Given the disgraceful actions in the last race, the administrators had the foresight to place extra cameras throughout the inside of this track," Blacc said. Jez let out a small yelp, producing a sneer on Blacc's face. "It seems the footage of the interior clearly shows these two half-wits attack their own team leader. Why they would want to harm their meal ticket out of here escapes me, but I believe their actions to be a shame to our Alliance."

"What does that mean, Chief Administrator?" Willis gestured to Jez and Toad.

"It means we have a predicament on our hands," Blacc said. "By rule, Red Team has won the right to represent the Alliance at this year's Chase. However, two of your teammates have proven themselves traitorous maggots. Not only that, they are too injured to continue running without the intervention of our doctors."

"You mean?" Willis prodded.

"I mean, these two will be recoded faster than a monkey on fire would jump in a river."

At the sound of the word 'recoded,' Jez's face shot up at Blacc, suddenly alert. She wrenched her body free of Kane's relaxed grip and threw herself toward Blacc.

"No!" she screamed. "You can't be serious."

"As serious as the plague, red runner. Back off."

"No! No!" Her frightened cries echoed in the spherical room.

"Get a grip, Jez," Willis said, but she didn't relent. Her body writhed on the ground as her terror overwhelmed her.

"What's her issue?" Perryn scrunched her face in disgust at the display.

"I'll tell you," Amber said, her expression smug. "It's been our little secret. Something I picked up from my previous alliance."

With that, Amber stepped over to Jez who was curled into a quivering ball on the floor. A swipe of her hand threw Jez's hair backward revealing her ear, which Amber yanked forward without being gentle.

"She made all kinds of threats about what would happen if I told anyone, but I don't see how that matters anymore." Amber spat on her thumb then she rubbed at Jez's ear next to her recoding number. A few moments later, Amber withdrew. "See?"

The group leaned in to take a peek at the still whimpering figure. Next to the number nine on her ear, still partially covered by the make-up Amber had been removing, was a second nine. This would be Jez's one-hundredth recoding. Silent seconds passed as the truth spread through the group. Willis let out a long breath, and the others followed, seemingly waiting for someone else to breathe first. He couldn't help the tiny spark of compassion developing in his chest for the sobbing Jez.

"So, Red Leader." Blacc squatted next to the still-seated Willis speaking in soft tones. "Who will be the lucky two?"

"Two?" Willis searched Blacc's face, confused.

"You're short two teammates. As team leader, you get to select their replacements for the Chase. Any member, any team."

Willis looked up at the other runners. He ignored Blacc's ongoing explanation and recommendations, which included Walker and Stone. His eyes stopped on Perryn's, which were wet with tears. He could tell she was trying to not appear too hopeful, but he'd made up his mind as soon as the question had been asked.

"Perryn and Jaden," Willis said.

"What? Who?" Blacc tried to catch up to what had happened.

"I choose Perryn and Jaden," he repeated.

Blacc's face darkened at the names. "Are you certain, Red Leader?"

"Absolutely, Chief Administrator. Perryn and Jaden will join Kane and me at the Chase this year."

Blacc jerked upright and addressed the group. "Officers, please escort these two sad excuses for Alliance runners to the hospital wing. Please remind the doctors that they have another chance to break the hundred barrier.

"Blue runners," he continued looking at Dex and Amber, "I'm afraid you will be going with them."

"Totally worth it." Amber smiled as she watched Jez. "I wouldn't miss seeing this happen for the world." Her comment renewed Jez's screams as the officers escorted her to the door.

She shook violently to escape their grip, but their hold was firm. Shouts of "no" and "please" could be heard for several seconds after the doors closed as the rest stood silent.

"Blue Leader," Blacc finally turned to Perryn. "As a team leader, you have the right to veto your own removal from leadership to join another team. Do you agree to this transfer?"

Her gaze never left Willis. For a long couple seconds, their eyes communicated silently. He could see the corners of her mouth begin to turn upward. Her lips trembled.

"Are you kidding me?" she shouted at Blacc, and she threw herself to her knees and wrapped her arms around Willis's neck. Willis held her, ignoring the sting of the cut on his shoulder, as her fear of recoding drained out with each joyful tear. Jaden cautiously stepped forward and crouched next to the two of them. He placed his hands on their shoulders and looked down. His body trembled, and Willis thought he might be crying. It wasn't tears, though, that caused Jaden to shudder. His smile was slowly broadening into a quiet laughter.

"Who would have guessed," Jaden said, smiling from ear to ear. His head shook in disbelief as breathy laughter welled up again. Soon, Willis and Perryn and even Kane joined him.

It wasn't a mocking laughter. It was not the kind that took joy in others' sadness. It was the quiet laughter of pure joy.

Chapter Twenty-Nine

The plush seat on the transport was as unfamiliar to Willis as the planet below. The Alliance-yellow upholstery felt like a guilty extravagance. He shifted to fight the inescapable softness cradling his body. For most of his life, Willis had lived in the barracks of one training center or another. His recent years were passed exclusively on the cold, hard surfaces of the space station. Now, he found himself seated on the luxurious Western Alliance transport that was to take them from the space station to the surface.

Blacc had given them one hour to pack up. Willis got the impression that he intended to get them off the station as soon as possible. The Chief Administrator would have a lot to answer for the last few weeks on the station. Creed was dead. Jez was useless genetic material. Zeke was who-knew-where.

Willis was shocked to discover that the hour was more than enough to pack everything he owned. The station had provided their every need, and he had little to call his own. He found two regular uniforms waiting for him in his quarters, which he packed. A special uniform for the Chase would be given to the team later. A few notes from friends from junior training that he'd kept, and all his Red Team notes were the remaining items he owned.

He rested his head on the back of the seat. Perryn had cleaned up and packed even faster than he did. She wanted off the station, and he couldn't blame her excitement. Her exhaustion over the last few hours had caught up to her, though, and she'd fallen asleep the moment she sat next to him and rested her head on his shoulder.

Willis felt the warmth of her fingers intertwined in his. He'd saved her life by selecting her, but she'd done so much more for him. He'd always taken his future for granted, but she'd shown him a new world. He always knew that he would leave the station one day, compete in the Chase, and return home. Perryn's story was different. She struggled for hope, and that made her hope all the richer. She'd experienced life without it. He understood now, and that was a form of salvation all its own.

Kane sat next to Willis on the other side. Huge and silent, he appeared to be enjoying his luxurious chair. Without this ex-convict, Willis would be lying dead on the track. A small shudder ran the length of Willis's spine as he considered it.

On Perryn's other side sat Jaden. He gazed out the window of the transport at the station. He couldn't imagine the conflict within his friend, who was likely thinking about his mother. Jaden's one hope was to leave his mother for a time to try to save her. The world was different seen through his eyes, and Willis would never be the same for knowing him.

Willis smiled as he considered the three people with him. His consciousness drifted as the transport jerked away from the dock. He slept all the way through reentry.

The sudden thump of the transport landing on the surface jostled Willis to consciousness. He rubbed his eyes to clear his vision.

Perryn was rubbing her eyes and muttering her disbelief that they'd landed already. She glanced over at Willis.

"What do we do?" She let out a long yawn.

He shrugged. "I don't know. I guess we sit here until they tell us to do something else."

"Whatever it is,"—Jaden spoke still peering out the window—"it's going to involve a lot of people. Check this out."

Willis leaned over Perryn to get a view out the window. His breath caught when he saw the crowd. A sea of people was gathered outside the transport. He'd never seen so many in one place. Here and there the glint of a camera caught his eye, but mostly there were endless pairs of eyes staring longingly at the transport and pressing in for a better view. An occasional sign welcoming them dotted the edge of the crowd. Reporters were already giving their opening words, no doubt building up to their dramatic exit from the transport.

"They can't be here for us, can they?" Willis moved to let the others get a view.

Jaden arched a brow. "There's no one else on this transport for them to see."

Willis found himself wishing that Sheila had been on the transport. She would know what this was all about, but she wasn't permitted on an Alliance transport. Her travel had to be arranged by her employer. Could she be out there? He scanned the crowd for her, but there had to be thousands of people.

A burst of light filled the compartment as a door opened, permitting the low rumble of thousands of voices to suddenly boom. A man wearing an expensive suit stood in the light, an opaque outline until their eyes adjusted to the new brilliance. He stepped closer revealing his perfectly combed hair, designer shoes, and Alliance pin on his lapel. He flashed a smile at the four racers, making Willis uncomfortable under the gaze of his unnaturally brilliant blue eyes. Nothing about this man felt genuine. He was all polish and shine, and he appeared far too happy to be there.

"My friends! Welcome back to your home in the great Western Alliance." He extended an arm, gesturing at his surroundings. "My name is Stan Jacobson, and I'll serve as your Alliance liaison during your time leading up to the Chase. I'm here to help you through the next several days."

The four of them stared in silence. Stan's eyes shifted back and forth waiting for some indication that any of them were impressed. For a second, his smile waned. Catching himself, he smiled fully once again.

"So, where shall we start? You," he said, glancing at his notes, "must be Kane. Am I right? I bet you're bursting with excitement to be here."

Willis chuckled to himself at the pathetic display. This man had obviously recently been assigned to them if he expected to get much conversation out of Kane. Seeing the flat expression on Kane's face, the man moved on undeterred.

"And you are—Perryn? And—Jaden?" He was reading his notes again. "How exciting to be placed on the Chase team last minute."

"We're thrilled." Perryn rolled her eyes. She must have been as unimpressed as he was with Stan. He made a note to tell her later that he liked her take on people. It agreed with his.

"And that leaves me with," he said, his smile broadening to the corners of his eyes, "the one we've all been waiting for—the hope of the Alliance—the son of the great Thomsons."

He leaned in to take a closer look at Willis as if fascinated. "You must be the ever-famous Willis. I can't tell you how honored I am to be one of the first to meet you."

His eyes were dazzled as if star-struck by Willis.

Is this how it's going to be with everyone? The thought made Willis ill. He was used to the relative privacy of the training facilities he'd been in all his life. This kind of gawking wasn't familiar—or comfortable.

"Yes, it is"—Perryn added dramatically, trying to hide her laugher—"so I wouldn't stare too long unless you want to offend the future hero of the Alliance."

Stan shot upright, his blue eyes wide with apology. The self-confident man suddenly appeared embarrassed. Perryn delivered an elbow to Willis's side, and he let out a small snort trying to hold the chuckle inside. On Perryn's other side, Jaden vibrated in his chair, silently laughing.

"Mr. Jacobson." Willis smiled to let him know it was a joke.

"Please, it's Stan to you." He held up a hand.

Willis sighed and glanced at his still smirking teammates. "Fine. Stan, if we're going to get along, you have to lighten up."

Stan nodded excitedly. "Certainly, Mr. Thomson."

"Willis."

"You sure?" The awe returned to Stan's face.

"Of my name? Absolutely."

At that, Jaden couldn't take it any longer. He guffawed so loudly that they momentarily couldn't hear the crowd outside. Willis and Perryn joined in the rising laughter. Even Kane smiled. For a moment, the stress of the crowds and the coming Chase melted away. Stan looked at the four of them, obviously not expecting them to be real people. He gave an unsure smile and tried to add a rather artificial laugh of his own.

"Okay, Stan," Willis said, composing himself, "what's going on out there? What are all the people here for? Us?"

"Of course. You four are this year's Alliance representatives in the Chase. Mr. Thomson—er, Willis, *will be* the next Law-changer." He smiled broadly and waited for the rest of the team to react.

"Law-changer," Willis repeated, his expression flat.

"It's the good Law that protects us all, isn't it? They're here to celebrate your arrival."

Willis gestured to his teammates. "So what are we supposed to do?"

Stan breathed a sigh of relief. These were the questions he had prepared to answer. Before they could ask anything else, they were handed laminated cards containing their schedules. Meetings with the press, various appearances, and check-ups with the Alliance doctors were all noted. For several minutes, Stan briefed them on the immediate details.

"But first," Stan held up a finger, "we must not keep your fans waiting any longer. If you'll follow me."

They stood and followed Stan to the doorway. Stepping out, he gave a nod to someone in the distance, and the music began. A loud voice squawked over the speakers. "Citizens of the proudest alliance in the World Coalition, we present to you the future champions of this year's Chase!"

The crowd's deafening roar overwhelmed Willis as he descended the steps of the transport. Camera flashes blinded him, almost causing him to miss a step near the bottom. Microphones were shoved in their faces, and journalists shouted questions. The four racers could do little more than stare at the crowds as they made their way to the narrow path cleared for them.

"Mr. Thomson, how does it feel to be back on the surface?"

"Any words for your fellow racers in the Chase?"

"Millions of young women want to know, is there a special someone in your life?"

"Willis Thomson, can you comment on the ethics of Alliance training methods?"

The tone of the last question stopped him. He glanced around to see who had asked, and a familiar face greeted him. To his left, Sheila stood there in a blue jacket holding a microphone toward him. Her face was turned away from her cameraman, and she winked at Willis. He smiled and moved on. *She wants me to know she's here.*

A minute later, Stan and several officers had pushed them through the crowd to a small building at the end of the landing pad. The doors shut behind them, comforting Willis as the noise of the crowd almost disappeared.

The building contained a hallway, at the end of which was an unlabeled elevator door. Stan ushered them inside and pressed the lone button. "You're at Alliance Headquarters in Central City," he told them.

"Kind of a small building to be the headquarters," Perryn remarked, a bewildered expression on her face.

"That's because the public front of the headquarters is a mile away at the center of the city. Much of the facility is underground. Lessons learned after the Great Collapse, you know."

Willis marveled at how big the facility must be as they descended for more than a minute underground. The sight that greeted them when the doors opened made his stomach sour. The hallway in front of them looked exactly like their barracks on the station, the red lights replaced with Alliance yellow.

"We've constructed your quarters here in the headquarters to look like the station to help you feel more at home. I can't imagine the shock the transition must be on you all," Stan said, trying to sound compassionate as he walked in front of them.

To Willis, it felt like returning to prison.

Willis jolted up in his bed. He'd lain down as soon as Stan had left them in their rooms, intending to rest his eyes for a minute. Noticing the clock, he was surprised to see he'd slept an hour. He might have slept longer, but someone was at his door.

"Come in," he croaked, his voice still sleepy. *Schwipp!* The door slid open revealing Stan, this time with two officers.

"Willis, there's been an alteration in your schedule," Stan said. He stared at his shifting feet. "I apologize, but you have a new appointment, and I've come to escort you there."

"Sure thing," Willis grabbed his jacket and gave the uneasy Stan a pat on the shoulder to let him know he didn't mind the interruption. In truth, he was glad for something to do.

An elevator took them to an unknown floor, a bit higher than the barracks. The hallway on this floor was twice as wide as theirs. Stan, Willis, and the officers climbed on a platform hovering in front of them. At the end of the platform, a panel display sat atop a small stand. Stan approached and placed his hand it.

"Conference Room D," Stan said.

"Access to this area is restricted," came an electronic voice. "Please enter authorization code." Stan punched in several numbers. "Code authorized."

The platform lurched as it moved down the white hallway, gliding effortlessly. Door after door passed them in a blur. Several other platforms passed with various official looking people going in other directions. Willis lost all sense of how far they were traveling as he took in his surroundings. They must be clear at the other end of the facility.

The platform slowed to a halt in front of a set of wooden doors. The trim-work and golden handles hinted at the ornate setting inside. The officers took position on either side of the door, and Stan approached placing his hand on the touch pad. A second later, the doors opened automatically.

"Your appointment is inside, Willis." Stan moved to the side.

"Aren't you coming in?" Willis turned to stare at him.

"Unfortunately, no. I haven't been invited." Stan's face showed his disappointment.

Willis stepped inside the room, the doors shutting silently behind him. The plush carpet under his feet felt foreign. The walls were a deep shade of crimson with yellow drapes framing panels meant to appear like windows, each displaying views from around the Alliance. A wooden table lay before him lined with expensive swiveling chairs. He reached out to touch the table, unfamiliar with its feel after years of the endless metal of the station.

Willis gazed at the other end of the room where a grey-haired man with wire-framed glasses entered, then sat at the table. His black robe was trimmed in the same crimson as the walls. He studied Willis for a moment, his hands folded on the table in front of him. "Nothing so natural as the grain of our planet's creation. Must feel exhilarating after years aboard a sterile space station."

"Who are you?" Willis pulled his hands from the table and straightened.

The man stood and stepped out from the end of the table, clasping his hands solemnly in front of him. "I am the humble servant of the World Coalition and the protector of the Law."

"Chairman DeGraaf," Willis blurted and then blushed. His mind raced. Part of him wanted to bow. Another to run. Still another to scream in anger.

"I see life in space has not completely shut you out of the comings and goings of life on the surface. I am pleased by that. Have a seat." He motioned to one of the chairs near him. Willis slowly made his way to the chair and slid into the seat. DeGraaf did not sit down.

"Sir, I wasn't aware that I would be meeting with you today."

"My young friend, the 'sir' is completely unnecessary. Please call me 'Chairman.'"

Willis tried not to show that he didn't see the difference as 'Chairman' seemed every bit as formal. The chairman's tone was one of polish as if he had used the line many times.

"I am sorry to interrupt what I'm sure is a very busy schedule," the chairman continued. "When I heard that you had returned to the surface, I felt compelled to travel here to meet with you."

"It's no problem. Is there something I can do for you, Chairman?"

DeGraaf circled around Willis's chair and crouched down on his right side. He smiled, the corner of his eyes wrinkling beneath his glasses.

"It is a wonderful sight to see a young person so willing to help another. It is people like you, Willis, that this world needs, people whose first question is how they can help another. Despite all our hard work to build a safe world under the protection of the Law, there are still those who would seek to advance their own desires."

The chairman spoke in a soft voice. Where was he going with his line of reasoning?

DeGraaf stood again and placed his hands atop the back of the chair next to Willis. He looked away as though in deep thought.

"My dear young man, you may have heard many call you 'the hope of the Western Alliance,' and I believe they are right in doing so. My hope for you is much bigger, though."

"Bigger?" Willis inquired.

"Yes. You bring more than hope for any one alliance. Your service to them is service to the entire Coalition. You serve all of us. You serve—me."

Willis shuddered at the last words.

"Young man, I asked you here today because I need to know that I can count on you. More than anyone, you stand to win the Chase this year. By the glory of our Law, I cannot tell you what to do, but I ask you to hear me."

DeGraaf spun Willis's chair toward him and knelt, clasping Willis's hands in his own. Willis admired that he could be kneeling and still be so in control of the room.

"Willis, despite the peace we have brought to the world,

there exists unrest in some of the alliances. People who wish to undo all that we hold dear, all that protects us from the dangers of the world prior to the Great Collapse. You can stop them."

"Me?"

"Yes, you. You, the symbol of hope for us all, will have one glorious opportunity to grace us with a new law. This year, more than any than I can remember, we must ensure the safety of the world. The Law has been a near perfect guardian against chaos, but I'm afraid it presently serves to tie our hands from doing what must be done."

DeGraaf took a long breath to let his point linger. His eyes grew sad before continuing.

"My one desire is to protect our people from ever again experiencing the horror of chaos and uncertainty, but I must admit there are limits to what the Law permits me to do. How can I serve my people when the very Law meant to ensure that service limits me?"

He pushed to his feet with his hands open in front of him as though wearing handcuffs.

"Those limits have prevented Coalition leadership from meeting peaceably with the voices of ignorance and showing them the value of order. We must be given the power to advance the protections of the Law, to convince the unconvinced."

Willis considered what 'convincing the unconvinced' might mean. The chairman's words were so certain. He spoke sounding so calculated and so concerned with the well-being of all, yet Willis couldn't quench the mistrust rising within him. It must have shown in his face because the chairman's expression switched from pleading to serious.

"Willis," he said, "I need to know that I can count on you. I need to know that you will do what is necessary to preserve the world we live in. Can you promise me that you will protect us all?"

Willis paused before uttering, "Y-yes, Chairman." It felt like the safe answer, but he couldn't help but wonder what the chairman meant.

A long pause filled the room, and DeGraaf stepped

backward. He clasped his hands again in front of him and walked to the edge of the table, sitting again in the chair where he had started.

"I'm glad to have met you, Willis," he declared. "It is good to know the extent to which you stand with us. I believe Mr. Jacobson is ready to escort you to your quarters. Thank you for your time."

With that, DeGraaf turned away from him. Willis stood staring at the chairman trying to decipher what he'd been told. He walked to the door and opened it. He could see Stan trying to catch a glimpse of the chairman before he turned to Willis.

"Shall we get you back?" Stan pointed in the direction they'd come the instant the doors shut.

"I guess so." Willis climbed aboard the platform.

"What a privilege. To meet the chairman himself."

"Sure. I guess."

"You must be the best racer in years, to get an audience with the chairman. To think, the World Coalition might be pulling for you in the race. It must fill you with certainty as to how the Chase will turn out."

"Yeah. Certainty." Willis was anything but certain.

Chapter Thirty

Three days later, Stan escorted Wills and the others to the transport, pressing through crowds even larger than the ones that welcomed them. Everyone pressed forward for a final glimpse of the team before they huddled around their monitors to watch the opening ceremonies that evening. The transport was headed to the Southern Federation of Allied States where the Chase was to be held this year.

Willis breathed a sigh to relief and readied himself for take-off. His conversation with the chairman had unnerved him, but Jaden had reminded him that he knew the truth about the world. The chairman could do little to stop him from passing a law to undo slavery, a law they'd discussed several times over the past few nights. Beyond that, their days in the Alliance headquarters had been an endless series of press conferences and appearances. All four of them were tired of answering the same questions over and over.

Perryn was always flooded with questions about her relationship with her teammates. She and Willis had agreed the first night to be careful about what they said as it became obvious the Alliance was anticipating another love story like Willis's parents. Still, she couldn't help blushing once or twice when a reporter hinted at a relationship between them.

Jaden had been particularly adept at answering questions about his background. Reporters seemed bent on trapping him into an unfair question, but he always managed to turn the situation around. He had an ability to joke with the reporters, and sometimes the entire group would erupt in laughter. Other times, he responded with a question for the reporters that would silence the room.

Kane was left alone for the most part. Willis guessed that his background was hardly something the Alliance planned to showcase. Kane acted more than content to sit quietly during the press conferences, and Willis envied him as a result.

Mostly, the journalists wanted to know how confident Willis was of winning the Chase. He'd been asked about his chances repeatedly. His standard answer had become that they "had not trained for a lifetime to lose." The response always brought applause. Currently, they sat on board the transport hoping for a few hours of peace.

"Guys, this is it. My time with you is almost complete," Stan told the group.

"What do you mean?" Jaden leaned forward. The group had developed quiet an affection for Stan. As plastic as he was, his excitement about the Chase was genuine, and navigating their schedules would have been impossible without him.

"The Chase is tomorrow. The opening ceremonies take place tonight, and I'll go back to shuffling papers for the Alliance."

"Really? I'm sorry to hear that," Perryn said genuinely.

"Don't be. These past few days have been the best I've had in a long time. How many people get to say they personally worked with the winning Chase team?"

Silence lingered between them all. Stan looked down and breathed a sigh as if letting go of his moments in the spotlight. "We hit the ground running when we get there."

Stan was not kidding. The second they were off the transport, the staff ushered them away to prepare for the opening ceremonies. Four rooms awaited them, each with a team of people ready to work. For the next few hours, Willis was trimmed, shaved, and dressed. He stood in front of the mirror staring at an image that was no longer familiar to him.

They'd dressed him in a perfectly tailored black suit and yellow shirt, complete with Alliance insignia cufflinks. His hair was perfect. His shoes were shined. He was ready to be paraded around before the world. *I look like a bumblebee.* Willis shook his head.

He stepped out into the empty hallway, occasionally tugging at a sleeve or smoothing the jacket with his palms. He wasn't used to these kinds of clothes. He wasn't sure he wanted to ever be used to them.

"Willis?" Perryn's voice came from behind him.

Willis turned around to see Perryn like he'd never seen her. Her sensible blue station uniform was gone. Instead, she stood there in a floor-length, golden yellow and black gown. Her nails were painted, and a delicate gold necklace with the Alliance insignia draped her neck. Her brown hair wasn't in its usual sensible ponytail. Rather, it had been expertly pulled together behind her head, allowing the remainder to fall in flowing curls down her back. Time froze as the rest of the room faded, and his lungs turned to stone, leaving him unable to breathe. What he loved the most, though, was that he could still see the same unsure Perryn beneath the perfectly applied make-up. Her well-toned arms and strong hands, betraying years of training, clasped nervously in front of her.

"You look incredible," he whispered after catching his breath.

"I feel stupid." She stared at the floor.

Willis stepped toward her and took her hand, which shook when he touched her. For several seconds, their gaze met silently. Her fingers slowly curled around his, and she searched his eyes. He couldn't imagine his life without her. He wanted to stay there in that empty hallway and never keep another secret from her again. He wanted to know her and to be known by her. They didn't say a word, but much was said in the silent space between them.

"Don't let us interrupt." Jaden laughed. Willis looked over to see Jaden and Kane standing there in similar formal dress.

"Shut up, Jaden," Perryn said with a smirk. Her cheeks flushed, a lingering trace of the moment they'd shared. "I'd wipe that smile off your face if I believed I had any chance of walking over there in these ridiculous shoes."

"And you are?" Jaden raised a brow. He held out a hand to

her, inviting a handshake. "I thought Perryn was going to run with us, but you don't look anything like her."

She swatted at his hand and missed, stumbling briefly in her heels. "I'm warning you. I'll hurt you if you get close enough."

"Remind me, Kane, to stay out of arm's reach, then."

Kane grunted a short laugh.

"So this is it." Willis placed his hands in his pockets.

"Yeah. In two days, this will be all over." Jaden bit his lower lip. He looked down as if considering the significance of what those two days might bring.

Schwipp! The door at the end of the hallway opened. Stan stood there in a suit that looked even more expensive than his others. Willis hadn't believed that possible.

"Okay, gang, here we go. You all look great. Getting you to the ceremony on time is my final task, and I'm not going to have you show up late." Stan tapped his watch with a finger.

He ushered them through the door to the elevator, which stopped and opened onto a hangar. The humidity suffocated Willis as he stepped out. Willis couldn't believe the thickness of the air in this part of the world. Talk among those helping him get ready was that the track had been built far into the jungle in an area formerly known as the Amazon prior to the Collapse. Willis had never been to a jungle, but at least he knew how hot it would be.

A hovering platform, similar to the one at Alliance Headquarters, waited for them, larger and decorated with a Western Alliance insignia on the front. Willis ran his fingers along the edge of one of the eagles. What would the days ahead hold?

"Your shoes are designed to hold you to the platform," Stan informed them. "Feel free to wave to the crowds. You won't fall."

"Don't count on it," Perryn said, giving another unsure glance at her shoes.

Jaden laughed.

"Hey, Stan," Willis said, climbing onto the platform beside this man who had briefly been a friend. "Thanks for everything."

"No," Stan said, "thank you, Willis."

Sure enough, as the platform moved, the magnetic floor activated, gluing their feet to the surface. Willis remembered the track on the station that had used the same technology.

It was the only race he'd ever lost.

It was not a reminder he needed right now.

The hanger they left was one of many that opened to a large roadway outside. Scanning up and down, Willis could see the other eleven alliance platforms emerging from other hangers, each bearing a team of racers dressed according to their alliance.

At the end of the road lay the exterior of a massive arena where the opening ceremonies would take place. The circular structure was made up of twelve gleaming metallic arches that extended from the top of the arena to the ground. Between the arches, multiple levels of seating allowed dignitaries and citizens of different alliances to gather in their own section, the most important seated at the point created by the meeting of two arches closest to where their racers would enter. The reflective surface between the arches glowed orange in the setting sun. Underneath, each contained a massive entryway through which one platform would pass, allowing all the alliances to appear simultaneously, symbolizing the cooperation of the Coalition. The roar of the crowd could be heard over the wall as the platforms positioned themselves at each archway.

How much did the construction of this monstrosity bankrupt this alliance? Willis gaped at the structure.

The chairman's voice resounded from somewhere inside. "Citizens of the World Coalition, our hosts, the Southern Federation of Allied States welcome you to this year's annual Chase. It is my humble honor to present to you the very best that each alliance has to offer. Each is prepared to advance the Law. It is the Law that protects us all!"

"The Law is good!" shouted the crowd, rabid to see their runners.

"The Law that preserves us all," DeGraaf continued.

"The Law remains!"

"The Law that saves us all."

"The Law is good!"

"Citizens, I present to you your racers."

The crowd launched to its feet as the platforms appeared through the archways.

Willis resisted the urge to cover his ears as the crowd's cheers swelled to a volume that vibrated the platform beneath his feet. Camera flashes came from everywhere. Flags were waving.

As they emerged from their alliance's archway, Willis could see the whole arch was framed in a sea of yellow and black dressed citizens and dignitaries of the Western Alliance. Here and there, shouts of his name could be heard. He found himself scanning the faces. *I wonder if my parents are here somewhere.*

Perryn stood wide-eyed as she scanned the arena. Their eyes connected, and her lips betrayed a small smile. He recognized her time on Blue Team had filled her with doubts that she would ever return to the surface. Now that she was here, he couldn't imagine her joy knowing that the next couple of days were all that were keeping her from home. Mandatory retirement awaited all runners who participated in the Chase. This procession was her victory lap. All she wanted, she had already won.

On his other side, he was surprised to see Jaden's face. His wasn't an expression of awe or joy. Willis wasn't sure, but he seemed saddened by the crazed stadium. He scanned the people filling the stands as if he was studying individual faces and searching for something.

The son of a slave must see this very differently. Willis reached up and put a hand on Jaden's shoulder.

He glanced over at Willis and breathed in a sigh of thanks. "People like my mother built this, you know," Jaden said over the thunder of the crowd. Willis nodded in agreement, but he privately chastised himself for forgetting the real cost of the Law and the Chase.

Their attention turned to the center of the arena where the

twelve platforms converged around a shallow circular stage where the chairman and the deputy chairmen and chairwomen stood. The other racers acted as awestruck as those on their platform, once their faces came into focus. That is, all but one. Willis's eyes caught one racer that appeared rather unimpressed with the entire scene. He stared until the platforms got closer and he could make out the racer's face. His breath caught when he saw who it was.

Antonio DeLuca stood on the platform of the Joint Mediterranean States. He was the racer who had fallen in the previous year's Chase, and the one person believed to legitimately threaten Willis.

But how? Willis's mind raced. *He raced last year. He can't race this year!*

"Willis, what is he doing here?" Perryn couldn't mask the worry in her voice.

"I have no idea." Willis shook his head. "He shouldn't be here."

Nonetheless, Antonio stood there appearing as determined as ever. He wasn't watching the crowds or hearing the fanfare. He gazed sternly over the floor of the stage at Willis's face, and an understanding passed between the two of them. Antonio had no thought of repeating last year's mistake. He was here to beat Willis and beat him soundly.

"Citizens of the glorious World Coalition,"—the chairman's amplified voice echoed through the stadium—"before you are gathered the hope and future of our world. The alliances of the earth have given up the best of their youth to compete, not for our enjoyment, but that they may shower all of us with their grace. For it is they who will shape the way the Law guides us."

At this comment, Willis was sure the chairman looked straight at him.

"First, let us as world citizens stop and remember those who paid so dearly during the Great Collapse. Please join together in silence to remember those who cannot be forgotten lest we forget all we have been saved from."

A hush came over the crowd, and the roar of thousands of cheering people transformed into a deafening silence. All over the world, Willis knew, people would be standing silently during this moment.

A sudden noise in the stands to Willis's right drew his attention. A woman pressed her way through the crowd. A murmur spread from that area of the stadium. Behind her, Willis could see uniformed guards closing in on her position. Reaching the edge of the stands, she took a frightened glance at the guards. Turning to the center she shouted in the common language of the Coalition.

"Slaves! The Law has made us slaves. Turn from it, all of you."

She was one person, but the total silence amplified her cries. The acoustics of the stadium carried her plea through the crowd. The guards rushed her position. Willis saw them insert a syringe into her neck, and a second later, she collapsed.

"We're not alone, Willis," Jaden whispered. Willis nodded. He wasn't sure what awaited the woman who was hauled away by the guards, but he didn't question her courage. The attention of the crowd returned to the stage.

"Citizens," the chairman said, clearing his throat. "While there are those who would mock the beauty of our Coalition, may we all be reminded this year of the peace and security the Law gives us."

Screens around the arena lit up with images from all over the world. Pictures of smiling children, celebrating families, dancing, culture, and art filled the frame. The video captured an idyllic view of the Coalition and was met with approving applause from the crowd.

"And now," he continued, "may you join us here tomorrow as we commence this year's Chase!"

The crowd roared. The fervor of the event returned. The woman's cries were forgotten.

Chapter Thirty-One

There had been more fanfare and cheers from the crowd, but the ceremony ended soon. Willis stepped down from the platform back at the hanger and wiped the beading sweat from his head with his sleeve.

"That was something," he said, stepping into the welcome relief of the air-conditioned elevator. He steadied himself as it lurched to return them to the barracks.

"That was nothing." Perryn crossed her arms. "Did you see how everyone went on as if it never happened?"

"Perr," Jaden spoke softly. "What she said wasn't a waste. For a moment, the world heard the truth. That woman gave what little she had, and for a second it outshined all the gloss and glitter the Coalition uses to dazzle everyone."

"What's going to happen to her?" Perryn looked back toward the stadium.

"I don't know." Willis shrugged. "Nothing good, I imagine, so we'd better make her sacrifice worth it."

They returned to their quarters, and Willis cleaned up. He laid down, certain that sleep would be hard to come by that night. His thoughts centered on the Chase, his parents, and all that the next two days held. A buzz at the door startled him. Climbing off the bed he opened it and was surprised by a nervous Stan.

"What are you doing here, Stan? I thought your job was done?" Willis leaned against the door opening.

"Sorry, Willis." He avoided Willis's gaze. "You have one more unexpected appointment."

"Who wants to meet me this time? The chairman's mother?"

"The doctors forgot to administer one test. Follow me."

Willis rolled his eyes. He'd been poked and prodded enough

that day, but he figured he would get to return sooner if he went along with it. The two of them walked to the medical section of their barracks. Walking into a room, a partially reclined chair sat in the middle of the space.

"Have a seat," Stan said flatly. "They'll be with you in a minute." With that, he left the room still staring at the floor.

The doors reopened. A man in a white lab coat entered flanked by two guards. These were followed by a short man with greasy black hair and an Alliance insignia on his jacket.

"What's going on?" Willis looked at the guards and started to get up.

"Calm down, Mr. Thomson," the man said. "These gentlemen are simply my escort."

Willis sat down, but he didn't relax. He stared at the four men who'd entered, the Alliance official studying him for a moment in silence. The man in the lab coat approached a table in the corner and began preparing something, his back shielding Willis's view.

"Mr. Thomson, I am the Administrative Liaison to the Coalition Chairman's Office."

"The what?"

"Let's say that I help carry out the chairman's needs in the Western Alliance."

"I was told this was a medical test."

"Mr. Thomson." He ignored the comment. "I'm here to provide assurance to our chairman of your loyalty to the Coalition. Too much has been invested in you to have the dangerous ideas of certain participants cloud your judgment on the matter." He stopped and stared at Willis to see his reaction to the statement.

Willis sat stone-faced. *He means Jaden.*

"We have—over the years—become very adept at planning ahead. When we discovered that your mother was pregnant with you, we perceived an opportunity that was like none we'd had before. We needed to be patient.

"You see, I share the chairman's concern that the Coalition exists on the knife-edge of peace. Tip off-center a bit, and we fall into anarchy again. He has called upon the Western Alliance to help him ensure that doesn't happen."

Willis pointed to himself. "And what does that have to do with me?"

"You will see to it that emergency powers are granted to the chairman to take whatever measures are needed to snuff out shameful displays like the one at the opening ceremonies today."

"What?" Willis laughed in disbelief.

The official sighed in annoyance and glanced over at the doctor, examining whatever it was he was preparing on the table. He turned back to Willis, his lips curling into a sinister smile.

"Many years ago, it became apparent that the Coalition couldn't function perfectly with the current model of twelve equal alliances. The Lawgivers were too idealistic in their belief that people from varied backgrounds and cultures could work together. The beauty of what we've created is threatened each year as the less worthy alliances fail to follow the leadership of the Coalition. Voices are growing stronger that challenge the very fabric of our world peace."

"You mean the authority of the chairman," Willis interrupted.

"Call it what you will." The liaison sighed. "They are one and the same. The will of the chairman is the will of the Coalition. He is the protector of the Law, and he won't see it cast to ruin by the agenda of alliances who insist on causing trouble. That is why he came to us for help."

"Us?"

"The Western Alliance. When your parents announced your coming birth, our wise chairman saw an opportunity. A great racer would be born in you, and you could restore our world back to order. The years since your birth have been spent preparing for your moment."

Willis swallowed hard. "Preparing? What do you mean?"

The man approached him, smiling. "Mr. Thomson, by passing emergency powers to the chairman, you're giving him the ability to use the resources of the Western Alliance to control the dissident alliances around the world. It took time to prepare these resources, but we are ready."

"Resources? You mean armies, don't you? To control the other alliances?" Willis was starting to understand the chairman's idea of "protecting his people."

"Don't be so short-sighted." His eyes narrowed. He walked the perimeter of the room and gestured as if giving a lecture. "This goes far beyond armies, though the use of Law-keeping forces will be necessary. We've compiled strategies and weapons. We've secretly placed key people in positions of leadership around the world. All the pieces are in place. As soon as you pass this law, the chairman will crush all opposition in one swift move and usher in the true perfection of the Law. The Western Alliance will become the World Coalition. We will have peace and prosperity like the world has never seen."

Willis couldn't believe what he was hearing. This official in front of him acted genuinely convinced of what he was saying. Willis shuddered at the idea of how many people would die opposing this move.

"There's no way I'll cooperate. You expected me to agree to do this?" Willis scoffed.

"Sadly, no." The liaison nodded to the doctor, and before Willis could react, a needle was in his neck injecting him with a solution.

"What are you doing?" Willis jerked away, but it was too late. The solution was in his blood stream.

"The chairman wasn't convinced of your loyalty when he met you shortly after your return to the surface. By law, we can't force you to pass any particular law. But like I said, we pride ourselves on planning ahead. You're aware that you were genetically recoded as a child?"

"Yes. So what?" He angrily rubbed the new wound on his neck. Willis thought better than to reveal his knowledge of his parents' intentions to keep him from training.

"Among other reasons for doing so,"—he smiled crookedly again—"your recoding allowed for two suggestions to be planted into your subconscious, which will be awakened by the neuro-stimulant the doctor has given you. The first was an unwavering desire to win the Chase, simple enough and part of why you have performed so well in training. The second was—well—let's say you're going to be far more open to passing emergency powers to the chairman. We won't have to force you to do anything."

Willis shuddered. He could feel it. He tried to focus his mind on all he and Jaden had intended to do if they won the Chase, but that idea grew distant. He strained his mind, reaching for the idea, but a haze kept it shrouded. It no longer made sense. Everything the chairman intended to do felt—agreeable—even admirable. In fact, Willis found in moments he was angry that he'd ever questioned the idea.

"I can see in your eyes the stimulant is taking effect. I'm happy to see you're coming around."

"What if I lose?" Willis was suddenly not sure if he was questioning the plans of the man or if he was afraid he wouldn't be able to help the chairman.

"Again, Mr. Thomson, we plan ahead. The Western Alliance was more than happy to support the Joint Mediterranean States in their appeal over the fall of Mr. DeLuca last year. In fact, it was our support that tipped the scales in their favor. You're not the only one prepared to give the chairman what he needs, even if the JMS doesn't understand why. We're confident you will win, but it doesn't hurt us to have a back-up plan."

Strangely, this news made Willis feel relieved.

Willis lay in his bed. He'd considered stopping by Perryn's room to tell her what had happened, but he stopped at her doorway.

Why would I tell her? She might try to stop me, and that can't happen.

He stared at the ceiling.

He had to win.

He had to help the chairman restore peace to the world.

Chapter Thirty-Two

"You okay?" Perryn approached Willis from behind. Willis started at the sound of her voice. He hadn't even noticed her. "Yeah. Why?"

"I don't know. You seem lost in thought."

She reached out a yellow and black sleeved arm toward him, placing her hand on his shoulder. Her eyes studied his for several moments as they waited for the elevator to take them up to the platform that would deliver them to the starting line.

"Just thinking about today, I guess."

"Willis, today is a big day. What you and Jaden hope to do will change everything, but I want you to know that I'm mostly glad I get to be here with you. I know I should care more about the plan, but it almost feels too big for me. All I'm sure of is I don't know what I would do if I was still on that station having to watch you from so far away."

"Perryn, I—" Willis couldn't get the words out. Something in him wanted to tell her about the previous night, but every time he opened his mouth to do so, the words wouldn't come. He hated keeping a secret from her and hated himself even more for doing so, but she wouldn't understand. He knew there had been a plan with Jaden and that he'd been convinced of that plan as recently as yesterday, but the chairman's intentions had rooted, no matter how hard he tried to convince himself otherwise. He rubbed at the injection site on his neck. The idea of betraying his friends made his stomach sour. Still, everything in him pushed to give the chairman the power he needed to right things.

She would never understand. He gazed at her in silence.

"What is it? You can tell me." She spoke as though she could see his inner thoughts, and she looked concerned.

"I'm glad to be here with you too."

She smiled and grabbed his hand in hers. The elevator doors opened, and they stepped aboard. Moments later, the hot blast of jungle air filled their lungs.

"You love birds ready?" Jaden smirked, elbowing Kane.

"I think so—and shut up with the 'love birds' talk." Perryn smiled and gave Jaden a sisterly shove.

"It's the day of the race, and Perr is trying to injure me." Jaden laughed, prompting Perryn to slug his shoulder. Jaden approached Willis, then placed his hands on his shoulders. "Friend, you ready for this? After tomorrow, the world will never be the same."

"Never the same," was all Willis could think to say. The statement was a double-edged sword to Willis. Giving the chairman what he needed would certainly change the world, but at what cost to his personal world? Jaden and Perryn might never talk to him again after today.

Thousands of cheering people, who had paid a premium for a seat at the starting gate, greeted Willis and the others as their platform turned the corner several minutes later. Twelve gates, like those on the station track, filled the space between two sets of stands rising almost vertical on either side. The image of people screaming and hanging over the edge of their stands overwhelmed him. Names of better-known racers were being shouted, and Willis was sickened by the display of hero worship.

Less worthy alliances. Willis pondered the words of the official he'd met the night before. *Tip off-center a bit, and we fall into anarchy again.* Seeing the crazed crowd convinced him of the words. The size of the multitude and the nearness of their endless screaming gave Willis the sensation that they were going to crash down and smother him.

Each gate was shadowed by a drone camera hovering over it, ready to follow the progress of each team. The video feed would be displayed on two massive screens bracketing the track, on which Willis couldn't make out the first obstacle. He could barely see a stretch of open track leading off into a fortress of tree-infested jungle.

Other teams had already arrived and were being announced one by one. Each alliance could be heard cheering their racers, but none more loudly than the Joint Mediterranean States when the name Antonio DeLuca was read. Willis could see him taking his place at a gate, his blue and white uniform in sharp contrast to the dark color of the track in front of them.

DeLuca appeared every bit the racer he'd been the previous year, though more determined. And calm—he was frightfully calm. Willis's mind returned to heated arguments with DeLuca when they were young during DeLuca's exchange program. He'd always had a short temper, but all signs of the hothead Willis knew from years ago appeared gone.

I wonder what thoughts they put into your mind, DeLuca. Willis quietly considered this. To his surprise, the emotion he felt was approval, not disdain. *Anything to help the chairman's cause.* The idea kept recurring until it was interrupted by the announcer.

"Led by the son of hall-of-fame racers, Max and Brenda Thomson"—boomed the voice over the speaker—"we present to you the team from the Western Alliance led by Willis Thomson!"

The throng rose to its feet to shout its approval.

"Willis, I think those are your parents!" Perryn exclaimed, pointing upward. High above the crowd on a platform between the two screens, a couple could be seen waving to the crowds. Willis looked up as he walked toward his gate. They were so far away that he couldn't see their faces, but their shapes seemed familiar to him.

They're here. They're actually here. Seeing them started to bring something to mind, but Willis couldn't focus on it. He sensed the thought or memory was important, but he couldn't force it to the front of his mind. All that remained was the will to win—the will to save the world from itself.

The team stepped off their platform and into their gate. Jaden turned and put a hand on Kane and Perryn's shoulders. "Ready, everyone?"

"I can't believe I'm here, but yes," said Perryn. She sounded almost out of breath as she took in the scene.

Kane nodded, his usual stoic self.

"Willis, you here?" Jaden tipped his head. Willis had returned his gaze to his parents way up on the platform. He was straining to remember, and the two people on the platform were the one stimulus that would bring him even close.

"Willis?" Perryn shouted above the crowd who was cheering the team from the host alliance.

He snapped his attention toward them. "Yeah. I'm ready to win."

"That's what I want to hear, bro." Jaden smiled.

"Per our great traditions, racers will run as teams this day to celebrate the birth of the twelve alliances after our forebearers gave us the Law. Final results will determine their starting time to run as individuals in tomorrow's leg to determine who will be this year's Law-changer." The announcer's voice disappeared, and the crowd quieted expecting the start of the race.

Willis could feel his body tensing as the countdown began. For most of his nineteen years, he had trained for this moment. Glancing to his left and right, he could see similar determination on the faces of other racers. *We've all trained our whole lives for this.*

Three. The final countdown echoed.

"For the benefit of the Coalition—" came the chairman's voice.

Two.

"—for the glory of the Law—"

One.

"—make us proud."

Tone.

Willis's legs found their familiar strength and sprang through the gate. Jaden matched his burst on his left. Kane and Perryn were on his right. He'd seen too many Chase events not to know that this was one of the most dangerous parts of the entire race. Forty-eight racers in close proximity could mean collisions.

As if on cue, a member of the Southern Federation of Allied States fell. Willis could see the flash of a blue and red uniform hit the ground out of the left corner of his eye. The 'boos' of the crowd confirmed that a member of the home team had suffered an 'accident' at the hands of another team. Before him lay open track as far as he could see. It would be a tight sprint to the first obstacle, whatever that was.

He chanced a glance to his right where he could see Antonio two teams over. He was shouting to his teammates as they sprinted down the track. *I have to get a lead on him.*

"Look out, Willis!" Jaden shouted.

He looked left to see the red uniform of a racer from the West Europe Collective somersaulting onto the track. Jaden was already airborne to clear the runner, but Willis had no time to react. He futilely launched himself upward, his foot catching the shoulder of the fallen racer.

The impact of hitting the ground expelled the air from his lungs. He could feel his skin burn as his hands, protecting his face from the ground, scraped the pavement in front of him, dirt and stone embedding in his skin. He kicked wildly, his feet searching for traction to get him upright again.

Get up, Willis! Get up! He shouted to himself.

Kane's grip on his arm suddenly yanked him to his feet. The giant man had barely broken pace to pull Willis up. Willis shook his head to clear the cobwebs from his brain. He ignored his gasping lungs and burning hands and willed his legs to keep moving. A minute later, the teams spread out. Willis cursed under his breath when he saw DeLuca's blue and white uniform ahead of him.

He guessed it was about a kilometer later that the track took a sudden left turn into the canopy of trees. The change in direction revealed a clearing in the dense jungle ahead, in the middle of which stood a monstrous pyramid. The blocks forming the pyramid were three-meter cubes, and he guessed there were at least twelve levels to the top. The two lead teams were already helping each other up onto the first level.

"Kane, this is you." Willis grunted between breaths.

Kane slid to a stop in front of the first block. Spinning to face them, he laced his fingers together. Jaden never hesitated. His foot found Kane's fingers in stride, and Kane's strength launched him upward. So efficient was the maneuver that Jaden was able to grab the edge and pull himself atop the block in one motion.

Perryn was next, and Willis used the half-second break to suck in a deep breath and find relief from his fall. Climbing up top, Willis turned to give Kane a hand up as Jaden was already lifting Perryn to the next level.

Chief Administrator Blacc did his job well. The maneuver to climb an obstacle like this one was second nature to all of them. Willis could see other teams struggling to get a rhythm as they climbed. Leaders were shouting instructions. In the distance, he could still hear the announcer relaying details to the crowd. Overhead, the camera drone designated to their team buzzed as it hovered, and he was sure the crowd could see the sweat beading on his forehead already.

Several minutes later he grabbed at the edge of the top block of the pyramid. He pulled himself upward in time to see DeLuca grab the handle of a zip-line and launch forward. To his left, he could see the emerald green color of a Central Asian Alliance runner pulling herself over the edge of the block.

"Come on! We're catching up," he cried as he rolled over onto the surface. He grabbed Jaden's arm and hoisted him upward. Kane was lifting Perryn to his right. Willis scrambled to his feet and grabbed the first of four handles on their designated zip-line.

The thick, hot air rushed at his face as he gained speed, drying his eyes out. For a second, he found himself enjoying his flight, knowing there was little he could do until he reached the end. Ahead, he could see Antonio gliding toward his teammates who were already at the bottom. Willis squinted to see them. They were waving frantically at Antonio from the top of a pillar at the end of the line, but it was too late. DeLuca crashed into his team causing the rear member of the team to plummet off the pillar to a net below.

As Willis approached, he could see that the race creators had dug out the ground for nearly one-hundred meters, leaving a series of narrow pillars sticking upward for each team to cross. Less than a couple of meters across, the pillars were hardly enough room for four people, a lesson DeLuca's team was too late in learning. Their teammate was busy untangling himself from the net below and making his way to the ladder rungs that would allow him to climb up the pillar.

Willis's mind raced as he approached the first pillar. His body jolted as the handle reached the end of the line, and he tightened his grip to avoid being flung over the edge. Letting go with his right hand, he spun to his left while still holding onto the handle as his shoe soles grabbed at the pillar. The effect left him at the corner of the pillar as Perryn appeared in view. He threw his free hand outward, wrapping it around her waist and slowing her to a stop. She grunted at the pressure on her stomach.

"Thanks," she said breathlessly.

"Jump over!" he yelled. She leapt to the next pillar, which was almost two meters away. She was in time as Jaden arrived. Willis caught Jaden, and the two of them turned to catch Kane.

"Nice move, Willis," Jaden blurted as he jumped to the next pillar, Perryn helping catch him.

"Go, go, go!" he shouted. Antonio was helping his teammate back atop their pillar, and it was the break they needed. Soon, they were jumping from pillar to pillar to cross the pit, their lead ever so slim. Other teams were beginning to land on their pillars, some able to mimic Willis's maneuver and keep pace. Willis could hear the cries of others falling to the net below and slowing their teams. Reaching the other side, they once again were faced with a stretch of empty track.

"Somehow, I get the impression the Southern Feds like to run a lot," Jaden said between breaths and gesturing to the track the Southern Federation had created.

"No kidding," added Perryn.

Willis stared at the door in front of them. It'd been several minutes of running when a right turn revealed that their path was blocked. The wall before them was several meters in height and too tall to climb. Each team had its own door, locked by a combination. A panel on the door was covered in lighted buttons which, when pressed, would switch several other lights on or off. The purpose was clearly to get all the buttons lit, but Willis couldn't make out the pattern. Glancing left and right, he could see that three teams had reached their wall and were maniacally working at the combination lock.

Perryn frantically pushed buttons as she had the most natural gift for these puzzles. Turning right, Willis noticed Antonio screaming instructions in his native tongue to two anxious-looking racers. Further up the line, he could see the United African Cooperative working on their door. The Central Asians were to the left, and they soon opted to cease pushing buttons and study the pattern of each one. Behind, he could see three or four other teams arriving, including the Southern Federation team, bringing cheers in the distance.

What is the pattern? It was driving him crazy. Each button lit a different pattern of lights around it, and the buttons didn't always respond the same way twice. The adrenaline of the start was keeping him from thinking clearly.

"Any help would be appreciated," Perryn announced, her concern poorly hidden.

"Sorry, Perr. I can't figure it out." Jaden sounded worried. "Willis? Kane?"

Kane shook his head.

An excited noise came from the African team as they had all but one button lit. They talked excitedly about which button to push. Deciding, they selected one in the corner bringing shouts of frustration as half the lights went out.

Suddenly, Perryn stepped back and stared at the door.

"Perryn, need me to take over?" Willis's voice dripped with urgency.

"Shhh," With two fingers, he could see her silently counting. The Central Asian team suddenly became excited and confidently lit up the buttons on their door.

"Perryn, if you don't have it, step aside."

"Quiet, Willis."

"I'm serious."

"Shut up. I've almost got it."

"Perryn, I—"

"Willis, give her a second," Jaden interrupted calmly. He was staring at Perryn's face, watching her calculate. The Central Asian door opened, and they burst through their door. Willis glanced over and noticed Antonio watching Perryn as well. He could feel the ball of stress forming in his gut.

I can't take this. He moved to take over. Perryn's hand on his chest stopped him. She quietly stepped up to the door and methodically pushed buttons. He could hear Antonio whispering, still studying Perryn. A second later, she hit the final button, and the last of the lights ignited. *Schwipp!* The door slid open.

"Yeah, Perr!" Jaden shouted jumping through the door.

Willis smiled and looked at her. He mouthed the word 'sorry.' She met his smile with her own.

"Come on," he said.

"After you." She punched his shoulder, and they took off running.

"Mr. and Mrs. Thomson?" Sheila tipped her head as she approached. The legendary runners stood before her in whispered conversation. In the background, cheers and boos could be heard as the massive crowds craned their necks for a peek at the closest screen. The Chase had already had its moments, and the matchup between Willis and Antonio lived up to expectations.

When she approached, the couple's words stopped, and they turned to Sheila. She'd sent the Thomsons another secret message to meet her after the race began in this hallway behind the stands. Max Thomson was an imposing figure. Still muscular and toned from his racing days, the gray streaks of hair on the sides of his head were the one giveaway that he was old enough to have a nineteen-year-old son. Brenda stood next to him, her wavy blond hair and striking features paired brilliantly with the faint wrinkles at the corners of her eyes.

Max placed his hand over his wife's hand. "We're the Thomsons. Who are you?"

"My name is Sheila Kemp."

"You're the one who contacted us about our Willis." Brenda stepped forward.

"Yes, I am. Thank you for agreeing to meet with me."

"You said it was about our son. How is he? They won't let us near him. The Alliance officials keep saying that Willis doesn't want to see us before the race, but I can't believe that." Brenda's hurried voice betrayed tears.

"I haven't been able to speak with him," Sheila said, "but I do know that there was little your son desired more than to see you."

"Do you mean to say they're keeping him from us?" Max's face darkened.

"Probably."

"I can't believe it." Max's voice caught. "After they stole him from us nineteen years ago, we're kept even longer from seeing him."

"Mr. Thomson, I know you're angry."

"Angry doesn't begin to describe it."

"I want to help. Something happened on the station you should know about."

For the next several minutes, Sheila recounted Willis's discovery of the slaves on the station, his friendship with Jaden, and Jez's attempt on Willis's life. Once or twice, she had to stop as Brenda's knees acted ready to give way. Max stood silent, supporting his wife with one arm, but the wetness of his eyes revealed his sorrow.

"So you see," she continued, "there's more at stake here than the Chase. Willis has a chance to change everything."

"So why come to us? Is something wrong?" Brenda squeezed her husband's arm.

"I don't know. I think so. Last night, I used my press pass to sweet-talk my way into the Alliance barracks. I stopped in to see the racers, and I was surprised to find Willis missing."

"Missing?" Max straightened.

"Yes. He was gone for some time."

"And you think they did something to him?"

"I do."

At this news, Brenda couldn't take it any longer. "Our son, our beautiful son." She sobbed falling to her knees.

"What can we do?" Max's voice shook.

"I think he needs to see you. He didn't appear himself at the start of the race. He was—distracted."

"And?"

"Mr. and Mrs. Thomson, I know Willis is your son, but if you could have seen him in training. Distracted isn't a word that could be used to describe him."

"We would gladly talk to him, but like I said," Max repeated and pointed a finger behind him, "*they* won't let us near him."

"Leave that to me. Meet me right here an hour after dark."

Chapter Thirty-Three

Willis's head hit the pillow. His body was exhausted, but his mind wouldn't permit him to rest. The team leg of the race had included two more obstacles once they passed the doorway. The first had been a series of cargo nets and balance beams, a simple enough task. The other had been a square platform resting on the apex of a small pyramid. The platform demanded the four of them carefully start from the edges of the platform and move simultaneously to the middle to strike a button, locking in their finishing position for the day.

Perryn had hit their button a second and a half ahead of Antonio DeLuca. It was essentially a dead-heat between their teams going into day two. Teams had finished one by one in the minute or two after that, except for the Central Asian Team. One member made a desperate dive for their button, and he failed to make it. The resulting misbalance of their team sent their team leader plummeting to the ground. Something tore in her knee on impact, ending her chances of winning. Outside of Willis and Antonio, she'd been the next most likely challenger. The rest of her team would be allowed to race, but at a thirty-second penalty for not finishing.

They're out of the race. Willis calculated the odds in his head. *It's between us and Antonio's team tomorrow.*

"Willis, you still awake?" Perryn whispered. He looked at her. Their quarters for the night were a simple square building with four beds and a bathroom. It served the dual purpose of providing them space to strategize the next day and sequestering them from any alliance influence. Two beds lined the walls on either side of the plain metallic room. The building stood right next to the starting line of the next day's track and bordered the buildings used by the other teams.

"Yeah, I'm up, but I don't want to wake the others." He winced as his whisper sounded louder in the small space than he'd intended.

"Don't worry about me," Jaden chimed in, "or about Kane over there." Kane was breathing heavily, already asleep. He seemed able to fall asleep instantly and could sleep through anything. "I don't expect that many are sleeping well."

Perryn pointed to herself, a nervous quiver in her voice. "Is it me, or does Antonio seem stronger this year?"

"Imagine training for a year knowing you'd be the first racer to ever get a second chance as a Chase runner," Willis said.

"I guess." Perryn turned her head to study the ceiling.

"Something bothering you, Perr?" Jaden inquired. He rolled over to look at the two of them.

"I never pictured the race being this close." She sat up. "With Antonio racing last year, no one was supposed to be able to compete with our Alliance."

"Every team wants to win."

"I know. It scares me. What if we don't win? What if one of you doesn't get the chance to change the Law tomorrow?"

"Perr, Willis and I are ready to do what we need to do tomorrow. Don't worry about it," Jaden assured her.

Willis held his breath. He'd been dreading this conversation all day. He could feel the battle inside of himself beginning to boil over.

"What if we're wrong?" Willis grimaced, unable to catch his words before he asked them.

"Wrong? Not funny, Willis," Jaden said, his annoyance shining through his words.

"What do you mean, Willis?" Perryn leaned forward, apparently not wanting to let the comment go unanswered.

Willis had done it now. He would have to make them understand.

"I mean, did you see them today?" He pushed up on his elbow. "All those people crazed over their own alliance? How is peace in the world possible with so many people pulling for their own interests?"

"Yeah, it's what the Law has done to them, remember?" Perryn tapped the side of her head.

Willis's mind fought the idea. He tried to remember why he'd agreed to their plan, but it wouldn't come to him. It no longer felt right. He couldn't send the world into anarchy, could he? Could he allow Jaden or Perryn to do it?

"I know we talked about it, but I think that freedom might be a bit dangerous. Imagine everyone making their own choices to do what is right or not. Do you think people will do anything other than look out for themselves?" The words tasted so agreeable as they crossed his lips. *They have to see the logic.*

"Are you serious?" Jaden sat upright on his bed. The room was too dark to see, but Willis could feel his anger in the blackness. "Do you know who you sound like?"

"Willis, what has gotten into you?" Perryn said, showing more deep concern than anger.

"All I'm saying," Willis said, realizing he was losing this argument. "Is that our plan could be too risky. What if we send the world into anarchy? What if we destroy everything? I think there might be another way to preserve what is good about the current Law."

"Okay, Mr. Chairman," Jaden mocked as he flopped backward onto his pillow. "I can't believe this. Did they do something to you?"

"No." The lie tasted sour on his lips.

"Willis?" He could hear the sob in Perryn's voice. "Please tell me you're joking. Please tell me you're not seriously considering this."

A war waged in his soul. Willis sensed he was breaking her heart, but the chairman's plan was so clear. Everything would make sense. They would see it soon, even if they didn't understand now. "Perryn, you have to trust me."

His words were met with silence for a moment, broken by the hushed sobs from Perryn's bed. Willis started to rise to go to her.

"I did trust you," she finally whispered.

"Perryn, I—" he started, pausing as his feet found the floor.

"Don't talk to me, Willis." She scrambled out of her bed. "Don't talk to me ever again." She ran for the doorway to the outdoors. Willis rose to follow her, but a hand caught his shoulder.

"Let her go," Jaden said firmly. "You've done enough."

Willis's heart ached. He knew they felt betrayed. He watched her unlock the doorway and disappear in the blackness outside. He sat down on the edge of his bed. He and Jaden sat in silence in the darkness.

Seconds later, he could hear hushed voices outside the still cracked doorway. The tones were very intense. The voices approached the door.

Oh, no! The Coalition officials have her. Willis pieced together a defense on her behalf. Confirming his fear, Perryn's form appeared in the door flanked by three people who were dressed as Coalition officers.

"Didn't want to let this one get too far before we arrived," one of the officers spoke into the darkness.

Willis shot up out of his bed. He knew that voice.

"Sheila?" he said.

One of the other two officers closed the door, while the third lit a small portable light. The florescent glow cast an eerie white blanket through the room, creating elongated shadows and dark corners.

"Willis, I brought someone to see you," Sheila said, stepping into the light to reveal her face. She grabbed the light and held it up. The two officers behind her removed their helmets. The faces of a man and woman stared at him in the pale light.

He studied them transfixed. They appeared familiar, but he didn't know them.

"Willis?" came the voice of the woman. The face was foreign, but he knew the voice. He once again tried to pry the reason out of his subconscious, but he could barely connect that he remembered her voice.

"Who are you?" His eyes searched her face, hoping for a clue.

"You don't remember us?" The man gestured to himself and the woman next to him.

Willis studied his face. "Should I?"

"Willis," Perryn spoke, tears still fresh on her cheeks, "they're your parents."

All at once, Willis gasped and staggered, his knees unable to support him anymore. He grabbed at the bed to keep from falling. Wetness clung to his cheeks, but not until he swiped at the tears did he realize he was crying.

"What? Who? I mean—?" Willis's head swiveled as he took in Sheila and his parents.

"My dear son," the woman said, "what have they done to you?" She rushed forward to embrace him, but he retreated, freezing her in her tracks. He could see the hurt on her face, but he wasn't ready to be that close.

"Give me a second," he said, hardly able to breathe.

"Of course." His father joined his mother and placed a comforting hand on her shoulder. Willis sat down on the bed trying to collect himself. Thoughts flooded his mind as he gazed at the floor. The Chase. The Law. Jaden's mother. Perryn's tears. Anarchy. The chairman. His parents. Once again, the memory he couldn't recall earlier creeped forward in his thoughts.

His desire to help the chairman railed against the memory, and he believed he might go mad trying to sort it out.

"Willis," his father said, "Ms. Kemp has brought us to you. She's concerned the Alliance has done something to you."

"I knew it," Jaden exclaimed, startling everyone.

A grunt came from the corner revealing that Kane had been watching and listening for some time.

"What do you mean?" Perryn spoke, her concern hopeful.

"We don't know," Sheila said. "All I know is that Willis wasn't there when I came to visit you guys last night."

"Willis?" Perryn looked at him. Her eyes showed fear.

"Son, did they do something to you?" His mother's voice pleaded.

The room spun, his wooziness making their voices sound muffled. He thought his mind might break from the war waging inside. The suggestions in his mind were so strong, he almost ran from the building. Slaves. Emergency powers. Antonio DeLuca. The neuro-stimulant.

His father knelt to gaze into his eyes. The strong, impressive figure before him wore an air of compassion. He allowed several moments to pass between them silently.

"Son, I know. Your mother and I have been there. We know what it's like to serve the Alliance and then question everything. We know how powerful they are and what they're capable of doing." His father spoke calmly. The words sounded so comforting, and yet so foreign. He couldn't remember the last time someone had spoken to him like this. "Whatever has happened—whatever you feel compelled to do—you need to know it doesn't change that you are my son."

Willis studied his father's eyes. Even in the dim light, he could see the sincerity. He wanted to scream. His mind wanted to throw them out the door, but his heart longed to embrace them. His soul was tearing in two, and it was almost more than he could bear.

"Willis, we love you, and we're so proud of you." His father's deep voice betrayed a hidden gentleness. He reached out and placed his hand on Willis's knee. The firm grip of this powerful man sent a shockwave of emotion through Willis. For a moment, the clouded memory cleared and the image of his loving father gripping his leg as a child came into focus. The tears in his eyes. The jerk of his arm. The sobs of his mother. The pain in his leg.

"Dad?" Willis whimpered. In that instant, the real memory shattered the artificial suggestion in his mind, and Willis crumpled into his father's strong arms. His mother fell next to them sobbing and wrapped her arms around both of them. For several minutes, the family embraced and wept.

"You tried to save me." Willis finally pulled back to examine their faces. Perryn stood near, crying. Jaden stood, his jaw hanging open. Sheila and Kane looked on silently. "I remember. You tried to keep me from all this."

"A racer's life is no life, Willis." His father gave him a warm smile. "Your mother and I lost our childhood. We were forced to train. We were forced to marry. We were forced to have a child. But even with all they made us do, they couldn't prevent your mother and me from falling in love. And they certainly couldn't keep us from loving you."

"We're so sorry we couldn't keep you from this." His mother had stopped swiping at her tears.

"Forgive us, Son," his father said, squeezing his shoulder. "I wasn't able to protect you in the end."

Willis placed his hand on his father's. "But you did. Just now."

"Mr. and Mrs. Thomson," Sheila suddenly spoke. "I'm sorry, but we need to be going before we're noticed."

"What do I do?" Willis was suddenly afraid, feeling like a small child in their presence. "What they did to me is still there, still fighting to take over. Maybe I should withdraw."

"No!" Perryn cried out. "You can't. No one has a better chance of beating Antonio than you."

"Your friend is right," his mother said, "You have to fight it."

His father nodded. "Willis, you will know what to do. We trust you."

"Time to go," Sheila reached for the door handle. She extinguished the light they'd brought.

"Goodbye, Son," his father said.

"Goodbye, Dad."

"We love you." His mother squeezed his hand.

The three embraced one more time, and Willis held his breath to control the welling tears as they slipped out into the darkness with Sheila. Sheila risked a great deal getting them in here, and he promised himself he would not forget.

Perryn slowly approached him from the side. She wrapped her arms around his chest and buried one side of her face in his shoulder. He returned the contact, not feeling a shred of embarrassment with Jaden and Kane looking on.

"And now we're supposed to try to sleep after all that? Yeah, right." Jaden spoke, breaking the silence.

Kane grunted a laugh and rolled over, and the others chuckled. They each climbed into their beds and drifted into sleep. Willis stared at the dark ceiling. What should he do? The conflict was still going on inside of him. The Alliance had done their work well. While they hadn't counted on his parents sparking his memory, the suggestions inside him were still there.

Win. Support the chairman. He shook his head trying to clear the jumble of ideas, but it wouldn't go away. It was as if he knew the truth, but his mind was not his own.

How can I trust myself to do the right thing tomorrow? It was the last thought before sleep finally took him.

228

Chapter Thirty-Four

The gate was much narrower than Willis was used to, but this was his first individual race in years. Along the new starting line, forty-eight individual gates stood side-by-side. The team had agreed that Perryn and Kane would be on the outside of their foursome. They wouldn't be able to keep up with Jaden and Willis in an individual run, so their first job would be to keep other racers away in the initial dash out of the gates.

Willis's thigh muscles trembled. He was trying to calm himself after the countdown restarted. A runner from another alliance broke through their gate early in anticipation of the starting tone, prompting massive 'boos' from the few who hadn't gathered at the finish and an immediate disqualification for the offending runner. Most of the crowd preferred to view the start on the screens rather than venturing into the jungle. The runners had to stand for several minutes as things were reset.

Breathe, Willis. He hadn't slept much, having spent hours battling the two opposing forces in his mind. Willing himself to focus, he took deep breaths and imagined the aches in his sleep-deprived body melting away.

"Willis, perhaps you would start early too, no?" came the thickly accented common language from Antonio DeLuca. Willis glanced over to his right. DeLuca's gate was two down from Kane's.

Willis pointed a thumb at his chest. "You mean disqualify myself and let you have it easy?"

"The Western Alliance will not be celebrating a win today, I assure you." He smirked. "Maybe you and your girlfriend should go home?" Antonio's teammates all laughed at the comment.

"Whatever, DeLuca."

"Willis, don't bother with him." Jaden shook his head.

"I have to, at least in the race. Remember, I lose to him, and the chairman still wins." *And if I win...* He shook his head to interrupt the chairman's suggestion.

"Then, it's up to one of us to stop him, isn't it?"

"Yep."

But who will stop me? Willis was still plagued by doubt. He didn't mind the desire to win except that it was so interlaced with the desire to support the chairman. He didn't want to worry the others, so he'd pretended to be completely clear-headed that morning.

"Chase runners, take your mark." The announcer's voice called them to attention.

The countdown. The tone. Coming in first on day one meant the Western Alliance gates turned green first. A second later, the Mediterranean gates did the same. Other teams waited longer, but the top teams were seconds apart.

Willis pumped his legs as hard as he could. Racers were going down everywhere. The individual race was so different and collisions even more commonplace. A grunt to his right drew his attention, giving him a chance to see Kane throw a runner to the side. The blue and white uniform tumbled to the ground having misjudged the behemoth size of Kane. Antonio had probably instructed his teammate to take a dive at him.

Two hundred meters later, the elite racers emerged from the pack uninhibited by needing to wait for their slower teammates like the day before. Antonio was a stride behind to his right. He could hear Jaden keeping up to his left. The corners of his eyes caught sight of a few other elite leaders, but they would not last. Barring a fall, this was a two-alliance race.

The track took a familiar bend into the trees. Willis suspected that the first obstacle lay beyond. What he didn't anticipate was how abruptly it would appear. Meters beyond the bend, the track disappeared, revealing another set of pillars similar to the previous day. These were smaller and further apart. He made his way to the narrow beam connecting the first two pillars in front of him and tiptoed across.

Whirr! Willis's stomach dropped as the beam gave way beneath him. He pushed off what was left of the beam's support and flung himself at the pillar. He grabbed at the edge, his fingers barely holding on. Pain shot through his fingers as they held his weight. He glanced below to see the beam fixed to supports that allowed it to raise and lower suddenly. A net filled the pit below.

"Willis, you okay?" Jaden shouted behind him. He and Antonio had stopped short of the pit. A second later, the whirring sound came again, and the beam shot up underneath Willis. He flexed his knees to prevent getting too much upward momentum as the beam supported his feet and he stepped onto the pillar, relief washing over him. He scanned the pit to see beams between the pillars rising and lowering in intervals.

Looking down, he timed the next beam and jumped forward to meet it before it rose fully in place. He ran to the next pillar, stopping again. Runners all over the pit crossed in staccato motions behind him. He may have nearly fallen, but his initial leap had given him a one pillar lead over everyone.

Jump. Stop. Wait. Breathe. He spoke instructions to himself as he crossed post to post. He could hear Antonio cursing to himself as he was forced to continually wait one pillar behind. At last, the other end of the pit came close, and Willis jumped off his beam, thankful to be on solid ground again.

"I will see you at the next stop, Willis," Antonio shouted confidently behind him. Willis ran, ignoring the comment.

I'm actually winning. Some part of him was surprised. Most of his nineteen years were spent preparing, and yet he still was in disbelief that he was winning the Chase. Trees and occasional spectators blurred by as he moved his legs trying to extend his small lead over the other racers.

He was the best in the world.

He was made for this.

Made for this. The thought scared him. *I am the genetically chosen and manipulated tool of the Alliance.* He shook his head to get the idea out of his mind, but he couldn't deny it. Even now, the will to win was overpowering. How overpowering would the will to support the chairman be when the time came?

He ran. He didn't know what else to do.

Four openings gaped in the front of the towering wall that spread across the track and disappeared into the blind of trees on either side. Running down a hill, Willis could briefly see the top of the maze structure beyond the wall. Huge metal spectator stands were built above the labyrinth, allowing crowds to watch the action from above. They appeared to Willis like upside-down staircases that extended from the left and right, meeting in the center and running the length of the obstacle. Each level had a row of people able to peer down on the passages below them. The air shook with the sound of screaming fans as the runners approached. Willis tried to examine each opening as he neared, catching glimpses of more walls and turns inside.

"Go farther! I'll take the first one." Jaden's distant voice called from behind him. The idea was agreeable as one or more openings could lead to dead ends in the maze beyond. He started toward the second entrance.

"Right behind you, Willis Thomson," Antonio called out as he ducked inside the maze behind Willis.

"Can't live without me?" Willis shot back breathlessly, taking a sudden right turn in the passageway. He tried to focus on drawing the maze in his mind as he ran to keep his bearings using the viewing platforms above as his reference. Right. Left. Left again.

Nearing a four-way intersection, Willis resolved to try to lose Antonio. He cut the corner to his right as close as possible hoping to get out of sight long enough to turn again.

He never saw the other runner.

The flash of purple and gold uniform filled his vision right before the impact. It'd occurred to Willis that the other openings might be passages that eventually intersected with his own, but his desire to lose Antonio overrode his caution. His vision exploded with light as his forehead collided with the jaw of the other runner. Both of them went down, the track surface jamming his shoulder.

Willis held his hand against his head as he stumbled to his feet. The other runner was crawling on all fours still dazed. Even with his blurry vision, Willis could see the blue and white of DeLuca's uniform streak by him. His mind screamed at his legs, but he continued to move sluggishly. The crowd above him roared so loudly from the turn of events that Willis's ears felt as if pierced by a sharp object.

Pull it together, Willis.

His mental map was gone, and he couldn't track where he was any longer. His one hope was to keep Antonio in sight, hoping his rival was as adept as he was at figuring out these puzzles. He forced his legs to move faster than even he believed he could, keeping the blue and white back of DeLuca in view several meters ahead.

His legs burned. His head ached. His shoulder throbbed. Here and there, he noticed other collisions. Occasionally, he would observe runners shouting at themselves in frustration as they'd gone in a circle or been forced to turn from a dead end. Once or twice, he guessed that Antonio had circled back on himself, but he unfortunately showed skills similar to Willis.

As Willis was ready to despair that they wouldn't break out of this obstacle, he could hear the crowd above rise to their feet cheering. Peering past Antonio, he could see why. Before them lay an opening in the wall. Beyond the opening, open track appeared.

"Thank God," Willis whispered between breaths.

The stuffy air of the maze was replaced by the slightly less stuffy air of the jungle. It brought some relief to his head. DeLuca was nearly twenty meters ahead of him. He glanced around him. On both sides, a couple other runners emerged from the maze. *Jaden, where are you?* To his relief, Jaden emerged a moment later looking around at the runners ahead of him and shaking his head.

Ignoring the pain that pulsated in every corner of his body, Willis fixed his stare on Antonio's legs. Silently counting Antonio's steps, he chose a slightly faster pace. He wanted to make up the distance without exhausting himself before the next obstacle. Above him a camera circled trying to find the best angle.

Left, right, left, right. Willis willed his feet forward. The space between him and DeLuca was closing. A glance either way failed to reveal other racers, but he could hear their footfalls. He hoped that Jaden was one of the nearest.

The camera suddenly hovered lower in front of him capturing his face. In the distance, he could hear a faint voice over a loudspeaker. This was followed by the general clamor of the crowd.

Here it comes. The next obstacle was near.

The level track turned sharply upward. The ground was rising underneath his feet, and he doubled his efforts. Ahead, Antonio panted, desperate to keep his lead. Willis had almost caught him when the slope lessened. The crest of the hill approached, and Willis took in the sight beyond.

The summit overlooked a gorge below. The sides of the gorge had been cleared of jungle vegetation and converted to nearly vertical stands on either side. Thousands of crazed people in the stands launched to their feet at the sight of Willis and Antonio cresting the hill. Cheers, songs, and flags were everywhere. Beyond, huge screens displayed the progress of the elite runners, and he caught a glimpse of Jaden running up the hill.

The center of the gorge caught most of his attention. A massive, black tower protruded like a single, upward fang jutting out from the mouth of the gorge. The four sides of the tower were slightly tapered, giving it an obelisk shape. The sides were littered with hand holds, ropes, and other means of climbing to the top. He raced down the hill toward the bottom of the gorge as a low rumble shook the ground beneath his feet.

The rumble transformed into a mechanical roar as he neared, and Willis blinked to be sure he was seeing clearly. The obelisk, sectioned into ten parts, spun on its center. Each section turned independently and at varying speeds and directions. Access to the base of each new section was blocked by a surrounding floor that rotated with the section and had one opening to continue the ascent. The design was ingenious and maniacal all at once. Runners could quickly climb a portion of the obelisk to find themselves blocked as the opening rotated away from their position.

Looking up, Willis saw the tower contained one zipline at the top. The first to reach the top would be the one to fly down to the finish line below. No photo finishes would happen at this Chase. Antonio spat a curse as he took in the tower. Willis didn't blame him.

So this was it. His entire life came to this moment. The desire to win surged inside of him, bleeding the pain in his body to somewhere distant. He would win this. He had to win this. He had to support the chairman.

The thought surprised him, causing his feet to momentarily stumble, giving another half-step to Antonio. Willis's eyes opened wide in fear. The growing desire to win had chained itself to the suggestion to support the chairman.

What am I going to do? Willis scanned the ground for answers that weren't there, but his legs continued to move as if on their own.

"Citizens of the Coalition, the first of our racers approach!" blared the voice over the speaker. Willis glanced at the screens before their view became blocked by the tower. One showed he and Antonio nearly astride. Another showed Jaden and a girl in green and black meters behind.

The shadow of the obelisk and the air at the bottom felt cool as his feet found the floor of the gorge. He scrambled to the first wall and climbed the handholds. Antonio scowled, a meter away. Willis watched the opening above and frowned. Their timing was all wrong, and they'd miss the first opening. Reaching the top, he and Antonio could only hang and wait as the opening rotated its way around the tower.

"Curse this tower," Antonio said to the air.

"No kidding." Willis glanced over at Antonio.

"Do not speak with me, Willis Thomson. This day does not belong to you." Antonio's words ended in a snarl.

"Can I join the party?" came a breathless welcome voice. Willis looked down to see Jaden and the girl reaching the bottom of the tower and beginning their climb. The Chase designers had done their job. There would be no distant second. This would be a close race.

The floor above continued its revolution, and the opening peeked into view. Antonio was the first to scramble through it. Two seconds later, the rotation gave Willis the chance to grab the edge. He kicked to get his feet on the surface and rushed to the corner. He wanted to time the next section better. Willis heard Jaden's grunt as he climbed through the gap behind him as he pursued Antonio. He guessed the girl from the other alliance wasn't far behind in ascending to the second floor.

The far side of the obelisk revealed a stairway. Glancing up, Willis saw the opening nearing, the feet of Antonio disappearing above to the next level.

No! DeLuca must have timed another side of the obelisk perfectly.

"Now, Willis," Jaden shouted, catching up.

The two of them ran up the stairs. Willis cleared the gap on his feet, but noticed Jaden was forced to jump for the edge, hoisting himself up to the next floor as Willis continued. Floor after floor they climbed. Ladders. Stairs. Ropes.

It was around the sixth floor that Willis heard the scream. The green and black girl failed to clear the top of the staircase a floor below, her foot getting caught between the edge and the top stair, crushing it. The crowd gasped in curious horror as she shrieked in pain. Still, he could not stop to help. None of them could.

"I'm doing no good following you." Jaden exhaled as they

reached the seventh floor.

"Right. Go left and stay with DeLuca. I'll see if I can find a better route." Willis snorted between heaving breaths as he ran off to the right around the obelisk.

Reaching the corner, he gripped the wall as the floor lurched below him. The movement threw his body weight outward, his firm grasp keeping him from plummeting off the side. In that instant, his head flung backward giving him a view above. His well-trained mind fired automatically as he took in what he could see of the next couple of levels. The section above, moving opposite to his, would line up perfectly if he could ascend quickly enough.

This is it!

Letting go of the wall, he took the first handholds on that wall and began his climb. The adrenaline-fueled moment gave him the strength to climb faster than he realized he was capable. His feet barely found their grip before his hands were searching for their next target, like a spider ascending a vertical web. Throwing himself through the hole in the next floor, he scrambled and ran up the flight of stairs.

The world spun as his foot slipped, not having found the edge of the stair squarely. He pushed his arms forward to catch himself and winced as his knee drove into the corner of a stair. A grunt of agony and frustration escaped his lips. The opportunity was passing. His window to gain a lead was closing. He launched himself forward up the stairs, but the gap had already bypassed him.

His mind raced. Waiting for the gap to come around could hand the race to DeLuca. Here he was on the ninth floor of the obelisk, the wire descending to finish barely out of reach, and his chance was drifting away.

Win, Willis! Win for the Alliance!

Without thinking, he threw his body into the open air toward the increasingly distant gap above. Willis almost didn't hear the gasp of the thousands below as the rush of wind filled his ears. For a moment, he flew freely. Then, his stomach dropped as gravity reminded him it was still there.

He strained his fingers forward. The sharp corner of the floor gap caught him below the second knuckle of the fingers on his right hand. His left hand never found its mark and flailed, grasping at air. A hush came over the crowd below as the most favored racer in the world dangled precariously near a fatal fall with one hand in mid-air. His muscles flexed, and he managed to secure his hand on the edge.

This is it, Willis. Pull yourself up and you'll win. Everyone is expecting you to win. Don't disappoint them. The voice in his head wasn't his own. Calm and reassuring, the voice of the chairman was urging him on.

He hung there, conflicted, as the obelisk continued its rotation. An angry voice broke into his thoughts as the section below him turned.

"I will not lose to you, Western scum!" Antonio shouted.

Approaching him, Willis could see DeLuca and Jaden hanging from vertical ropes awaiting the arrival of the gap. Jaden grunted as he tried to keep his grip. DeLuca was kicking wildly with his feet at Jaden's fingers. Suddenly, Jaden's hand gave way, and Willis saw the fear in his teammate's eyes as the imminent danger of falling flooded his mind. DeLuca worked on the remaining hand, not noticing Willis.

Time slowed down to a crawl as images engulfed Willis's mind. His well-trained brain hunted for a solution, and the world around him blurred to a standstill. Then, the world was gone. Memories of training exercises shot through his consciousness like the pages of a book being flipped, until they stopped on one.

All at once, he was standing in the training center on the station. Before him stood a tower, and a group had gathered at its base. They were standing around a body on the floor.

Creed's fall. The memory filled Willis's mind.

He walked over to the body obscured by the small crowd. Looking around, the faces were not those of the trainees on the station. As they came into focus, they looked up at him, and each spoke words he remembered them saying.

"I need to know that you will do what is necessary to pre-serve the world we live in," the chairman's words echoed in the room.

"I did trust you," Perryn's tearful voice intruded.

"Emergency powers," reminded the Administrative Liaison's voice.

"We've got to take care of each other," Kane breathed.

"Hope of the Alliance," Chief Administrator Blacc's voice boomed.

"Cannot change my hope," Jaden's mother whispered.

The group gravely stared at the body on the floor. Willis's gaze followed theirs. He remembered Creed's twisted frame ly-ing on the floor after his death, but this body was different. It was too slender to be Creed. His eyes made their way upward taking in the details of the racer on the floor coming to rest on his face.

It was Jaden.

Willis stepped back in horror at the scene, confusion over-whelming his senses. The faces looked up at him silently. He wanted to run—to cry—to scream.

"What does this mean?" he shouted. "What am I supposed to do with this?"

Their silent gaze deafened him—judged him.

"My fault? No, this isn't right. It was Creed that fell that day," he pled with the group. "Creed fell because Stone-zee let him. He let him fall. He let—"

His breath caught in his panic. He turned to flee when a hand caught his shoulder. Turning, it was the face of his father. Willis crumpled to the floor in tears. His father knelt placing a hand on his knee. Willis looked down at his hand.

"You are my son—you will know what to do," his father's voice broke in.

The words washed away the tangled vision, and Willis shook his head to clear it. DeLuca coiling his leg for one last mighty kick at Jaden's fingers. He could see Jaden's despair over his loosening grip. Sweat dripped in large droplets from his fore-head. He appeared ready to give in to his screaming muscles.

Jaden's words earlier on the station filled his mind. "You're the hope for the Alliance, the *real* Alliance." The genetically imposed will to win for the Alliance blazed inside him, but the meaning of that Alliance had morphed.

Willis relaxed his grip on the ledge, focusing on the rope below. His body plunged and reached for DeLuca. Antonio's eyes widened as Willis filled his vision, and he thrust out a defensive hand. Grabbing at Antonio's rope below his remaining hand, Willis raised an arm to block the kick aimed at Jaden.

He missed.

His momentum still forward from the turning floor above, his feet flew freely out in front of him, flattening the angle of his body. A chill shot through his spine as his intended block met empty air, the already committed kick from DeLuca connecting with Willis's jaw. The flash of pain and crunching of teeth sickened him, and his fingers involuntarily loosened their grip on the rope. Antonio, not expecting his kick to connect so soon, shot backward as the force of his kick transferred up his body.

He was falling. They both were.

Chapter Thirty-Five

"Willis!" Jaden shouted as he regained the grip on his rope. The wind was expelled from Willis's lungs as his body slammed into the floor at the bottom of the ropes. His head exploded with pain as it struck the metal surface. The shock travelled through his body to his extremities with a burning numbness. For a second, he couldn't move, see, or hear. With a rush like a wave, the roar of the crowd filled his hearing. The scene cleared, and he turned his head to look at DeLuca.

Antonio was stirring next to him, a deep, bleeding gash on his head. He was turning over in a daze. By some miracle, neither had fallen to their deaths.

"Must win. Must serve Chairman." Antonio muttered to himself in a drowsy half-speech.

"Willis!" Jaden slid down the rope and landed at his side. "You okay?"

Willis tried to get up, his body sluggish. His limbs wouldn't respond to his will. A new sound filled his ears, and he realized other runners had arrived and were making their way up the obelisk. Jaden must have noticed too because he peered over the edge to glance below. DeLuca was on all fours reaching for a rope, but he was going nowhere quickly.

"Come on, friend. You have a race to win," Jaden said, pulling at Willis's uniform to sit him up.

The war inside him surged to the forefront. His will to win. His will to support the chairman. His will to free the slaves. His will? He realized he had no idea which thoughts were his own. Did he ever have a free will in his life? Then, a new idea occurred to him.

Yes, I do. He smiled to himself.

"It isn't my race to win," he said staring Jaden in the face.

"What do you mean?" Jaden's forehead furrowed. "Hope of the Alliance, remember? Your father said you'd know what to do when the time came."

"He was right. I do. My whole life has been about other people's choices, and it's time I made one of my own—to exercise my own will," he whispered with certainty. "One of us hasn't been tampered with by the Alliance. One of us hasn't had his brained scrambled." He grabbed the collar of Jaden's uniform, pulling him close. "One of us can be sure to do the right thing. I *choose* not to win."

He let go of Jaden, who straightened up, realizing what Willis was saying. Willis smiled at the thought of making his first free choice.

"I get what your mother was saying, 'What they did to me cannot change my hope.' I am a slave like she is. I didn't know it. For the first time in my life, I have hope. And now, you'd better get going before someone else catches up."

Jaden's expression turned resolute at the words of his mother. He placed a firm hand on Willis's shoulder. "My friend," he whispered, and ascended the rope. DeLuca protested in quiet mumbles, but he no longer had the strength to continue.

Willis heard the noise of the crowd swell as Jaden made his way to the top of the obelisk. He sat against the side of the obelisk and imagined Jaden taking a deep breath and grabbing the line. Thoughts of his mother were surely filling his mind as he flew down to the finish. Willis peered out at the crowd hoping to catch a glimpse of his parents.

We are so proud of you. His father's words came to him. Willis noted he'd said 'are' and not 'will be.' His parents were proud of him, and it had nothing to do with winning the Chase.

The screams of the crowd went wild. Watching the screen to his right, he smiled as Jaden crossed the finish line, collapsing to all fours. Whether it was from exhaustion or relief, Willis couldn't tell. He guessed it was both. The announcer proclaimed the victory for the Western Alliance. Alliance flags were waving.

Anthems were sung loudly. Somewhere, the chairman was cursing to himself.

Willis didn't notice any of it. He closed his eyes and smiled. He was finally free.

Perryn, where are you? Willis scanned the crowds, his brow furrowed in worry.

Once the race finished, officials quickly ushered Jaden into a holding room right next to the finish line to ensure the Alliance couldn't have any last-minute influence on him. Any minute, he would be escorted on stage to pass a new law. Willis desperately wanted to find Perryn before that happened. They needed to witness this together.

Crowds were pressing in upon the stage. A section up front lay roped off and reserved for the winning alliance. If Perryn was anywhere, he guessed she would be there. He pushed and shoved his way through the masses of people, two Law-keepers by his side escorting him. Occasionally, people would recognize him, shoving autograph books or cameras in his face. Finally, he reached the yellow and black tape designating his Alliance.

Reporters and cameras were everywhere. Dignitaries were mingling and exchanging enthusiastic and congratulatory handshakes. More people knew him here, and getting a clear view became impossible as the crowd pressed in.

"Willis Thomson, how does it feel to lose the Chase after so many years of training?" A reporter shoved a microphone in his face.

"Is the Thomson family doomed to always be second place?" The question turned his stomach.

"Rumor has it that the Alliance paid you to lose. Is that true?" He ignored this question all together.

"Mr. Thomson, can you comment on the ethics of Coalition access to the racers?" The voice nearby warmed his heart. Sheila posed the real questions. He caught her eye and smiled. She didn't return the smile with the cameras on but gave him a knowing glance. He saw her gaze move to peer over his shoulder.

Willis turned around and saw them. Through the crowds, he caught a view of his parents. Perryn was with them. Pushing aside the microphones and abandoning his security, he forced his way through the mob. Cameras and flashes followed him, but he didn't care.

Seeing his goal, the last few people parted to clear his path, and he ran to Perryn. She started to speak, but he gave her no chance. He threw his arms around her, his emotions somewhere between laughing and crying. For a long time, they held each other, relieved to have it all over.

"I knew you'd do the right thing." His father placed his large hand on Willis's shoulder. He turned to regard his father.

"I almost didn't. What they did to me is still there inside." His lips trembled as his eyes watered. He sniffed to hold back tears. "The doubt is still raging, but I realized what it would cost me." He clutched Perryn's hand a little tighter with his final words. She squeezed his in return.

"The chairman doesn't appear happy." Perryn chuckled.

Willis looked over at the building where Jaden was being held. The chairman and administrative liaison were both there, clearly wanting access to Jaden, but the multi-alliance guard detachment stayed true to their orders. The chairman settled for giving the liaison a tongue-lashing as they stormed out of sight.

Perryn breathed in deeply. "What do you think Jaden is doing?"

"Not much. They barely give the winner time to clean up and dress before announcing them." Willis stared at the wall of the building as if he could see through it if he tried hard enough.

On cue, the Coalition anthem began. The chairman started his ascent up the stairs to the stage. His face was contorted and still red from his tirade off-stage. His black clothes appeared darker than usual, matching his expression. Flanked by the usual deputy chairmen and chairwomen, Willis couldn't help but notice the difference between them. Some of the representatives acted upset, while others stood oddly calm. Today's Chase already had its divisive effect. Jaden ascended behind them dressed in a suit.

Perryn chuckled."You think Stan selected that outfit?"

"You think he'd let anyone else do it?" Willis said. Both grinned at the thought of a very proud Stan insisting on selecting Jaden's wardrobe.

Jaden clasped his hands behind his back. He was a picture of confidence, the resolve that came to him on the tower still apparent. In that moment, Willis had no doubts about his decision. Jaden was ready to change the world.

But how would he do it? Willis couldn't help but wonder. They'd discussed many possible options that could alter the Law from the outright freedom of the slaves to more subtle laws that would force the culture of the Coalition to change over time.

Chairman DeGraaf made his way to the podium, taking a second to compose himself. He wiped the sweat from his shiny forehead, and pushing his oversized glasses into place, peered down at his notes. He fiddled for a few seconds with the sweaty handkerchief which wouldn't go in his pocket properly. Willis noticed that he appeared to be trying not to look at Jaden.

Things not go according to plan, Mr. Chairman? Willis laughed to himself.

"Greetings and welcome to the loyal citizens of the World Coalition." DeGraaf began in his usual manner, his voice cracking on the word 'loyal.' "This year's Chase once again serves as a reminder of the humble burden I carry in my love for our global people. That burden is tempered and made bearable by the greatness and purity of our Law, handed down to us by the Law givers. The Law that protects us all."

"The Law is good!" the crowd responded.

"The Law that preserves us all."

"The Law remains!"

"The Law that saves us all."

"The Law is good!"

"This year's winner shows us that world-changers can truly come from anywhere. As the Law-givers graced us even amidst the anarchy of the world after the Collapse, so too this year's winner came out of nowhere among his alliance to serve us all with wisdom that will carry into future generations.

"Our Law is perfect. It cannot be changed except at this one moment, by one found worthy through the trial of the Chase. As such, we as a people must persevere. We must be slow to change. We must be patient."

The chairman looked right at Willis with his final word as if to admit he was down but not beaten. New plans would certainly be put into place.

"Representing the Western Alliance," DeGraaf continued, "this year's winner will grace us and demonstrate the blessing of the Law."

The chairman stepped aside and motioned for Jaden to step forward.

Jaden strode across the stage to the podium. He scanned the crowd in silence until he found Willis and Perryn. He smiled. "On this day, I stand here representing more than my alliance." DeGraaf's brow furrowed at these words. "I represent all people, both free and oppressed. Nations, both privileged and disadvantaged. The rich and poor. The great and least."

At these words, a few quiet cheers rose from some of the smaller alliances. The rest of the crowd was deathly silent. The deputies on stage squirmed and glanced at each other.

Do it, Jaden, before they stop you. Willis silently urged him on.

"All of us are bound to this Law," Jaden said.

At this, the chairman stepped forward. "Son, I urge you to be careful of the words you choose to describe the goodness of the Law." He attempted to cover the microphone. "Lest people misunderstand what you mean."

"There is no misunderstanding." Jaden's voice resonated with confidence.

"I don't think you understand. You are not properly prepared. I believe we should take a recess—"

Boos from the crowd interrupted the chairman's words, and he started as he realized the crowd was listening. Cries of "let him speak" rose from the back of the crowd and swelled forward. "As chairman, I believe it is my humble duty to protect us in the event of a misinformed law being passed."

A shout came from the crowd. "No, it's not!"

"You're as *bound* to the Law as we are." came another dissenting voice.

Get it out, Jaden, before it's too late. Willis silently shouted.

"Citizens, please. Let us take a short recess—"

"It is done." Jaden's voice boomed into the microphone. The crowd hushed at his words. The chairman stared at him in shock. "As of this day, I hereby declare the Law fulfilled and complete. It has served its purpose, and all citizens no matter their status in the Coalition are all free from it."

Thousands of people stood frozen, astonished as the gravity of Jaden's words were realized. Jaden didn't change the Law. He'd ended it.

No more Chase.

No more chairman.

No more Law.

The people of each alliance were free to govern themselves.

DeGraaf stood indignantly and stared at Jaden. His face turned bright red and his anger boiled. "Who do you think you—" he blurted, but the crowd wouldn't have it.

A roar arose, igniting the no-man's-land between anger and excitement, as people surged forward. Several of the smaller and poorer alliances pressed toward the stage, starting panic in others. People scattered as the crowd rushed the podium.

"We're free!" Shouts echoed from the crowd.

Others chanted. "No more Coalition!"

Guards surrounded the chairman and ushered him from the stage with the Deputies. At a motion of DeGraaf's finger, a guard grabbed Jaden's arm to take him as well. Twisting, Jaden freed himself, and Willis saw him race off the other end of the stage, disappearing into the crowd.

"Willis, what to do we do?" Perryn shouted above the growing noise.

"I don't know," he said. "I never thought this far."

"One thing is for sure," his father said, "we can't stay here. They'll be searching for you, Willis. Come on. We have a private transport waiting."

"Halt!" a uniformed Law-keeper commanded as if on cue. "By order of the chairman, you're to be taken into custody." The officer ran up with three others, pointing his firearm at Willis. His father stepped between the officer and Willis.

"You'll do no such thing." Max held up both hands. "My son has done nothing wrong."

"Stand aside." The officer cocked the gun in his hand. "We have orders to take this traitor into custody by force if necessary."

Max stepped closer until the pistol was inches from his head. He spoke calmly. "You can't have my son." The air froze as the tension of the moment surged. Willis would not see his father killed.

"Please—" Willis started when the officer suddenly lurched to the side, his pistol skidding along the pavement. His body crumpled to the ground from the force of Kane's blow, who proceeded to strike the next officer in the jaw.

"Get out of here!" Kane bellowed as he turned to flee, the remaining two officers following him. He shoved his way through the surging crowd beyond Willis's vision.

"Come on." Max led the way, and they ran.

The four of them scrambled away as the crowd reached the stage, which was promptly turned over. A few climbed the wreckage and incited the rest of the crowd. Cheers were shouted. Fists were thrown into the air. Coalition and Alliance flags were torn in protest. The Thomsons and Perryn ran through the mob to a corner of the property. There, they jumped into a car that waited.

"Whose car is this?" Willis studied his parents' faces for answers.

"I told you, Son, that I know what it's like to serve the Alliance. Your mother and I came prepared. Let's get to the landing pad before this gets out of hand." Max Thomson fired up the engine. The tires screeched as the car tore out of the area. Narrowly avoiding the still running throng, Max turned down onto a utility ramp that exited on the non-public side of the grounds. Willis looked out the window at the chaos of the crowd until it was finally obscured by the buildings. Tendrils of smoke curled into the air—someone must have lit something on fire.

"Wait, we can't leave without Kane and Jaden." Perryn leaned forward in her seat.

"We'll never find them in this," Brenda spoke breathlessly. "Kane bought you time to escape, and I think he'd want you to take it."

Willis remembered to the way Kane had looked at him on the station after the officers tried to arrest him. "He would. I hate the thought of it, but he wouldn't want us to go back for him."

"And what about Jaden?" Perryn held her breath, waiting for his answer.

Willis thought about Jaden's intentions after the Chase. Willis knew Jaden would have one thing on his mind, and it wasn't running away. "He's got his own plans."

He sat down, feeling the need to catch his breath. He noticed Perryn was equally electrified and wide-eyed. Half an hour later, they sat aboard an Alliance jet provided to the Thomsons. Willis's parents sat silently together facing him.

Perryn leaned up against him, her head on his shoulder. "What does this mean for the world now?"

"I don't know. People are going to have to make a choice. I guess that's the point. They get to choose," he said. "They're not slaves to the Law anymore."

She looked up at him, studying his face. "What about us? What does it mean for us?"

"Rest, I hope." He returned her gaze. "I'm tired."

"I could go for that." She settled back into his shoulder.

She closed her eyes and moved closer to him. Willis glanced at his parents who smiled approvingly. A few minutes later, she was asleep.

"They won't leave us alone, will they?" Willis whispered to his father.

"We have a secluded place we can go. We prepared it years ago, knowing the day would come when you would return. We'll see how this plays out and decide when to come out of hiding."

"Why come out ever?"

"Willis, your friend changed everything. He gave the world a chance for a new life. The Coalition will do its best to keep that message from getting out. What do you think that means?"

"It means someone has to tell them."

"Someone?"

"We do." He breathed deeply, thinking about his words. "We have to tell them." Willis sensed his father was right. They would hide for a time, but eventually they would have to tell the world what Jaden had done.

Willis peered out the window of the jet at the horizon. He couldn't remember ever seeing a real sunset. The colors were breathtaking hues of red and purple as the sun sank into the cloud cover below. He took in the sight and thought about the station and his years of training. He considered Jaden and how he'd stop at nothing to return to his mother. He quietly thanked Kane for rescuing them and hoped he had himself escaped. He thought about Perryn and their future together. He thought about tomorrow.

And he thought the sunrise might be still more beautiful.

Epilogue

Sheila Kemp sat in her seat aboard the Alliance jet on the way to see her sister. A blinking cursor on her computer stared at her, daring her to start her article on the Chase which had ended in chaos two days earlier. Flights worldwide were delayed due to the event, and she was finally able to return, choosing a route that would let her visit her sister.

She and Tony had done their best to capture the images of the brief riot. It'd been mostly the damaging of property and a lot of anti-Coalition clamor, but nothing like that had been seen in many years. Rumor had it that the last two days had been filled with small outbreaks of unrest in some of the poorer alliances, but the Coalition was keeping a tight rein on the media.

Coalition officers had rushed in about twenty minutes after the uprising began and made several arrests. The riot hadn't been planned and was carried out mostly by law-abiding citizens unused to being in trouble. A couple of visible flashes of handcuffs and most dispersed quickly.

"I can't believe they took my camera," Tony muttered to himself a couple of seats over. Officers had been waiting near the tents of the journalists. Every camera with footage had been promptly confiscated.

"Tony, it was a live feed. Even without the footage, the world still saw what happened." She tossed him a smile.

"Still, that camera was my baby." He crossed his arms, pouting in his seat.

Leave it to Tony to miss the bigger picture.

Chuck had been madly filling her inbox with requests for the article saying their print was the single one "in a million miles" that hadn't released anything from their people on the scene. The truth was she'd attempted the article several times simply to scrap the effort. She couldn't find the words to say what she meant to say—what she needed to say. She flipped her screen over to the article released by Coalition headquarters.

WESTERN ALLIANCE GOVERNMENT ATTEMPTS COUP OF COALITION

Coalition Intelligence has uncovered the subversive efforts of the Western Alliance's attempt to take over leadership of the world. Leading the attempt, Deputy Chairwoman Judith Marion was arrested while returning to Western Alliance offices, upon eyewitness testimony that she intended to assassinate Chairman DeGraaf in the ensuing chaos. DeGraaf issued "humble praises" for the officers who rushed to his aid at the Law-passing Ceremony.

A Coalition spokesman assured the public that an all-department manhunt was already underway for the fugitive known as Jaden. Coalition enforcement has charged him with assaulting two Chase runners, Antonio DeLuca of the Joint Mediterranean States and teammate Willis Thomson of the Western Alliance during the race.

"Jaden is clearly a confused young man who has been made the unfortunate pawn of a corrupt alliance," said DeGraaf, adding his heartfelt desire to see the racer found so he may receive the "obvious psychological care needed to undo the damage inflicted by his alliance."

Sheila shook her head in disgust. The rest of the article did little more than quote the new Western Alliance deputy chairman's praise for the glory of the World Coalition and the bravery of the chairman. It closed with an understated call to end any further unrest around the globe.

"Do they think anyone will believe this garbage?" She glanced around, realizing her open dissent.

Come on, Kemp. If you can't say that, how do you expect to write this article?

No one knew where Jaden had escaped, but rumors flew everywhere. Some said that he died in the riot. Others claimed that he'd altered his appearance and was living openly in a city somewhere. Still wilder was the notion that the Coalition already apprehended him, and the manhunt was a ruse to test the loyalty of various Coalition officials.

Sheila knew better. Jaden had one goal. Somehow, he would attempt to travel to the orbiting station to free his mother.

She placed her fingers on the keys of the computer in front of her. The ideas were there, but the words wouldn't come. Her fingers fumbled as she typed out a few words. She crammed down the backspace to delete the words and hung her head. Reaching for the screen, she started to shut the computer when her message alert chimed.

Sighing, she opened the screen and looked at the message. She held her breath as her encryption software began working on a coded message. A second later, the words appeared—

Safe. W. and P.

She smiled to herself. Willis and Perryn had safely hidden themselves away from the eyes of the Coalition.

"Okay, guys. You all did your part," she whispered. "The gloves are coming off—as promised."

She slowly typed a single word, *Truth*, and stared for a long moment. Taking a deep breath, she began to write.

Author Note

I still sit in shock that this project has come to life. What began as a way to direct my energies when I lost my career is now the book you hold in your hands. Thank you for being one of my readers. In so many unintentional ways, Willis's story is my own. His journey is my journey. For so much of my life, I felt the burden of others' lofty expectations for me and did my best to live up to them. My life halted in burnout, and writing this book was part of my recovery. Willis became the embodiment of all that I felt during that season of life. Whether you bear the weight of expectations like Willis, are a survivor like Perryn, or live as an optimist like Jaden, I hope you connected to a character.

I wrote *The Chase* knowing the beginning and the end, but the middle was a discovery process as I got to know the characters along the way. Jez and Sheila underwent quite the metamorphosis. Jez started as a one-note villain, but her tale opened up as I questioned the 'why' behind her actions. When I realized she was motivated by her fear of death, she struck a chord of compassion in me to the point that I mourned the end of her story in the book. Sheila's role was far smaller, but her place in the story grew thanks to my first reader, Lauren, who insisted she needed more of Sheila. Expect more of Sheila in book two.

You may have guessed that many of the principle characters had intentional names. Willis, for example, refers to his need to overcome his will to win. His last name Thomson serves as a reminder of the disciple Thomas who is famous for his moment of doubt. Perryn's name could either mean 'wanderer' or be a feminine form of Peter, meaning 'rock.' Choosing which path to take is her struggle, one you will follow more through the rest of the series. Sheila Kemp translates to 'female champion,' and trust me, her moment to speak up is coming. Even many of the side character names hinted at the role they played: Blacc is short for his 'blind acceptance' of the condition of the World Coalition;

DeGraaf means 'chairman' hinting that his person is entirely wrapped up in his position; and Jaden translates 'God has heard' as he is the catalyst to begin the changes on the space station. I would love to connect with you and hear about which character mimicked your story. Follow the links below and drop me a note to let me know your favorite scene or the biggest surprise or where you guess the story might be going. Sign up for my newsletter to get ALL the insider information and get a free download of *Kane: A Chase Runner Story* to learn how the silent giant made it to the training station.

Website and newsletter (and your free book): *BradleyCaffee.com*
Facebook: *facebook.com/bradleycaffeeauthor*
Instagram: *@bradleycaffeeauthor*

PLEASE LEAVE ME A REVIEW AND TELL YOUR FRIENDS. The greatest help you can give to any new author is to leave them an honest review. Amazon and Goodreads are the place to start, but any review helps. Better yet, tell your friends about *The Chase* and get them hooked on this series along with you. Thanks, my friend.

And Now, a Sneak Peek at Book Two in
The Chase Runner Series

Chapter One

Buzz.

The cell door opened with a metallic clang to reveal a uniformed guard on the other side. "Prisoner 513, you have a visitor." He spoke in a monotone, not moving his eyes from his notepad.

Sheila stared at the stone wall across the room. Six months had passed since Chuck had published her article. He had been so eager to get her words about the riots following the Chase uploaded online that he had not even glanced at them. If he had, he never would have sent them to print. It took an hour after her words hit the internet for the Law-keepers to arrive at Sheila's door.

"Prisoner 513, on your feet," the guard said more firmly, looking at her.

Sheila's dirty fingers curled on the floor around her as she turned to glare at the guard. Her dry, cracking lips parted as she sucked in enough air to speak. "I told you I'm not interested in seeing anyone." Her voice creaked from disuse.

He rolled his eyes. "No choice this time, I'm afraid."

"Oh yeah, who's the special guest?"

"The Administrative Liaison to the Coalition Chairman is here to see you."

Sheila's stomach turned at the title. She remembered the greasy-haired man she had last encountered on the space station. Her half-starved existence in this isolation cell seemed far preferable to ever laying eyes on the weasel again. She was about to protest when she noticed the two other guards standing outside the door.

"Wow. I've gotten popular, haven't I?" She smiled. Sarcasm was not going to win her points with the guards, but she had to admit that it felt good in the moment. She turned over on her knees to stand, her arms shaking with weakness. "Don't suppose your friends could offer me a hand."

A nod from the guard brought the other two inside. They roughly grabbed her upper arms, hauling her to her feet. The cell spun as she adjusted to standing again. All at once, she thought she might vomit or pass out. She opted for the latter. The guard's cursing was the last thing she heard before losing consciousness.

"Ms. Kemp?" The tone was soft, almost pleasant. "Ms. Kemp, can you hear me?"

Sheila squinted as light poured into her eyes. The smell of disinfectant and clean sheets roused her from semi-consciousness. She was lying on a bed in what appeared to be a hospital room. Monitors beeped beside her, and an IV was delivering fluids into her arm. Otherwise the tiny space was empty of furniture.

"There you are Ms. Kemp," came the voice again.

She turned in the direction of the speaker. A middle-aged woman sat in a chair next to her bed. She was dressed modestly in a gray, professional-looking skirt and jacket. Her perfume, a sickening fruity aroma wafted in Sheila's direction with each movement. Her eyes creased when she smiled at Sheila as she reached out a hand to the side of the bed. Several golden bracelets jingled as she touched Sheila's arm, which she withdrew the second she saw the Alliance insignia on the woman's lapel.

"Who are you?" Sheila eyed her suspiciously.

"My friends call me Penny," she said, smiling again. "You gave us quite a scare when you collapsed, and I insisted that you be brought to the infirmary at once. I have longed to meet you. I serve humbly as the Administrative Liaison to the Coalition Chairman."

Sheila's eyes widened. She bolted upright in bed, finally noticing the guard at the door. She turned to the woman. "I don't want to talk to you. And I'm not your friend."

"Oh, honey. I understand."

"Somehow, I don't think you do."

The woman glanced down as if embarrassed. "I know you had dealings with my predecessor."

"Dealings would be a polite way of putting it." Sheila's forehead throbbed—with anger or pain from sitting up so quickly, she could not be sure. "He sent me to that station. He threatened my sister. And he put me in here. I wasn't aware he was no longer in office."

"After the Chairman uncovered the shameful coup attempt of the Western Alliance, many officials were—" She paused before finishing, "—replaced."

Sheila shuddered as she considered the meaning of *replaced.* "You mean, they were—"

"Sweetheart, it doesn't matter." Penny returned to smiling sweetly. "What matters is I'm here to help you."

"Help? How?" Sheila lay back down to ease her pulsating temples.

"For starters, a hot meal and a shower. I honestly had no idea how you were being treated here, or I would have come much sooner. You were severely dehydrated. It's fortunate we found you when we did, or things might have been worse."

"I'm sure that was the idea of your—predecessor." Sheila doubted her, and she wanted this woman to know it. "Don't get me wrong, a meal and a shower sound great, but why the sudden change?"

The woman's smile instantly disappeared. "All in good time," she said flatly, her eyes not giving anything away. She brightened again as if a switch was being thrown on and off in her mind. "But for now, we need to get you cleaned up. I am afraid you are still at the prison, so you will be under guard. That is, until we can do something about your sentence. You leave that to me." A glance at the guard caused him to step aside and rap on the doorway. Two female nurses, dressed in yellow Alliance uniforms, entered.

Sheila must have shrunk backward because Penny was quick to add, "Oh they are here to assist you. I'm assuming you do not want the guards helping you clean yourself."

Sheila nodded.

"Very well." The liaison held her hands out in front of her as if ready to embrace the room. Her bracelets jingled with each movement like they were trying to celebrate the sterile environment. "I am pleased with this. Is there anything else I can do for you?"

"New clothes would be nice, if it's not too much trouble." Sheila continued to take in this woman. She could not make up her mind about whether to trust Penny. "And if I'm going to get out of here, I'd like transportation somewhere."

"Oh really? There are things, dear, that we must attend to."

We? Sheila did not like the sound of that. "Yes." She straightened her posture to show the seriousness of her request. "I need to go see my sister."

Penny's face darkened at the mention of Sheila's sister. "Very well." She frowned. "You can see your sister, and then when you are ready to appreciate those who have helped you, you will get around to seeing me. That is—if it's not too much trouble." Penny spoke the last few words slowly, clarifying that it was not a request. Without another word, she exited along with the guard leaving Sheila alone with the nurses.

The door clicked behind Penny, and Sheila let out a long breath. The hair on her arms still stood at attention, and she could not help feeling like an animal might after a predator had left her cage.

Made in the USA
Monee, IL
11 February 2023

27588973R00148